Dawn Of Devotion:
Beller Ties
Book 3

Lee Dawna

LeeDawna Books

First edition

Cover design by Premade Ebook Cover Shop
www.premadeebookcovershop.com

ISBN 978-1-949192-11-7 (paperback)
ISBN 978-1-949192-10-0 (ebook)
ISBN 978-1-949192-12-4 (audiobook)

Published by LeeDawna Books www.leedawnabooks.com
leedawnabooks@suddenlink.net

~

This book is dedicated to my sister Billie. Our adventures are never dull, and your friendship is a cherished blessing.

~

~1~

Whenever I forget what my laugh sounds like, I think back to that day. The one when Dad and I left our lakeside house, hand in hand and skipping along the trail that led to the park on the far side of the lake. I'd just gotten a pretty rainbow-winged butterfly kite the day before, when my best friend and I celebrated our ninth birthdays, and Dad was taking me to fly it in the open field beside the park. We giggled the whole way there and I squealed with delight when those wings finally soared through the air over our heads.

The very last drop of joy I've ever experienced is forever frozen in that small space of time, when big rainbow wings cut across the sky above me, a tail of white satin ribbons cascading behind my butterfly.

Dad gave me control of the line and I let out too much, sending the kite diving into a mass of brambles along the lake's edge. "Don't worry, cupcake. Daddy will get it." He ran to where the kite's tail tangled in the thick underbrush and picked his way through the dense mass of bushes and briars.

Wanting to help, I dropped down and crawled on my hands and knees, thorns pricking my skin and hair as I pushed through his khaki-clad legs. Just on the other side, through a small opening, I saw something that didn't look right. Crawling closer, the toes I was staring at came into focus. "Daddy," I tugged on his pant leg. "Who is that?"

Every day of the last eight years I've remembered that moment. The sounds, smells, what the earth felt like under my palms. With agonizing detail, I remember Dad pulling Kira from the shallows, a sound I've never heard a human being make before or since ripping out of his chest. Kira's peach shirt clung to her throat, her lower half naked, knees bloody and face so caked in mud I barely recognized my best friend. While Dad wailed and rocked her in his arms, I counted the gravel pieces embedded in her cheek.

1

~

"You're seventeen, Dani." Dad glances up from his tofu eggs, checking the hallway for his new wife. He met Evette last year and married her seven months ago so they're still in the honeymoon stage, meaning he's pretending he doesn't mind converting to veganism. "You should be focused on making friends, going to parties, and meeting boys I can run off."

I chug a glass of juice and pop my bread out of the toaster. "For the last time, Dad, I'm not obsessed with death. I'm obsessed with bringing child killers to justice."

His mouth turns down. "It's the same thing, sweetheart."

"Hardly." I slather the toast in ghee, one of the few non-vegan products left in the house. "And aren't you supposed to tell me to spend my time focusing on grades? And college?"

"You already have perfect grades. And I'll pay for your college if…" I look at him and he shoves the tofu around his plate again. "You're spending too much time staring at screens of kids none of us can help. That's what the police are for. They'll handle the missing kids while you handle being a teenager starting her senior year of high school."

According to the FBI, 365,348 children went missing in 2020. By sheer numbers alone, law enforcement doesn't have the resources to find them all. I've explained this to Dad before and though he'll admit it's a problem, he insists that I stay out of the citizen sleuth business. Then there are the *stings* I've conducted on my own. He absolutely forbids those. My mistake was not knowing the police would contact him when I gave them the first sex offender's name. I was only twelve then. Now I set up fake social media profiles using burner phones and once I have a predator hooked, I send the login info to a cyber tip line. All completely anonymous.

Grabbing my backpack from the counter, I kiss his cheek. "You're in luck, Dad. After senior orientation, I'm going to the library, also known as the perfect place to meet boys. One might even be nice enough that you won't have to run him off." I slip my toast onto his plate. "Eat the butter, it's good for you."

Before he questions *why* I'm going to the library after school, I rush out the door. Exiting before Evette makes an appearance is a daily goal.

If I don't get out in time, she'll lecture me about animal fat, then I'll be forced to lecture her about the number of animals murdered in large-scale government farming practices. That debate always ends with her eyes glazing over and her mouth complaining to Dad that I'm being *difficult.*

I'll give Dad credit though—while he loses every attempt to stay neutral and Evette is just as superficial as my mother, she's twice as old as my egg donor Susan. So, Evette disliking me simply because she can't understand why any female would choose to wear sneakers and have a perpetual ponytail is a pill her age appropriateness makes easier to swallow.

"Want a ride, Miss Madison?" Henry calls out to me like he does every morning.

"I'm good!" I wave to the garage where Dad's driver stands ready and waiting. "He's having tofu."

Henry gives me a nod and a wink. "He's got a meeting later. I'll run him by the bagel shop on the way. Text if you want me to pick you up, I'm already coming to the school anyway."

I eye William's second-story window. "I'll double whatever Dad's paying you if you leave Evil Step stranded. A three-block hike won't hurt anything but his ego."

William is a nauseating mix of prep-school snobbery and only child syndrome. When I think he can't possibly whine any more, he morphs into Baby King Three Thousand. Because of it, he always gets his way; thus he struts around like he owns the world.

At school, William picks on anyone and everyone, and no one says a word to him. Except me. And we were butting heads long before our parents met. If I'd known volunteering for the clothing drive would bring Dad to the school, I would have just made a donation and prevented him from meeting Evette. No Evette, no me being forced to live under the same roof as William.

Before Evil Step moved in, I didn't have as many problems as I do now. At school, I'm not the richest kid in the private institution but Dad is wealthy enough. That afforded me some leeway to be *fundamentally different*, as my old biology teacher dubbed me. A difference stemming from being too detached from other kids to be a trendsetter, a nerd, a math geek, emo, or any of the other labels people who despise labels use to describe themselves.

Since William now has my dad's ear, he gets to tell dear ol' dad all about my lack of social inclination. I wish they understood how hard it is for me to play the part of the bright and interested student to pacify the teachers, and then the marginally engaged friend to appease the other kids. I might appear normal enough on the outside, but on the inside, I'm defective. I don't care about the latest gossip, the hottest new band, or where a boy who supposedly likes me wants to go for a date. The only thing that holds my interest is finding out who raped and murdered my best friend.

$$\sim 2 \sim$$

Senior year orientation is basically the same as junior year. More of a social gathering than an informational one. Since attendance is required, I'm here. I'm signed in and have my class schedule in hand. The very hand that's pushing open the emergency exit.

I don't skip school, but I *have* used this exit several times. It opens into the faculty parking lot and there's no alarm on the door because it's what teachers use throughout the day. The parking lot itself is fenced and you have to have a code to get in. Unless you're on foot and simply duck under the bar because someone didn't think this whole secure parking lot situation all the way through. And I'm glad they didn't.

The library is four blocks away. I hurry along the sidewalk until the library's stone exterior comes into view. I won't be paying attention to any boys who also might be skipping orientation, but I'll muster the enthusiasm to be as excited as my peers about school starting on Monday when one of the librarians inevitably asks about this supposed milestone year. I'll give a fake smile and make it connect with the rest of my body language by thinking about the day when I'll finally track down Kira's murderer. The year in which *that* day happens will be the milestone. It'll be the year when my life begins again.

As I search the aisles for books on how a criminal's mind works, I think about Dad's words from this morning. I've poured my heart out to every overpaid therapist he's sent me to, but nothing makes me want to engage with the world the way he tells me I should. The way all the other girls do. I don't want to giggle when some boy throws out a cheesy pickup line to gauge my level of interest. If a boy wants me to take him seriously, he should be direct. And you can forget about me *dressing to impress.* Both Evette and Susan have the mentality that a woman's sole duty in life is to keep herself polished and groomed for the benefit of landing and then *keeping* a man. I say my duty is to make my own body comfortable, and on a warm end-of-summer day like today, that means cut-off jean shorts and a blue camisole paired with my favorite pair of sneakers.

"This all for you today?" The round-faced librarian lowers his glasses as he examines my selections.

"Yes, sir," I reply. He's asked me ten times to call him Dave, but I have a hard time doing that.

"This is some heavy reading for your senior year. You excited about school starting back up?"

I plaster a broad smile on my face. "I absolutely can't wait for the day it all starts."

~

"You're home early." Dad meets me in the hall outside my bedroom.

I make a show of the stack of library books in my arm, keeping the titles hidden. "Orientation was boring so I went ahead and got a head start on some of the extra reading I'll be required to do this year."

His throat bobs. "That's…nice."

I eye him suspiciously. "What's wrong?"

He rubs the back of his head and motions for me to go ahead of him into my room. I measure my steps as I walk across the black and pink Bohemian rug that Evette picked out. At the foot of my bed, I gently place the stack of books on the comforter and position my backpack in front of them so the titles can't be read.

I turn back to Dad, heart dropping when I see his face. Before Evette and William came along, Dad and I were close even though he's never quite understood me. The years after Kira's death were brutal, and forasmuch as it tore us apart, it also drew us together. Dad was always there when I had night terrors, panic attacks, and such a fear of water that he moved us out of the lake house and into the heart of suburbia.

Before Kira died, I never had a fear of water. I'd been a fish. All of the yards in the community where we'd lived ran down to the lake. On our ninth birthdays, we had one big joint party with tables and decorations set up between my house and Kira's, and inflatables Dad rented floating on the surface of the water for all the kids to enjoy. The next day she was dead.

"Dad?" I whisper.

His body stiffens, mouth blurting out in one quick breath, "I think going to live with your mom will open you up."

"Excuse me?"

His arms fold over his chest. "Name your best friend. One who is alive."

I assume his posture and lift my chin. "It would be rude of me to single out one friend as *the* best."

He loosens his arms. "Who did you talk to at orientation today?"

I shrug. "Our entire class was there, and all of the instructors."

"No one," he bites. "You spoke to no one, because you have no friends. And you have no friends because you refuse to try."

"That isn't true!" I defend. "I talked to both Sherry *and* John today." I name the first people who come to mind. "And Jenny was walking me home from the library until Henry pulled up and begged me to get in the Cadillac. You do know that still embarrasses me, right?"

"What I know is that ninety percent of the kids in your school have drivers, yet I have to beg mine to track you down because you insist on ducking him. And Jenny is older than I am! She might be a sweet old lady who loves to tell you stories, but she isn't a friend, Dani. You *need* a friend. Someone your own age to talk to."

"And your solution is Susan? The woman who wasn't much older than I am now when you married her?"

He sits on my bed with a sigh and I glance at my bag, it's still concealing the books. "Your mom was in her thirties when I married her and she has custody rights. She's asking to see you."

I sit beside him with an eye roll. "That's new."

He nods, hand sliding to mine. "She wants you to come stay with her. For the school year."

The earth begins to tilt, tiny splinters shattering through my universe. Dad's left eyelid is spasming, the way it always does when his mind is made up. "You want me to *live* with *Susan*? I haven't even spoken to her in years."

He looks down at his brown leather shoes. "She calls you every year on your birthday and you two always have a…nice chat."

I launch off the bed and stand over him. "Because I have to pretend that I like whatever ridiculous gift she sends while listening to her tell me how much she paid for it, which breaks every rule of gift-giving."

He swallows. "Still, she has a right to see you, and she's exercising that right."

"Then I'll video chat her," I snap.

He stands and places his hands on my shoulders. "The arrangements have been made. The school you're transferring to starts on Monday also, and they've only just had their orientation which was probably much like the one you half attended today."

A tremor shakes up my legs. "You're serious? You're sending me away?"

His moist eyes dart away. "You're leaving after dinner. I've already arranged for a plane to meet us at the airport."

Air sucks from my lungs as if the room is being vacuum sealed. He places a cold hand on my cheek. "I know this is a shock, cupcake, but your mom and I have been discussing it for a while and well, Evette and I think—"

"You and Evette think?" The words break out of my chest in a rush of grief and rage. "More like *Evette* thinks! And you're going along with it so you don't upset her *delicate* constitution."

"That's not fair."

"Fair?" I spot my luggage in the corner. "Fair would be getting to go through my senior year with Kira!" I throw open my closet doors. Almost all of my clothes have been packed. "Fair would be having a father who doesn't want to forget he has a daughter all to please his new wife!"

He reaches for me but I dodge his hands, tugging open my dresser drawers. They're empty, too. Tears stream down my face. He knew this morning he was shipping me off but he never so much as uttered a syllable. He waited for me to leave, then packed my life into those suitcases. "Where are my journals? My research?"

He clears his throat. "Incinerated. And I haven't told your mom about your infatuation but if you don't change your life around... Cupcake, you need a fresh start. And I'm hoping you can get that with your mom because I don't know how to make you get over this obsession. When you tell me you've quit, that you've found other hobbies, all you're really doing is getting better at hiding things from me. This can't go on. It isn't healthy."

My tears drip into the empty drawers. "You burned all of my journals?"

He sighs. "Your mom will expose you to new things, open you up, and you'll see in the end that this move was for the best."

"What if I refuse to go?"

"Then you don't go to college. I'm not paying for you to go isolate yourself on some campus."

I spin around. "But I didn't apply for any scholarships. We agreed that since you can afford to pay, we'd pay, and leave the scholarships for those who can't afford to go to college without them."

His face hardens. "And now I'm telling you that you have one year to prove to me that I can trust you to engage with other human beings because I won't always be around and I'm worried that when I'm gone, you'll be all alone in the world. I won't be able to rest in peace if that happens to you."

I move away from him and affix the lone duffle bag to the top of the largest piece of wheeled luggage. I don't want the rest, he can burn it, too.

I drag the two pieces to the bed and throw my backpack over my shoulder, leaving the books in full view. I face him. "You're not sending me away for my benefit. This is happening because you're embarrassed of me. Well, now I'm gone. Congratulations on your new family. I hope William is the child you always wanted."

~3~

I didn't say goodbye to Evette or William, and I refused to sit down for that *one last family dinner* Dad tried to sell. For once, I willingly let Henry give me a ride. He dropped me off at the airport, a tear in his eye as we muddled our way through an awkward goodbye. He's always been kind to me and it isn't his fault that my own father just dumped me.

The airport doors close behind me and I glance backward, giving Henry one last wave. He throws up one hand and wipes his eyes with the other. I turn away, allowing one single tear to slide down my face before I force all of my emotions away. If I start allowing myself to feel anything but anger now, I'll end up in a sobbing, hyperventilating mess on the floor.

I tug my luggage toward the first airline counter I come to. "Hello, can you tell me what airport is closest to Huntington, Pennsylvania?"

If Dad wants to send me away, he doesn't get to make himself feel better about it by sending me off in style. I had to empty the pouch I keep tucked inside my backpack with all my allowance money to buy this coach ticket that will take me from Washington state to Pennsylvania, but I'd rather fly the red-eye on a cheap airline than get banished via private jet.

Dad's leaving frantic voice messages and he does seem worried that I never showed up for the flight he arranged for me, but he's also not at the airport looking for me. He's also the one making the decision to send me to live with Susan. He knows she has a long list of grievances when it comes to me and never holds her tongue about how disappointing I am, so he can't be *that* worried about my well-being. There's not a single memory I have of Susan that doesn't end with some part of my body being ridiculed. The woman had me on a diet at the age of three!

Turning my phone off, I shove it into my backpack and run my sweaty palms over my legs. Legs that are no less chubby now than they were when I was a kid. Great.

I lean my head back and look up to the airport's beams that are far overhead. My chest hasn't felt this tight in a while. My last full panic attack was over a year ago, and the previous one nearly ten months before that. One. Two. Three. I begin counting the bolts in the beams. One of my therapists taught me this counting technique and it's been helpful. It might also be helpful to just get up and walk out of here. I've already turned my wheeled suitcase and the duffle over to the airline, but I still have my backpack. It's stocked with one journal, some pencils and highlighters, two granola bars, and what's left of my life's savings—which isn't enough to even rent a room in a cheap motel. And even if it was, where would I go?

I'll be eighteen in under four months and have a high school diploma in nine. If Dad pays for my college like he's always agreed to do as long as I keep my grades up, I'll be off to study criminal law and no longer subjected to Susan. If he doesn't pay, well, I've got nine months to figure out another way to move out of her house.

I barely know the woman anyway. She was already gone before Kira died and when I called her crying, wanting my mom in the devastating hours after I'd watched my friend's remains get stuffed into a bag, Susan told me that people die and to grow up and stop being a baby about it. That was the last time I voluntarily spoke to her. Dad calls her every year on Mother's Day and hands me the phone, and he sends her a gift in my name. On my birthday, she calls me and Dad doesn't allow me to ignore the call, but that only proves that she doesn't know me because there's been nothing happy about any of my birthdays since I was nine.

~

I can't say I'm surprised that Susan didn't pick me up from the airport. I sent her a message with my flight information, and I assume she told Dad because I didn't receive any more messages from him after that. But alas, the woman who refuses to call me Dani like everyone else, didn't bother to even send a car for her daughter *Danielle* who she's supposed to be just dying to see.

Exhausted from not being able to sleep on the overly long flight because of toddler-aged twins who didn't stop screaming for the entire last leg, and that after a three-hour layover in a too cold airport, I ordered my own car and used the credit card on file so Dad gets to pay for *this* part of my banishment.

Unlike William, I don't carry a physical copy of Dad's credit card. I rarely need to make purchases and when I do, it's usually something I don't want Dad knowing about so I just take an allowance and pay cash for whatever I need. Now I have a feeling that refusing the plastic was a big mistake. I should have taken it and kept it on me for a time like this. But I never even considered a life where Dad wouldn't be there when I needed him.

The driver plops my luggage onto the sidewalk in front of Susan's house. This isn't the largest home in the gated community, but it's close. Which makes me wonder how much she actually took Dad for in the divorce. Guessing *why* she needs a house this big isn't hard. It would take something this grand to accommodate her ego.

"Hope it all works out," the driver offers, jogging back to her door and disappearing inside. I don't think she appreciated my candor when she asked how my day was going.

"You know what they say—there's always hope," I mutter as she pulls away from the curb, leaving me standing alone on the street with everything I own sitting next to me. Once again, there's no Susan anywhere in sight.

Taking a look around, just in case Dad's hiding in the bushes and this is just one big joke, I note the cul-de-sac beyond Susan's house. It's overgrown and undeveloped, essentially making hers the last home on the street. Worst case scenario, I set up a tent over there and live off the land.

Hefting my backpack onto my shoulder with a groan, I stack the duffle onto the rolling case and tug the two pieces up the sloped driveway. When I reach the three small steps, I drag the luggage up them and then just stand underneath the New England eyebrow awning, studying the oversized onyx corbels. In front of me, there's a diamond-shaped doorbell. My stomach tightens into a knot as my finger presses against it. An opulent gong resounds and I can't help but let out another groan. This place is exactly like Susan, a bunch of fancy stuff all plopped together to construct something that doesn't make any sense. If someone told her the sound of a sneeze was expensive, her doorbell would sneeze.

Susan throws open the door. "There you are! You're late!"

"I sent you my flight details."

"Flight? Oh, yeah." She waves her hand, flustered. "I meant the party. We're half an hour late already, and if I know those *Bellers,* they won't consider it fashionable." She walks to a side table and picks up a handbag. "Well, don't just stand there. Go change!"

"Into what?" She's wearing a sarong. "You do know I'm underage, right?"

She walks by me. "Your room is upstairs, the first door on the left. Your outfit is on the bed. I'll be waiting in the car."

It feels as if a thousand bees just descended upon me, jabbing their tiny spears into every part of me. "Nice to see you too, *Mom.*"

~4~

Hefting my luggage up the flight of stairs, I push open the door to the room on the left. The walls are painted a soft lilac and the white satin bedding has lilac flowers embroidered all over it. The carpet is white and the furniture itself is a dark oak. It's pretty. And very clearly my room because my name is embroidered on the pillows.

A part of me would believe Susan set this room up because she actually wants me here if the *outfit* she left on the bed didn't dissolve any inkling that this woman even knows what kind of person her own daughter is. Somewhere in her twisted mind, she thinks she's influenced me enough to make me turn out just like her.

I hold up the itty-bitty black bikini. Technically, it will fit *on* my body. But even with the lace cover-up, there's absolutely no chance I'd be concealing anything.

Still in my jean shorts and blue camisole, I head outside to where Susan's idling in a Porsche near the end of the driveway. I lean into the passenger window. "Thanks for the highly inappropriate attire, but I think I'm going to sit this one out. You go have fun, though."

Her painted nail wiggles up and down. "You have to go. The party is for you."

"Me?"

"Well, all the kids in Michael Beller's class. Which you are now in." A smile twists over her features. "It's his annual end-of-summer back-to-school pool party. *At* the Beller house."

"Cool." I nod. "But I'm still going to pass because even if the bikini you got me wasn't one hundred sizes too small, water isn't really my thing. Neither are parties."

14

Her face hardens and her words come out in a low hiss. "Danielle, get in this car right now."

"Bu—"

"I said now!"

~

The winding road leading away from Susan's gated community is isolated. There's a steep cliff on one side and a forested mountain on the other. I close my eyes and hope the soft purr of the engine will lull me to sleep. "Here we are. Sit up straight." Susan's words slice into my tranquility.

I do as she says and sit up. "Tell them to put in a sidewalk and we could just walk here."

"Not in my shoes." She glances at my feet, a line deepening at the corner of her mouth as we pull up to the gate at the mouth of the driveway.

A giant of a man exits the guard house. I slink back down into my seat while Susan gives the enormous brute an *I know you want me* smile. His head tilts, the scowl on his oversized brow making my heart race as he eyes me. I turn away and focus straight ahead as Susan's singsong voice says, "Susan and Danielle Madison."

"I know who you are." His flat tone makes me glance his way. He's still staring at me.

"Isn't she beautiful?" Mom bats her lashes and whips my ponytail over my shoulder. "Like mother, like daughter."

His scalding blue eyes sear across my face. "Miss Madison, you're approved to enter. But you'll have to exit the vehicle and let my partner escort you to the main house because," his eyes burn into Susan, "*Mrs.* Madison is not approved."

Susan's face blazes red. "I happen to know that *every* parent is invited to this party, so if my daughter is allowed in, so am I."

The man speaks into his earpiece, eyes never leaving Susan's. "Tell Mr. Beller the problem showed up, and she doesn't want to let her daughter stay if she isn't permitted inside."

I slide over the console and look up at him. "No problems here. Her daughter doesn't want to stay. We'll just leave."

One day, I'll have a say in my own life. In particular, I'll get to say where I go and when. Because Susan arguing with a guard who is completely ignoring her while whoever is on the other end of his earpiece listens in, makes me want to jump out of this vehicle and try my luck at being a survivalist. "I need to learn how to fish."

"What?" Susan snaps, grinding her gears as the gate finally opens in front of us. "John Beller is *not* going to ostracize my daughter just because of his stupid wife. When we get up there, if anyone tries to make me leave, let them know we're a package deal."

"Since when?" I mumble as a house comes into view on the horizon.

Susan parks, sliding around to face me. "Since you enrolled in the class of the most eligible bachelor in Huntington. Michael Beller just turned eighteen. I can't be sure, but he probably got access to at least part of his trust fund. If not, he'll get it soon enough and it isn't like he even needs it. Mommy and Daddy aren't going to let him do without *anything*."

So *this* is why she called out of the blue and demanded Dad share his custody. She wants access to these people and I'm her way in. "Too bad I didn't wear the lingerie you bought me."

Her lip cocks in disgust and her eyes roam over me. "Yes, it *is* too bad. You'll have to work extra hard on having a personality that will make you stand out."

"Shucks." I snap my fingers. "I left my personality on the plane. I guess we might as well go."

Her hand clamps around my wrist. "Now that your dad is remarried, don't you think for one second that his well isn't going to dry up. Not just for me, but for *you*. Evette didn't blink an eye over sending you away. She was all too happy to get rid of you, and that's just the tip of the iceberg, honey." She releases my wrist and plasters on a smile. "Now, you get in there and mingle. The Bellers have the highest price tag, but they aren't the only catches at this party. Take your pick, *after* you make sure their wallet will keep you comfortable."

~5~

The miniature scuffle I was having with Susan while she attempted to pry me out of her Porsche ended when a raven-haired woman appeared just outside the intricately detailed floor-to-ceiling doors on the front of the expansive ranch house.

Susan stopped pulling and instead, shoved me. "For goodness sake, Danielle. You can't live your life expecting me to do everything for you. Stand up straight and make yourself as presentable as you possibly can in that…whatever it is that you're wearing."

"They're called clothes, *Susan*," I bite. "And I quit expecting you to do anything for me when I was nine."

Not keen on having an audience any more than she is, I clamp my jaw shut and traverse the stairs, moving my eyes from the beautiful woman in the doorway to the wall of a man at her back. Towering behind her, hands secured over her shoulders, he has death rays fixed on Susan. Who is either worse than me at reading social cues or just plain doesn't care that these people can't stand the sight of her. She gives me another push, a smaller one, while her voice lifts into a jubilant lilt for them. "Isn't it wonderful that our kids will be in the same class? Just think, if we had put them in kindergarten together, Michael and Danielle would probably be engaged by now!"

The woman's words are as cool as her demeanor. "I'm sure your husband had an excellent reason for keeping your daughter with him all these years."

"*Ex*-husband." Susan winks at the man. "I hear divorce is in the water these days."

"I also hear you can drown in water," the woman retorts. The man smiles, one of his hands sliding down her arm, moving around her waist and pulling her back against him as a growl rattles through the air. She smiles up at him and he smiles back, a dog ready to bite every hand but hers.

This would be a great time for them to kick Susan out. She's already lost a little of her poise. "Hi." I hold up a hand and wiggle my fingers. "I'm too young to be engaged. Too tired to attend a party. And pretty terrified of drowning. So, it was nice to meet you, but we're just going to go."

Susan grips my elbow. Tight. The woman scans the grip and Susan releases it, a laugh on her lips. "Danielle is shy. See why she needs to be here?"

The woman moves forward. "Danielle, I'm Mary. This is my husband John. We have lifeguards on duty so if you'd like to stay, you're welcome in our home. You can probably get some rest in one of the loungers by the pool."

"Sounds perfect." Susan's shoulders scrunch as she moves past them into the house.

"Susan." The man's chest thunders. "You're only crossing that threshold because my *wife* is allowing you to. But you *will* know your place in our home or I *will* personally remove you."

She waves a nonchalant hand over her shoulder and proceeds deeper into their house. The interior is roped off so no one can meander down the halls. A good move considering Susan seems bent on snooping.

I glue my feet to the porch as the three of us watch her until she disappears out the back doors to where the party is happening. Mary's head slowly turns back to me. John's head snaps around, looking as if it's going to detonate at any second. I swallow. "I'm sorry. I can try to get Susan out of there, or you can just call the big guy from the gate and have him drag her out. Whichever you think will cause less of a scene. Which will probably be the security guard because she clearly doesn't listen to me."

John's eyes narrow. "You're her daughter?"

I shuffle my tennis shoe-clad feet. "That's what Dad tells me."

Mary laughs. "Well, even so, we're delighted to meet one of Michael's new classmates."

My eyebrow hitches. "As long as the apple fell far from the tree?"

She motions for me to enter the house. "Apples don't get to choose what tree bears them. Now go on inside, we'll introduce you to our son and he can acquaint you with the others."

The stone patio behind the Beller estate sprawls out in every direction. To my right is a cozy area of bright red cushions surrounding a fire pit. Beyond that is a gleaming row of banquet tables from which an enticing aroma wafts above the fray. To the left, a more modern sitting area with chairs and benches is set up with custom chess boards and dainty refreshment trays. But it's what's straight ahead of us that steals the show. I rest my eyes on the in-ground pool and study the teenagers twisting down the slide that flows into the deepest end. A lifeguard stands below, coordinating with the lifeguard at the top of the slide to keep the kids jumping off the diving board from colliding with the sliders.

Lounge chairs and various intimate seating configurations encircle the water's edge, one of them focusing on the hot tub that's sunk into the patio. Fifteen girls are making use of the bubbling water, each string bikini smaller than the next. The entourage of buff flesh passing a Frisbee next to them tells me those are the *it* girls, the boys making a show of catching their flying disc when they think one of them is watching.

Before Mary opens her mouth, I know who her son is. Michael Beller sits on the edge of a lounger near the hot tub, but that lounger might as well be a throne. He's their king. Heir to their tiny miserable worlds. He's William, only amplified by a few zeroes judging from the way Susan chose an outfit for me that wouldn't be out of place among the girls buzzing around the king.

"Michael!" Mary's hand takes to the air.

Raven hair like his mom's falls over his forehead as he looks our way. With fluid grace, his body lengthens. Tall like his dad, with the same long and lean muscles filling out his Adonis form, he strolls toward us. I can't help but think the bikinis around here are itty-bitty for more reasons than one. This full-grown man has a jawline that can cut glass as easily as it can break a heart.

He approaches with long, determined strides and I study the tattoo flowing from his shoulder. Two ropes of thick black liquid wind down his arm all the way to his wrist. From there, my eyes flit across his hips. His sculpted abs. To the place where a trail of hair starts below his belly button and disappears under the band of his board shorts. I look up from the blue fabric and meet his eyes. They're creamy caramel. His dad's emerald daggers must have diluted his mom's rich dark earth. "Shame."

I didn't mean to utter the word aloud, but Mary's creased brow and John's glare tell me I didn't keep a lid on how I feel about their son's eyes not matching his mom's. I pick at the hem of my camisole. "It's a shame I didn't bring a bathing suit. The pool looks nice, but I haven't even opened my luggage yet. Mom dragged me over here as soon I stepped foot on her property."

Mary sighs. "I see."

"I see, too." The sovereign one stops in front of me. "You have to be the new girl."

"This is Danielle," Mary answers for me.

"Dani," I correct. "My mom's the only one who calls me Danielle. I prefer Dani."

"Dani it is, then." He smiles. "Most people call me Mikey, but I'll answer to Michael when it's my mom yelling it." He winks at her. "Unless she's yelling it because she's mad at me."

"Good thing you're a perfect little angel." She pats his jaw. "Apparently, Dani just stepped off a plane and came straight to our door. Show her around and introduce her to your friends, then make sure she eats."

"You've got it." He grins, holding his hand out to me. "May I?"

My stomach somersaults and my teeth clench. Mary nudges me. "Go with him. And if you want to swim later, I might have a suit that will fit you. Just come find me whenever you're ready."

"Okay." I move forward but ignore Mikey's outstretched palm. He turns and I follow along beside him, running a nervous hand over my ponytail. It hangs halfway down my back but our pace is slow so there still isn't enough hair to keep fiddling with in an attempt to avoid speaking to him.

He glances at me. "Where did you transfer from?"

"Washington state." I keep my answer short.

"I've been camping there a few times. Pretty state."

I let his words hang in the air but he plows ahead with another question. "Do you have any siblings?"

"No." William is *not* my blood. I don't have to claim him.

"I have a younger sister. She's around here somewhere, and goes to our school. Sort of."

He's trying to bait me into conversation but I know how this works. I'm new, so he's feigning interest. Once the newness wears off, or if I say the wrong answer to his questions, I don't only get dumped, I get dumped on.

Putting two extra steps between me and his shirtless body, I plant my feet. "You can go back to your friends now. I'll mingle and meet everyone on my own."

His head tilts. "Are you sure? I can take you over to the girls." He points to the hot tub. "One of them might have an extra suit you can borrow so you don't have to wear one of my mom's."

I cross my arms. "I don't swim. And I'm *sure* I'm perfectly capable of walking around on my own. I can probably manage talking at the same time, too."

I see the green flecks in his eyes now. His gaze is as intense as his dad's when he's ruffled. I don't care. I stand my ground. His lips part and he waves his arm around with a dip of his head. "Make yourself at home and enjoy the rest of my party, Dani."

~6~

The grounds of the Beller estate are massive. I roam along the temporary fencing that's in place to mark the boundaries of how far partygoers are allowed to wander. While the confinement section is large, it isn't so big that it should be taking me this long to find Susan. Though she'd jump on the first chance to stray beyond the boundary, I doubt she'd climb over the fencing. Most of what lies beyond is all woods anyway, and there would have to be a whole pot of gold out there to make her walk into nature.

The party is segregated. Not too many adults are mingling with the teens, and the teenagers are doing their best to pretend their parents aren't here. It makes me wonder why the parents *are* here. I must have moved to the land of helicopter parents.

"Hello there." A bubbly blond woman waves to me from the corner of a table where she's sitting with seven other adults.

"Hello." I give her my most polite smile.

She smiles back. "I'm Kim. And you're Susan Madison's daughter, right?"

"Yes, ma'am." I wish Dad would have made Susan give up his last name.

Kim leaves her seat and stands very close to me. "Mary Beller is my best friend, and I'd hate for anyone to ruin her son's party."

I nod. "*Anyone* being my mother."

Her posture shifts and she rubs my arm. "Such a smart girl, you're going to fit right in at the academy. And what a cute little top you're wearing. I'll have to see if Mary carries anything like that in her store. Another place where just *anyone* isn't welcome."

I stand in place as Kim whips around and goes back to her table, the eyes of all the adults around her shifting between us. If the road between

22

here and Susan's wasn't narrow and curvy, or if it had a sidewalk, I'd leave. Then instead of giving me lame threats, they could do the job of hunting down Susan themselves.

My to-do list now has one more item. Get a driver's license.

Moving away from the adults, I continue my search, eyes floating to the hot tub where all the girls are standing and looking out toward the pool. I follow their gaze. Mikey Beller flips off the end of the diving board. He hits the water so smoothly that the surface hardly seems to ripple, his long form slipping under the water as if he's part of it. My stomach does a flip of its own and I look away. The sooner I find Susan, the better.

Ignoring the entire end of the party where my future peers are congregated, I move out across the part of the lawn where a stone path leads to a gazebo. The heads of six men are visible above the trellis, and one lone swath of blonde hair. When I was four, Susan used to ramble on about how much I looked like her. The plus-sized version of her. I hated the truth of it then just as much as I hate it now.

"Susan!" I call from just outside of where she's holding court. "It's time to go."

"Don't be silly." She slides between two of the men, making eyes at one and intentionally rubbing against the other. Her arm slips around my waist, her fingers clamping on my side and forcing me forward. "This is my daughter that I was telling you about. Danielle will be going to school with all of your handsome sons this year. And," she whispers conspiratorially, "she's single."

All of them begin sizing me up, and I'm not sure if it's for their sons or for them. What I do know is that it's creepy. I pry Susan's hand from my hip and cross my arms over my chest. "Are you coming, Susan? Or am I walking back to your house?"

She laughs. "See how funny she is? And these days I hear men like a girl with a sense of humor."

I glare at her. "Yeah, my age-appropriate boyfriend tells me every day how much he loves the way I make him laugh."

She shrugs. "Long-distance never works. You'll soon put that Washington boy behind you and choose a man from our fine Pennsylvania stock." She winks at the men in her private little circle. "Just like I'm doing."

It's impossible to penetrate her skull. I turn around and stomp back to the patio. If I survive walking the winding road without getting crunched by a car in a blind curve, it's no telling how long I'll have to sit outside and wait for her to get home. Once I leave, maybe the Bellers will kick her out.

My stomach growls as I pass by the food. I really don't want to help myself to the hospitality, but I'm starving. And if I'm going to be locked outside Susan's house for an undisclosed amount of time, I should probably eat.

While I attempt to decide if I should partake of food that clearly wasn't meant for my mother or me, I wander aimlessly along the shallow end of the pool. It's the neutral ground between the adults and the teens. The only other person in this zone is a girl who is also wearing shorts and a tank top instead of skimpy underwear masquerading as swimwear. I walk up beside her. "Mind if I sit with you?"

She looks up with a smile and scoots over even though there's plenty of room without her moving. "Go ahead."

I sit next to her and take off my shoes, dipping my feet into the cool water. "I know that smile. You must be Mary's daughter?"

She tucks a strand of copper-blonde hair behind her ear. "Everyone says I have her smile, so at least I got something from my mom."

"Take it from me, the less we get from our parents, the better."

"Uh-oh." She laughs. "Are you in the midst of teenage angst?"

No, I just resent the idea of being anything like my mom. And at this point, I don't even want to be anything like my dad. "Susan Madison is my mother. Everyone here seems to know and hate her, so go on, start judging me."

Her eyes go wide, then fall back to their normal size. "I was going to tease you but I don't actually know who Susan Madison is. I'm sure people don't hate her, though. At least my parents don't, or she wouldn't be here."

"Think again." I sigh, watching the ripples from where our feet gently move through the water. "If this is your house, it's your party, too. Why aren't you swimming?"

She stares at the crowded end of the pool, green eyes like her dad's watching the other kids. "I don't like to wear a swimsuit in front of them. I'm not built like the other girls."

I lean on my knees, looking toward where the girls are now out of the hot tub and sprawled out on loungers, the boys still vying for their attention while Mikey sits on the end of the lounger I first saw him on, reaping the adoration of all his court. "*They're* not built like them. Nose job. Boob job. Orthodontist bills that could have fed continents." I shrug. "I guess they're all right if you like the fake perfection look."

She kicks her toes out of the water. "The boys definitely like it."

"Boys?" I act shocked. "How old are you?"

She blushes. "I know I look twelve, but I'm fifteen."

She does look like she hasn't quite gone through puberty yet. But she isn't ugly. Her sharp features are the kind that grace magazine covers. Watching her head dip is like watching one of those modeling shows where all the girls are super insecure because in real life they get made fun of for being lanky and awkward, then the camera gets a hold of them and the world gasps. "I'm seventeen, and if it weren't for the boobs, boys wouldn't look at me either. So count yourself lucky. If and when yours sprout, you're going to miss the days when people used to look at your face."

Her head lowers even further. "Right now, they don't even look at my face."

I put my arm around her. "Trust me, they do. But I have a feeling that dad of yours probably has this entire state scared to breathe when they're near you. I'm not a boy and I'm half terrified to be sitting next to you."

She laughs. "Everyone is scared of Dad, but he's really nice."

"To you, maybe. But let a boy walk over here and see what happens." I lean in. "I'm pretty sure I heard him growl. Like actual throat-rumbling dog noise."

She giggles. "You probably did because he does that a lot, but he never does more."

"He doesn't need to." I shiver. "The sound is enough."

"Speaking of growling and being vocal," she pats my stomach, "your body is trying to tell you something."

"More like it's screaming that it's starved."

Her brow knits, head nodding toward the buffet. "We have food."

I swallow. "Yeah, but your parents only let Susan in because of me, and I feel weird about eating their food when I'm only here because…"

"Because?" she questions.

Because my dad is forcing me to live with Susan. "Because I'll be starting school with your brother on Monday. I don't know anyone here so it's just…weird."

She climbs to her feet and pulls me up with her. "I'm Lily. So now you know someone. And this someone orders you to go eat because you're also starting school with *me* on Monday and I don't want to be responsible for you starving to death before then."

Following my stomach to the buffet, I slip a plate off the stack and contemplate diving headfirst into the baked macaroni. It looks *and* smells like real cheese. Not the non-dairy imitations I keep telling Evette can't be cheese because by definition, cheese *is* dairy.

"You're allowed to come back more than once." Mikey pops up beside me, tossing a handful of almonds into his mouth and eyeballing my now overflowing plate.

I look him in the eye as I plop a scoop of macaroni overtop the sweet-and-sour meatballs. "Why have a buffet if you don't expect people to eat?"

Dimples crush his cheeks. "It's a test. You pass."

I turn away from his perfect face and glance toward the shallow end of the pool. Lily is gone. Just as well, it *is* her brother that I'm trying to get away from. She might be offended that I'm not fawning all over him.

There's zero chance that I'm going to sit at one of the already occupied tables, so I make a sharp right at the end of the buffet and move to the side of the patio where a stone wall rises just tall enough to sit on. I plant my backside firmly on the wall and dig into my food, starting with dessert. Or what I think is dessert. It's some kind of fluffy white cookie-looking thing with a dollop of what I think is lemon curd. I bite into it and close my eyes. It *is* lemon curd, and meringue that's chewy inside and melts in your mouth. *So* good.

"Pavlova." Mikey sits next to me, refusing to take my not-so-subtle hints. I stare at him. He points across the patio to the puff of white hair hanging on his dad's arm. "My dad's the baker in the family, but the one thing Grandma makes is pavlova." His caramel eyes scan the sugary pillow I'm biting into. "That's her recipe. Do you like it?" I nod, adding in an eye roll because it's obvious I was enjoying my dessert before he rudely interrupted. He chuckles. "Good, because I made those. I'm practicing for Christmas so I can have a bake-off with my dad."

"You win my vote." I stuff the rest of the treat into my mouth and go back to minding my own business.

His finger grazes along my lip. "You got a little something right there." I scoot away from his touch. His eyes narrow. "If you want to hang out with my sister, she's in her room. I saw her duck away and thought I'd let you know. I'll tell security to let you into that part of the house if you want. And I'll also get you a napkin if you'd rather not use my finger."

"Very funny." My stomach tenses. I was too worried about eating to bother with grabbing a napkin.

He holds his hand out to me. "My fingers don't mind. I'll keep them right here in case you need them."

I nudge him with my elbow just as Susan's voice scrapes over me. "Honey!" She pinches my cheek. Too hard. And then throws a smile to Mikey while her hand latches onto the edge of my plate. "You two are just adorable together. Why don't you go take a swim?"

"I'm eating." I stab a meatball with my fork, tugging the plate back toward me as she pulls it away.

Her nostrils flare. "You're finished, Danielle. Go let Mikey teach you a swimming stroke. He's quite the swimmer."

"I don't like water." I glower, not relinquishing control of my plate to her. She gives it a hard tug and I feel the edge slip from underneath my grip. My hand scrambles forward but it's too late. Susan's momentum pulls the plate upward, sending an avalanche of ooey-gooey goodness straight into her. Potato salad splatters across her chest and macaroni oozes down her torso. I plop the one meatball I managed to save into my mouth and use it to hide my smile.

Mikey doesn't attempt to hide his. Or the chuckle. "I'll get a towel."

He jogs off and Susan lowers her voice, the decibel vibrating straight through my skin and shaking its way down into my bones. "Get. Up."

I push myself off the wall and pick up the plate she dropped, beginning the process of shoveling the spilled food off the patio. Her hand clamps around my forearm and she drags me up to face her, words hissing through her clenched teeth. "You are an embarrassment."

I shrug. "Isn't this what you wanted? The two of us to be the center of attention?" I motion around us to the spectators who haven't yet gone back to their pre-food-spill activities.

She spins around, tugging me along in her death grip as she stomps across the patio. Mary meets us halfway to the door, her guard dog at her side as she extends a towel to Susan. "You're free to clean up in the guest bath. After that, you're free to leave." Her eyes flit to mine. "You're welcome to stay, Dani. We'll see to it that you get home safely."

I shake my head but don't launch a response as Susan lets go of me, ripping the towel from Mary's grip and lifting her chin. She waltzes out the front door. "Sorry," I mutter to the Beller's and follow Susan's trail. She's in the Porsche and it's already in motion. "Hey!" I bang on the passenger window. She slams her brakes and the door unlocks. "Thank you," I snap as I get inside.

"Why can't you just be normal?" she attacks. "Did you see any other girl in there stuffing her face like a pig?"

"Most of those girls probably have an eating disorder, and I don't know why you're mad at me when *you're* the one who spilled the food."

She slams the car into gear and speeds down the driveway. "Michael Beller *noticed* you. He singled you out among everyone else and all you could do was sit there stuffing your face like a fat little pig!" Her chest heaves. "I try to help you *again* after already dropping a gift in your lap and what do I get? Food spilled all over me by a selfish, ungrateful brat!"

She slows down to pass through the gate and I open my door. "Finally." She huffs. "Walk back up to that house and make sure the person who brings you home is Michael Beller. And don't you dare put one more thing in your mouth unless it's *him*."

Tears burn against my eyes. "The Bellers don't want us here!" I scream at her. "They don't want *you* here. And I'm guilty by association even though you wouldn't know me if you passed me on the street because *you're* the selfish one. You're a selfish, self-centered, nobody and I am *nothing* like you!"

Her eyes narrow. "Wait until I tell your father how you're speaking to me."

"Call him right now," I dare her. "I'll tell him exactly what I said to you, right after I tell him how you're trying to sell me to the highest bidder. He'll put me right back on a plane and bring me home, and I'll *never* have to see you again.

"Home?" Cold laughter flows from her lips. "Your house is *gone.* Sold. And your father is on his way to Europe as we speak. Didn't Daddy Dearest tell you?"

The hard glint in her eyes tells me what she's saying is true but I call her a liar nonetheless. Her lips curl into a smile. "William wanted to do his senior year in Paris, so their little family packed up and boarded a plane this morning. Right after they got rid of *you.*"

~8~

Normally, when I close my eyes at night, I relive the last time I saw Kira. Both dead and alive. I replay all of those moments over and over, willing my mind's eye to look beyond what I remember seeing, to where a strange man might have stood watching us, or a familiar one looked at us in a way he shouldn't have. Last night was different. I spent every waking hour trying to figure out exactly where I went so wrong that it made my dad stop wanting me. And when I closed my eyes, I dreamed of all the pictures William has been posting to his social media. Ones my dad looks really happy in.

I've had all of William's accounts blocked so I wouldn't accidentally hear anything from him. What I endured at home and school was bad enough. But now that I've purposefully trolled through his posts, I see everything so clearly. William is documenting his journey abroad. One he didn't even rub in my face that he was getting to go on. The three people I was living with were so covert that I never had a clue how far I was outside of their family.

Dad has never approved of my involvement in Kira's case. He never wanted me to so much as listen to a news report in the days following her death. When it came to the first sting operation I orchestrated, he nearly had a stroke. But as far as I know, I kept all the others well hidden. I even appeased him by joining the yearbook staff and volunteering for community service projects. And I never let my grades slip. If he ever found out exactly what I was doing to help law enforcement put an end to human beings who have no business walking among the rest of us, I didn't want him to view it as a hindrance to the regular parts of my life. But none of my efforts mattered. They were in vain because the real issue has always been that *I'm* not good enough to be his daughter. Same as I was never good enough to be Susan's.

31

Wiping steam off the bathroom mirror, I stare at my reflection. I feel like the same person I've always been, but so much has changed. I pick up my phone and dial. "Hey, Henry. It's Dani." Tears sting my eyes at the sound of his sleepy voice answering. "Sorry I'm calling so early, but…um, are you at our house?"

He sighs. "No, honey, I'm not. Your dad flew to London right after you left."

I swallow back the sobs. "So it's true, then? He sold the house and left?"

There's a long pause before he finally answers, the emotion in his voice ringing clear. "I didn't know what was happening. Not until after you left. I guess your dad knew I'd tell you about his plans, so he kept me in the dark, too."

Tears slide from my eyes. "I guess neither of us was good enough to take with him."

He clears his throat. "Your dad did ask me to go with him, Dani. I declined. I'm going to stay here and help my daughter out at her flower shop. She's been needing a delivery driver."

I lean against the sink, my tears dripping down into the bowl. "Dani," he whispers. "I don't know what's going on with your dad, but how he played all this out with you was wrong. I told him that when we parted ways."

I wipe my face. "Yeah, well, maybe if I would have stopped ditching you and making you hunt me down all the time, he would have treated me differently."

"Maybe." A soft chuckle drags from his lips. "I kind of liked having to figure out if I could find you or not. I'm going to miss that part the most."

I close my eyes. "I'm going to miss everything about you, Henry."

"Young lady," his voice cracks. "I'm going to miss everything about you, too. And I'm always here if you need me. Just a phone call away. You hear?"

"Yeah, I hear." I lower myself to the floor. "Bye, Henry."

Before he can hear what's coming, I hang up, emotion splintering bone and breaking skin as it explodes from my chest. Dad really did toss me out of his life. If I'd known, I would have been better. I would have forced myself to be someone else.

~

Puffy eyes on my first day as a senior in a new school is the least of my worries. Susan's attitude toward me hasn't changed and if it wasn't for the neighbor's poodle getting loose, I wouldn't have had a ride to school. Helping catch the big white fluffball prompted a conversation that led to the middle-aged couple asking if they could give me a lift on their way out. Since Susan was still in bed and showing no signs of getting up anytime soon, I took them up on the offer.

Unsure of where I should go, I enter the brightly lit halls of Virginia Williams Academy and step to the side of the door. My cried-out eyes sting under the force of the sun's rays as it spills through the rectangular windows lining the top of the corridor in front of me. One hundred yards ahead, this corridor intersects with another, their meeting place marked with plush seats that surround an atrium. Above the foliage is a glass dome where yet more sunlight filters into the building. It's beautiful, and much fancier than my last school. Wealth practically bleeds from the mural-decorated walls around me.

Hoisting my backpack onto my shoulder, I walk to the first set of doors on my right. There's a carved wood plaque above the door marking this as the administration office, and administration sounds like the place I need to report to first.

This office is as nice as the hallways outside. I silently applaud their use of solar lighting while forcing my lips to curl up into what I hope is a normal-looking smile as the mousy but fashion-forward woman at the desk greets me. "You must be Danielle Madison. I've been waiting for you."

"Yes, ma'am. And sorry if I'm late. I had…car trouble."

She adjusts her glasses. "Well, hopefully you get your car fixed. But you're not late yet. First bell is about to ring soon though, so let me grab your welcome packet."

She shuffles to her desk, picking up a folder but stopping to answer the phone before coming back to the counter. I look down at the marbled tiles and add getting a car to my list of things I need to do. Not that I'll be able to afford a car. I opened Susan's refrigerator door last night and she acted as if she'd have to mortgage her house in order to afford to feed me.

That means I need to feed myself, and I doubt she'll be offering to give me any spending money. Especially if she knows it's going toward food.

It's unlikely Susan would even pay me an allowance for doing chores. She's already told me that I'm responsible for cleaning up after myself because she's not paying her cleaning service any extra. I informed her that I'm not a slob, but I don't think she has the ability to hear anything I say. Unless what I have to say has to do with my willingness to throw myself at the feet of Michael Beller.

"This is your welcome packet. Your class assignments are here." The secretary, Mrs. Stilton according to the nameplate on her desk, hands me a blue and silver folder, opening it and tapping the top sheet of paper on the left. "A student aide will be here shortly to show you around and answer any questions. And our door here is always open so if you need anything, let us know."

"Thanks," I mutter, rubbing one sweaty hand against my blue jeans while using the other to tug the class assignments from the folder. There's a map of the school behind the list. I study it while I wait for the student aide.

"Hey, Dani." Mikey sidles up beside me, winking at Mrs. Stilton, whose cheeks are suddenly rosy and lips fully expanded into a wide smile.

The last thing I need this morning is his ridicule over what happened at his party. I slough my backpack off my shoulder and on the way down it manages to snag my gray t-shirt in its zipper.

Mikey looks across me to where I'm fighting my bag. "Need some help?"

"Nope." I yank the shirt free, putting a tiny hole in the hem. I dig into the bag and pull out the towel Susan took from his house. "Here. I was going to give this to Lily but I haven't seen her yet."

"Unless you get here early, you probably won't see her."

"Well some of us can't manage to be early," I snap unnecessarily. His caramel eyes narrow a fraction and I turn away from him, focusing back on the secretary and wishing I could just fade away. "There's a map in my packet so I don't need a guide, I'm sure I can manage on my own."

"This map?" Mikey plucks it from my folder. "I drew this freshman year. Some of the rooms have changed."

I snatch it back, stuffing it into the folder and tossing my backpack over my shoulder, ignoring the stupid smile on his face. "Like I said, I can manage on my own."

I spin toward the door, my escape blocked by a petite redhead wearing a yellow fifties-style dress that's cinched around her waist with a red leather belt. To complete her ensemble, there's a red scarf with yellow flecks tied in her hair. She thrusts out her hand. "Hi! You must be Dani. I'm Madge. I didn't get to introduce myself at Mikey's party." She nudges him, her bubblegum lips turned up to him. "I missed you this morning, handsome. Swim practice?"

He nods. "A few of the guys wanted some extra coaching. But Dani here doesn't like water and she also doesn't want a guide. She thinks the map in her packet will do a better job than you will of telling her everything she needs to know."

"Hardly." Madge quirks a brow like I'm a moron. "Do you want to be lost all day?"

I glare at him. He knows I only said no because I thought *he* was the guide, and the humor dancing over his face makes me want to unleash all the anger I've been feeling the last few days and smash it straight into his stupid dimples. His fingers slide behind the desk and pick up an old-school microphone. "Good morning, V.W.A!" He keeps eye contact as he begins morning announcements, making sure I'm fully aware of my mistake. His presence in this office has nothing to do with me.

~9~

Madge escorts me through the halls, her shiny flat shoes tapping over the tile as Mikey's voice fills the space around us. "Don't you just love listening to him?" She stares up dreamily. "That deep voice, and he's *so* cute."

I don't offer a response but she isn't deterred, announcing proudly, "I'm going to the winter formal with him."

"Congratulations," I reply.

She leans into my shoulder, lowering her voice. "He hasn't asked me yet, but he will. Just you wait and see."

I pull out my class assignments. My locker information is at the bottom and there's a bay of shiny black metal up ahead. I walk toward it, scanning the numbers and praying one of these is mine because if I wanted to talk about Michael Beller all day, I would have just stayed at Susan's. "I think this is me." I point to a top locker that's three in from the end.

She looks at my paper. "Lucky you. This one is Mikey's." She taps the first locker on the end of the row. It's a full, not half like all the rest. "Mine is all the way on the other end of the building. Want to trade?"

"Are we allowed to?"

Her shoulders lift. "The administration frowns on it, but who cares?"

"Me." I sigh, relieved when the bell rings even though I have no idea where my first class is. "I'm not looking for trouble, and I want to get to class now because walking in late makes the new kid even more of a spectacle."

She grins, fingering the freshly torn hole in my shirt. "Your cameo at Mikey's party made you a spectacle. And your outfit today leaves a little something to be desired. I have a sweater in my locker if you want to try to make yourself look better."

"I'm good in what I'm wearing, thanks."

She raises a brow and slips her hand onto my arm. "A girl who's confident enough not to care what the rest of us think? I like it."

"Good." I point to my locker. "I'm going to make sure my code works, and then I'm sure I can find my class. The school is basically a three-story 'x'."

Her hair swings over her shoulder. "A drab attitude to match your drab clothes. The building is designed like a plus sign, because we're extra."

"If that's what makes all of you feel better." I nudge around her and enter the code written on the paper into the keypad. Instead of a whole number set, there's only zero through four. The perks of being in a small private school. "How many students are in the academy?"

She rolls her eyes. "Too many. I can't wait to graduate and get out of here. I already have my college acceptance letter and I can't wait to move. My dorm is co-ed." She wiggles her brows. "I'll pledge a sorority, but first I want to live that dorm life."

"You do know there will be more people in college, right?"

She shrugs. "It won't be these people. I just wish Mikey would come with me. He's so stubborn sometimes."

I close the locker and begin to walk in the direction of where I think my first class is. Calculus. Madge is right in step with me so I offer the only advice I can think of. "All relationships have their problems. I'm sure you two will work it out before you leave."

"Doubtful." She groans. "Did you see how Taylor and Wendy were *all* over him at the pool party? I swear if those two get any thirstier, he's going to have to get a restraining order."

I pick up my pace. "Sounds like a problem you should discuss with your boyfriend. Especially if he isn't doing anything to dissuade them from crawling all over him."

My room number comes into view and relief floods through me. "See ya, Madge."

I stroll ahead of her and remove myself from the topic she's determined to harp on. Walking into the classroom, I hear him before I see him. "Dani!" Mikey calls out from the back of the room, tapping the seat next to his. "I saved a spot for you."

My face flushes, all eyes in the room are on me. There's an empty desk in the front right corner. I hurry across the open space and drop into the seat. The atmosphere around me goes deadly still. I have no doubt not a single person in this school would dare sit someplace other than where Mikey told them to, but they're soon going to learn that I don't care about stroking his ego.

~

As soon as calculus ends, I rush out the door, having already consulted my map to figure out the best route to my novels class. Mikey catches up to me, his long strides easy compared to my frantic dash. "I didn't know if you were going to make it to class."

"I'm not an idiot. I can read a map and a schedule."

"I wasn't implying that I thought you couldn't, Dani." His tone is flat. "I figured Madge would talk you into sneaking into the cafeteria with her. A local bakery delivers fresh pastries and she swears they're always stale by lunch." He stuffs his hands in his pockets. "She doesn't like to eat alone and you seemed to really like dessert the other day, so I thought you might be easily persuaded to go with her."

"You thought wrong." My stomach grumbles at the mention of food and I swear his mouth just twitched in amusement.

"So did Madge get you all straightened out, or do you want me to be your guide for the rest of the day?"

I halt my pace and turn toward him. "What I want is for you to stop talking to me. Why is that so hard for you to understand?"

He removes his hands from his pockets and holds them up in front of him. "Sorry for trying to be welcoming. I'll stand right here while you leave so I don't accidentally feel compelled to speak to you again."

"Thank you," I snap, turning back around and continuing on my path.

In my novels class, I sit in the back corner. Half the seats are still open and I hold my breath, praying Mikey doesn't show up. If he does, surely he won't sit in one of the empty seats next to mine.

"Dani!" A voice crawls across my skin. But it isn't Mikey's, these deep tones belong to a boy with nearly golden eyes and natural curl to his dark hair. He struts toward me, as tall as Mikey and just as chiseled, but my stomach doesn't flip when I look at him.

He plops down next to me with a grin spread over his perfect teeth. I recall seeing him at the pool party, he was sitting on the lounger next to Mikey's. "I didn't get to talk to you at the party the other day, but Mikey said I should holler at you."

My gut sinks. "You always do everything he tells you to do?"

"Yep." He chuckles. "He and I roll like that. More like brothers than besties."

"How cute." I give him a patronizing smile. "Do you have matching bracelets and carry part of each other's hearts around, too?"

"Yes to the hearts, no to the bracelets." He grins. "I like you, girl. And that's a good thing. Because we have a lot of classes together."

"How do you know?"

He makes a show of tapping his heart, wiggling his eyebrows at me. I have no idea what that's supposed to mean so I pretend to organize the papers in the welcome packet so I'll have something in my hands. Books are being assigned this week and I'll feel better when I have a wall of them in front of me.

My neighbor leans his arms onto my desk. "I'm Angelo."

I motion for him to remove his arms. "Angelo, since we're going to have a lot of classes together, let's make a deal. You don't invade my personal space *or* bring up Michael Beller anymore, and I won't stab you in the neck with this pencil. Okay?"

~10~

Angelo wasn't lying. He's in all but my calculus class, and constantly talks about Mikey just to annoy me. On the bright side, Mikey hasn't attempted to speak to me since our encounter this morning. Madge has, and some of it actually had nothing to do with her boy toy.

I wouldn't have bothered to speak to Angelo or Madge if it wasn't for the hot tub girls who were in my classes in varying numbers, and somehow trolling me in the halls just to keep making loud jokes about my food faux pas with Susan. Angelo was always kind enough to shut them down and Madge engaged, which also succeeded in making them stop. While I don't relish letting someone else fight my battles, I'm too tired to engage a bunch of dimwitted girls.

Trudging outside the school after the longest first day in history, I take my phone from my backpack. I have no idea if Susan is picking me up or how she expects me to make it back to her place if she doesn't.

On my screen, there's a message from Dad. *Hang in there, kiddo.* Four words. That's all he bothered with after the pages of messages and the voicemails I left him last night. I delete the message, an ache soaking deep into my chest. He boiled my whole life down into those four single words.

Is someone picking me up? I text Susan.

Figure it out. She manages to dismiss me with even fewer words than Dad.

Tears straining against the barrier I put in place, I walk down the street away from the school. If I look like I have someplace to go, maybe no one will realize how miserably untrue that optic is.

A block away from the school, I send Susan another message. *While I'm figuring it out, I'll try to avoid being raped and murdered. I know how you'd hate to be inconvenienced.*

40

At this point, I have nothing to lose. Nothing to hold onto. No reason to be nice to her and certainly no reason to rush back to her house. According to the map on my phone, the one I'm surprised Dad hasn't cut off yet, Harper Road is the center of this town's universe. All the shops and eateries feather out from there. I set the map for a walking route and take off on the course it directs. I'll reach the heart of town in three hours and twelve minutes.

~

Forty-five minutes into my walk, I stumble upon a public bus stop. Two men and one woman are standing at the curb, a bus lumbering to a stop in front of them. It's times like these that I realize decisions made in anger are rarely good ones. I wish I hadn't spent the bulk of my life savings on a plane ticket. I should have been more frugal. More normal. Less prone to spend money on burner phones, too.

I've never actually been on public transportation before. I've never had a reason to be. Up until recently, I lived where everything I needed was within a two-mile radius and where there were ample sidewalks.

Standing in line behind the others, I watch as each one of them slides a ticket into a little slot. I dig in my pocket for the change I received after buying one of those pastries from the school cafeteria. I took my goody into the library and tucked into a quiet corner, eating my sugary lunch alone.

"On or off, honey?" the bus driver calls, her sunny face trained on me.

"I'm going to Harper Road. Does this bus run downtown?"

"Yep." She waves me forward.

I climb the two steps, glancing back at the annoyed faces of the other riders. I jiggle my change and meet the driver's gaze. "How much does it cost to ride?"

Her head tilts. "You're not from around here, are you?"

"No, ma'am. I just moved here from Washington state."

She chuckles. "You came all that way just to ride on my bus? Well then today, your ride is on me." She slips a card into the slot and winks at me. "Go on back and find you a seat."

I do as she says and make my way to the back of the bus where four seats are arranged as a bench seat. One lady got off the bus when it stopped and she exited via the second door that's back here. I assume when it's my stop, I should get off through this same door.

"Where you headed to?" a man on the far side of the bench asks.

I shrug. "Nowhere in particular."

He points at my backpack. "Did you just come from school?"

The hair on my neck raises. There's a fine line between being polite and divulging too much information to a predator. I meet his eyes, committing each line of his face to memory. "I'm coming from the place I came from, and going where I'm going. How about you?"

His hand comes up, patting the air as if to tell me to calm down. "Just trying to make conversation."

I scoot a little closer to my side of the bus and wait two stops after his exit before I wave to the bus driver and step out onto the sidewalk. The creepy man from the back row went left when he got off. I turn right.

Though miserable and practically homeless, I'm taken with the beauty of this town. The buildings are mostly interconnected and the sidewalks are wide, benches and shaded tables conveniently spaced and inviting. I make my way along the streets, stomach growling when I pass by restaurants. There's a street vendor up ahead. I might be able to afford something from there.

Standing far enough away to peruse the menu without being in the customer line, my eyes keep diverting to the building across the street. Scoopz is the name of the ice cream shop and there's a hand-painted platter of ice cream treats stretching across the front window. I need real food, but I also need something comforting, and there's nothing better to soothe a soul than ice cream.

Ditching the sidewalk, I dart through the nearest crosswalk and enter Scoopz. Proving that decisions made in hunger are also rarely good ones.

"Step right up," a boy calls from the counter, his honey-colored hair long enough that his bangs half cover his eyes. He's pop-star cute. Not remotely my type, though I've never really considered having a type until Mikey Beller and his perfect face stood in front of me.

I walk to the counter, looking at the many items displayed on the menu. "Um, I'll just have a small cone, plain."

The boy leans on the counter. "What flavor?"

I shrug. "Any. I'm not picky when it comes to ice cream."

"A girl after my own heart." He winks, straightening. "But if you like ice cream, you can't just have a plain cone. Let me make you something special."

I bite the inside of my lip. "No thanks, I'm kind of on a tight budget so just a plain cone, please. Small."

He pulls a large sugar cone from the case. "We're having a special today, pretty girls eat free."

I raise a brow. "And who decides what constitutes *pretty*? Inappropriate boys?"

He grins. "Yep. And this one has just the treat for you."

I was going to walk out, but then he dipped the cone in chocolate and my feet wouldn't get on board with leaving. More of my body decided to stay as he piled two scoops of ice cream into the cone and hit the whole thing with strawberry glaze. He watched my face as he drizzled chocolate over his creation.

"You're going to want a spoon for this." He sticks one into the dessert and hands me the cone. "That's a coconut vanilla bean ice cream with strawberry chunks mixed in, and the glaze brings out the strawberry flavor even more."

My mouth waters. "How much do I owe you?"

"Nothing." He hands me a napkin, waving at some kids filtering into the shop behind me. "Come back and see me some time. This after-school rush will die down in a couple of hours and I'll be free."

My cheeks heat up, the noise in the shop increasing as yet more teens fill the space around me, calling ice cream boy Zach and shouting out their orders. I recognize some of these kids from the academy. Zach's attention draws away from me and I take this opportunity to ditch the shop without having to reply to Zach's invitation. Either the people in this town are overly nice, or the boys here are severely in want of fresh meat. My money, the little of it I have, is on the latter.

~11~

An ornamental white church sits on a corner not far from Scoopz. I take up residence on a bench in front of the elegant building and begin devouring what's likely to be my dinner. As the ice cream slides deliciously down my throat, I stick the toe of my shoe into the kaleidoscope of colors from the stained-glass windows that are playing across the ground beneath my feet.

"Let me guess…coconut ice cream with strawberry glaze and loads of chocolate drizzle?" Mikey slides onto the bench next to me.

My stomach drops. "Did you follow me?"

Dimples roll over his cheeks. "My cousin works at Scoopz. I just dropped by there to see if he needed any help with his after-school rush and he told me this really hot girl he's never seen before skipped out on him without him getting the chance to ask her name. Even before I saw you sitting here with the cone, I thought you were probably the girl. But don't worry, I didn't tell him about my suspicion, so your identity is safe."

Cute guy explained. I should have known they'd be related. "Inform your cousin that if the unknown girl hears him talking about any of his female customers' physical appearance again, I'll have no choice but to report him to management."

Mikey leans on his knees. "Zach doesn't just work at Scoopz, he owns it. But I'm sure he'll be fair in reprimanding himself."

I roll my eyes. "He might manage the shop but he doesn't own it. He can't be any older than me."

"He's sixteen," Mikey answers. "My aunt and uncle homeschool their kids and encourage a creative drive, so all of my cousins have some form of business. Zach's brainchild was the ice cream shop, and he's been

44

open more than two years now." He looks at the mixture melting down my hand. "He works hard to keep Scoopz successful, but I don't doubt that his motives in opening an ice cream café had something to do with luring girls into his web."

I don't say anything. He sits up, stretching his arm across the back of the bench. "I'm kidding, Dani. Zach did get pretty excited telling me about you, but he's usually not so animated. He just went through a breakup with a girl he's been dating for several years, so he's casting nets and figuring things out."

"Don't worry," I groan. "I wasn't feeling special. You don't have to hammer in that Zach is having a crisis."

His hand moves over my shoulder, his eyes locked on mine, searching for my reaction to his touch. "You like dessert, you don't like water, you're prone to overreacting, and you're most definitely special." He stands. "See you around, Dani. Maybe over ice cream?" He walks backward toward the street. "Before you say no and yell at me for continuing to bother you, just think about it. Me, you, and a private after-hours tour of Scoopz."

I clench my fist as he jogs across the street. *No.* I internally scream at the giddy butterflies yearning to gush from my depths. Boys like Mikey know exactly how to make a teenage girl crush, and I refuse to be his next conquest. He and Zach can shove their free ice cream.

Trashing the cone, I walk in the opposite direction that Mikey went. I'm so sick of not being able to get away from the Beller family. If I'm not seeing one of them, I'm hearing about them, and I've had enough of it to last a lifetime.

~

Huntington's library isn't as nice as what I'm accustomed to, and it's a shame because everything else in town feels modern and updated despite the age of the architecture. The library is still using old computers and while they do have an online presence, the website isn't user-friendly. It kept timing out whenever I tried to search their catalog for the books I'd checked out before being forced to move here. I really hope Dad had the good sense to return those.

My phone pings and I tug it from my bag, expecting it to be Susan growing a conscience. *You look so good. What I wouldn't give to have your mouth on me.* I drop the phone onto the table in front of me. It pings again. This time a photo of me scrawls across the screen. From just now, when I was on the bench craning my mouth wide to get a full bite of the ice cream.

"You dirtbag." I pick up my phone, shocked at the audacity of Michael Beller. *I don't overreact, you're just a jerk. Stay away from me.*

Life in this town is going to be harder than I thought. I text Susan. *Do you think you can be bothered to pick me up from the library? Now. Before it's pitch black outside and the place closes.*

Surprisingly, she answers. *You're lucky I'm already out in town. I'll be there in half an hour.*

I click her message away. There's no sense in pointing out that she has a parental obligation to come get me; she's coming, and that's good enough. While I wait, I poke around on the internet until I manage to find the public bus routes and the prices. It's not very expensive and technically I have enough money to buy a monthly unlimited pass, but then I won't have enough money to eat on. I need to get a job.

The phone pings again and I cringe. Susan better not be backing out on picking me up.

It's another photo of me with the white church silhouetted behind me, my tongue enjoying a big spoonful of ice cream. *I always liked watching you and Kira lick your cones, it made it so hard to decide which flavor of little girl I would like best.*

~12~

I had a panic attack last night. Not the worst one I've had but far worse than I've had in two years. It took everything I had to keep a semblance of composure as I left the library, scared to walk outside on my own until I knew Susan was there, and afraid to fall apart in front of her. Alone in my room, I fought the stampede of fear until I had nothing left to fight with.

This morning I came up empty when I tried to find out who sent me those pictures. Even if the messages came from a burner phone, there's one thing I know—Kira's killer is in Huntington. And he messaged me because he *wants* me to know that.

He could be the man from the bus yesterday, or any number of people I passed on the sidewalk. He could be living right next door to me or teaching in Virginia Williams Academy. I could have bumped into him accidentally or he could have followed me here. Not knowing is terrifying.

I knock on Susan's door for the tenth time. I'm going to be late for my second day of school if she doesn't get up, and I haven't seen the poodle running loose next door. Not that I'm confident enough to take a ride from the couple this morning. What if the woman decided she didn't need to go out and the man is Kira's killer? He could abduct me and no one would even know I was gone. I'd never be reported missing, at least not in a timely fashion by either of my parents, so killing me is almost the perfect crime. All he has to do is not leave any DNA, the same way he didn't leave any on Kira. "Susan!" I knock harder.

"Go away!" she shouts back. "I need to sleep. I'll take you to school when I get up."

"By then school will be over!"

I storm away from her door, hand clutching my chest, breath coming out shallow and tight. The public bus doesn't run nearby and even if it did, there's a killer out there. One who is watching me.

On the other side of my fate coin is the fact that if I don't go to school, my grades will slip and Dad won't pay for my college. So if I stay here to avoid the killer, I might as well be dead.

Opening Susan's front door, I slowly move outside, eyes darting around my surroundings. Everything seems quiet down here at our end of the street. Clutching my phone so I can at least attempt to call the police if someone grabs me, I trudge out to the sidewalk, scanning all around me and occasionally looking back to be sure I'm not being followed.

I should be happy that Kira's killer is stalking me. Catching him is what I've always wanted and using myself as bait has crossed my mind at least twenty-five thousand times. Only I was always safe in those scenarios, the one calling the shots and stalking *him*. Not this.

"Hey, Dani." I freeze as a car pulls up behind me. I can see the gates of the community from here. Where there are people. I could make it there, unless this car decides to drive on the sidewalk.

Turning slowly, the voice registering in my brain as not only familiar, but female, I'm flooded with relief. "Hey, Madge."

She eyes my backpack. "Are you going to school?"

"Yeah, I'll be there in a few hours."

She laughs, unlocking her door. "Get in."

I slide onto her sedan's leather seat and tuck my backpack between my feet. "Thanks. I wasn't looking forward to becoming roadkill."

She pulls away from the curb, eyes darting between me and the road. "You weren't really going to walk all the way to the academy, right?"

I sigh. "I don't have a driver's license *or* a car, and Susan doesn't get out of bed this early so yeah, I was going to give walking a shot."

Her eyes bug out as she hits the gas. "Just call me if you need a ride. I live over in the original part of the neighborhood, where the homes are older but the lots are larger."

"I'll have to check it out sometime. I haven't been too far beyond Susan's at this point."

"Why do you call your mom by her first name?"

I shrug. "I've never been around her enough to consider her a mom, she's basically just my dad's ex-wife."

She grins at me. "Well, you better plan on being with her a while because I was at Scoopz last night and Zach couldn't stop asking about you."

I shrink down in the seat. "His ice cream is good, but I'm not interested in him."

"Too bad." She smacks her lips. "Lauren was there, too, and she has a huge crush on Zach so she was *livid*. She recounted your whole food spill situation for everyone in Scoopz, and that led to some internet searches. The Bunny Clique is out to get you."

"Wait, what?" My blood runs cold. The girls she's referring to are the same girls I had problems with yesterday. The same ones from the hot tub. "What internet searches? And did they text me last night?"

Her shoulders bob. "It wouldn't surprise me. They've done that to me before, trying to bully me. And once they were actually dumb enough to text me as if it was Mikey. Like I don't know his phone number and can't tell you what he's going to say before he even says it."

I don't want to get caught in any teenage drama, especially over boys. I also don't want to be so foolish as to think a murderer contacted me after all these years. Would an internet search on me somehow connect to Kira's murder? "This Bunny Clique, I'm pretty sure I know who they are, but can you point them out to me today so I don't miss one?"

"Yep. They're all the girls at my lunch table so just come eat with me and you'll get to evil eye every one of them."

"And you eat lunch with them because?"

She shrugs. "They're bunnies. Where Mikey goes, they go. And if he isn't around, they hop after Angelo and just keep jumping down the line of boys until someone pets their furry little thirsty heads."

"But you're Mikey's girlfriend, right? Out of respect for you, shouldn't *he* stop them from chasing after him?"

She waves off the comment. "We don't do labels. He can do what he wants with them because in the end I know I'll always be the one he comes back to."

I sit quietly, my interaction with him on the church bench yesterday turning those would-be butterflies into a bubbling cauldron of poison. I let him affect me and even at my lowest point last night, I couldn't shake his face in my mind's eye. When it jumped from images of Kira's death to his dimpled face, a dose of stillness would sprinkle over my sorrowful state and calm my fear. Now it's acid in my veins.

"Madge, do you know of anywhere around here that's hiring?"

"Like for a job?"

"A paying one. If I'm going to take rides from you, I'll help buy your gas."

She signals and cuts in front of a car to turn into the school parking lot. "I don't need gas money but if you're looking for extra cash, Mikey and Ang detail cars at a dealership. I drop by sometimes and watch. Always seems like they could use another set of hands. Not *my* perfectly manicured hands." She wiggles her fingers at me. "But your chipped nails might do."

Working in close proximity to Mikey Beller is a huge no. "I doubt I'd be able to do a job like that. I was thinking more along the lines of working in one of the shops in town."

"Oh!" Her face lights up as we get out of her car and head toward the academy entrance. "I bet Zach would give you a job. Lauren would be so ticked off. It's perfect!"

"I'm not interested in having drama with your Bunny Clique. I just want to get through this year and move on with my life."

I part ways with her as we enter the school, avoiding my own locker bay so I don't have to chance running into her unlabeled boyfriend.

Sitting in the front right corner of my calculus class, I watch the clock, praying the seats around me will fill up before Mikey gets here. They do, and I relax into my seat. "Good morning." Mikey leans his hands on my desk, his forearms flexing as his head dips down. "I can't decide how I best like your lips. With or without the chocolate sauce."

My eyes snap up but he's gone, his arm brushing against mine as he moves past me to take his seat in the back of the class. I flash back to the library mirror that told me I'd made a mess with my ice cream and still had chocolate on the corner of my mouth. Mikey saw it and didn't tell me. I turn around and look at him. He's in his seat now, watching me. He winks. I face forward. There's absolutely no chance I'm eating lunch with Madge, I'd be embarrassed to have nothing but one little measly muffin anyway. The instant we walked into the school I could smell fresh bread baking and if the halls hadn't been loud, everyone in here would know how hungry I am.

$$\sim 13\sim$$

I walk the streets of Huntington with much more caution today than yesterday. The public bus driver, whose name is Sally, had me sit behind her so we could chat while she drove. That made me worry about the man who was in the back of the bus yesterday but when I asked her about him, she said he was a distant cousin of hers and had lived around here all his life. I asked about trips he might have taken but she laughed at the thought that he would have enough money to travel to the next county, let alone out of the state.

Sally's information doesn't entirely rule out her distant cousin, but he also doesn't fit the profile I've been developing for Kira's murderer. The person who took her blended into my old lake community. He could have been a laborer of some sort, but my gut tells me he lived there. Or knew someone who did.

If yesterday's messages were actually from the killer and not catty teenage girls, they confirm another thing I've felt sure of—the monster was watching us long before he grabbed Kira.

Moving slowly along the sidewalk, I scan the face of each passing male, looking for an inkling of recognition. It's hard to say how old the man would be now. His crime against Kira was so fast and clean that it makes me think he was older. Seasoned. An old pro at the atrocities he inflicted. But how old? How seasoned? All the questions I read books to answer because I don't know how someone took my friend right out from under everyone's noses. Kira didn't fit the typical profile of a neglected child or one from a low-income neighborhood where crimes against children are statistically higher. Her killer chose prey that was harder to get to, and I need to understand the psychology of a predator who goes after the difficult victims.

I also need a job, and in the bottom left corner of the window display in front of me, there's a help wanted sign. The lacquered wooden board is partially tucked into a layer of fabric, not exactly prominent, but it is on theme with the rest of the cozy display so it might only be a prop. I move closer to the glass, studying the rustic country vibe of the furniture positioned atop a woolly white rug. Wooden gameboards sit between small round tables. Outfits, jewelry, and shoes are highlighted among the furniture. Without mannequins, the display still makes you feel like you're watching a family at play on game night.

I peer past the window display and into the heart of the store. Men's and women's clothing intermingles with furniture, armoires serving as racks while coffee tables are adorned with accessories. There's even a children's section with shoes displayed on large wooden blocks. It's cute, and probably not a place murderers shop.

I'm met with a delicate mix of scents when I open the door. Sweet like cherries but perfumed like dozens of bouquets of deep-red roses. A middle-aged woman with short dark hair and smile lines permanently creased into her cheeks approaches me. "Hello. Can I help you find anything in particular?"

I point at the window behind me. "I'm here about the job? There's a sign in the window."

She looks me over, taking in my ripped jeans and sneakers. "We don't really carry your style here. You might be happier someplace else."

I take a deep breath. "I'm not trying to get a job that gives me a clothing discount, I'm looking for one that pays. And I didn't intend to apply for a job today or I would have dressed differently. I just got out of school and happened to be walking by, and I thought I'd check to see if that sign is real."

She stares at me. "Where do you go to school?"

"Virginia Williams Academy."

Her arms fold, mouth turning down. "Uh-huh. And you just happened to stumble in here wanting a job."

Her words are a statement, not a question. I adjust my backpack strap. "I'm sure I don't look like I belong in that school any more than I belong working here, and probably I don't actually belong at the academy, but I have better clothes I can wear to meet whatever is required for this job. And I swear I shower every day, even though I'm sure I don't look like I do that either."

Her lips hitch. "So you just walked down the street and saw the sign? No other reason to walk through those doors?"

I hesitate. Something about her demeanor is off. "No other reason than being strapped for cash. So if the sign is real and not a prop, I can start today. Like, right this very second."

She laughs. "Go on up to the counter and tell Davina to give you an application. We'll start with that."

~

I sit in the corner of Carpenter's Boutique on a stool meant for those trying on shoes. Behind me is a glass wall that allows shoppers in this store to see into the woodworking shop where the furniture sold here is made. It's pretty cool, and now the name of the place makes perfect sense.

Davina is middle-aged, same as Pam, who Davina informed me is the store manager. Despite my age, I'm hoping Pam's willingness to give me this application is a sign that I made a decent enough impression to actually be considered for the job. The boutique has clothes and shoes for all ages and while the Bunny Clique might not find anything skimpy enough for themselves in here, someone like me could shop here. Not that I have enough fashion sense to pull an outfit together. Hopefully, that skill isn't necessary in this job, or it's one that can be learned.

I approach the counter, heart stopping as the door behind the counter opens and John and Mary Beller walk in, hand in hand. The application slips from my fingers and floats to the floor, the words of the short blonde woman at the pool party crashing into my ears. She mentioned Mary having a store.

"I'm sorry," I mutter.

"For what?" Mary asks.

Pam points at the application in the floor. "She came in looking for a job but she didn't mention she knew you. Said she *happened* on the sign and decided on a whim to come and apply."

My mouth goes dry. Now I know what Pam's earlier questions were about. "I didn't know this was Mrs. Beller's store. If I did, I wouldn't have come in here." I meet the thin line of Mary's lips, her husband's demeanor mimicking hers. "I honestly had no idea who owned this place. I just thought the window display was cute, and then I saw the help wanted sign."

"Dani, where is your mother?" Mary asks.

I lower to the floor and scoop up the useless application. "I don't see her much so I don't know what she does all day."

Her head tilts. "Then how did you get here?"

I shift my weight. Might as well be honest with these people; John looks like he can sniff out a lie a mile away. "I walked to the bus stop after school and rode it into town."

"What bus stop?" he asks.

"The public one," I answer, ignoring the shock crossing their faces.

"That's nowhere close to our school." Mikey strolls out the same door his parents came out of, sidling up to his dad's shoulder and adopting the man's posture. "I thought Madge was giving you a ride."

I hold tight to the strap of my backpack. "I rode *to* school with her, but then I figured she had better things to do than run me all over town so I took the bus here *from* school." I ignore the narrowed eyes of his parents. If he doesn't want me to be flippant with him, he should leave me alone the way I asked him to.

"Look, obviously you're not hiring me because of whatever it is that Susan did to get under your skin, so I'm just going to go and we can all forget I was ever here. Shouldn't be hard."

I crumple the application but Mikey plucks the ball from my fist. "I'll add you to the schedule, Dani, and *personally* show you the ropes."

"You're not *personally* showing her anything," John bites.

"Fine." Mikey winks at me. "Pam can train her. I'll just supervise."

"*If* she's hired it will be *me* who hires her," Mary snaps at her son. "Dani, if you rode the bus here, how are you getting home?"

"Car service," I lie, hoping John doesn't call me out.

Mikey nudges his dad. "Cool your jets, big guy. I already asked her out and she said no."

Air rushes from my lungs. "I did not!"

He smiles. "Then we're going on an ice cream date?"

My gut rolls. After yesterday's texts, even if they do happen to be from one of the bunnies, I don't think I can ever eat ice cream again. I spin on my heel and rush out the door. "Dani!" Mikey calls from behind me. I push my feet into a run, dodging through people and making a hard left down an alley. I run until I hit the street on the other side and duck into the first store. It's a kitchen store, with big shiny pans and lots of knives. I walk as casually as possible to the back of the store and pretend to look at cheese graters while watching the windows out front. If anyone comes after me, I hope it's Mikey and not a murderer.

~14~

If there's anything good in my life at this moment, it's the fact that my dad's credit card is still active on the app I used to call for a car, making the one lie I told to John Beller not a lie at all. Not that it matters. I'm sure his whole family is having a big laugh over how much of a weirdo I am.

I feel like I've been hanging on by a thread these past few days, and now that thread is frayed. "Susan?" I call out as I enter her house. There's a Mercedes parked in her driveway, so she either has company or bought a new car. Either way, since I'm home much earlier than I was yesterday, giving her a heads-up that I'm here seems like the right thing to do.

She doesn't answer and the soft music playing in the background makes me think she might be up in her room with whoever drives that new car. As gross as that is, my stomach is going to take advantage of this situation. If Susan notices the missing food, I'll tell her to add it to my tab and I'll reimburse her after I find a job. Maybe she has connections that can help me find something that doesn't require me taking my clothes off for money.

I pass through the living room to be sure she isn't in there and cross to where the space opens to the dining room. Beyond that is the coveted kitchen where an unfortunate pantry is stocked with rice cakes. I step around the corner and slam a hand over my eyes. A half-dressed Susan is on the table with a disheveled man enjoying a meal that did *not* come out of that pantry.

"Danielle!" she screeches.

I retreat to the stairs, dashing up to my room and slamming the door. Of all the horrible visuals I harbor in my head, I didn't need that one.

It's no wonder I'm messed up. Even without the trauma of what happened to Kira, I was bound to have mental problems.

Digging through my backpack, I find the packet of crackers I snatched from the trash in novels class. The can was beside my desk and I stared at the unopened crackers the whole time. When the bell rang, I pretended to trip and drop my notebook into the can, retrieving it *and* the crackers, and stuffing everything into my bag before the person who threw these delicious fake cheese crackers away noticed they were now in my possession.

"Danielle." Susan throws my door open. "Did your father not teach you any manners?"

"Me?" I huff. "You're the one who was sprawled all over the table. They make bedrooms for that sort of thing."

"I was entertaining a guest in the privacy of my own home, and I don't need permission from *you* to do so."

"Forgive me for thinking it was safe to walk into a common space in the house I'm supposed to be living in."

"Well, I hope you learned your lesson." She snatches the crackers. "You'd be so pretty if you'd just lose fifteen pounds."

~

Tonight's nightmare was the same as what I've always had. Kira crying and screaming for her life, trying to get free of the man attacking her. In every dream, I run toward her screams. In every dream, I'm always too late.

Tonight, there was a twist at the end. The monster was still there when I reached Kira, the shirt around her neck balled tightly in his fist as he strangled the life from her. I lunged for him but he turned a second before my hand clamped over his shoulder, the blade of his knife sinking deep into my stomach.

I press my nails into my palms, focusing on the present pain. The *real* pain. *One. Two. Three.* I inhale fully, my rib cage expanding as I stare at the ceiling, doing everything I can to drag air back into my lungs. *Four. Five. Six.* My body shakes, lungs fighting the air I'm trying to force into them. Even with all the therapists I've seen over the years, I've never found a better way to calm myself. All I can do is count, and inflict enough pain to give my brain something else to focus on.

~

I'm not sure how much time has passed. I only ever count to ten and then start the process all over again. But I've been lying in this bed long enough for the sheets to be soaked in sweat. Crawling off the side, I wash my face in the bathroom and then chance tiptoeing downstairs. I'm sure the stabbing from my dream was a subconscious jab of hunger.

As quietly as possible, I open the pantry. Surely Susan doesn't keep a head count on her nonperishables. "Danielle?" A man's voice whispers from behind me. I freeze. A light flips on above the bar. "It's me. Randall. Your mom's…boyfriend. We didn't get to formally meet earlier."

Slowly, I release the jar of peanut butter and turn to face him. He smiles, pointing at his ham sandwich. "Looks like we both had the same idea."

The muscles in my stomach spasm. "Why were you sitting in the dark?"

He looks down at his plate, as if that makes it seem like he didn't hear the sound of my hunger. His sandwich is piled high with ham, and the mayo and tomato smear the plate where he's already eaten half of it. "I didn't know if you were a light sleeper so I was trying to be quiet down here. I figured I'd done enough damage to you with my earlier behavior."

"A light being on a whole floor below me isn't going to wake me up."

He clears his throat. "Yeah, I guess I preferred to sit here in the dark. I needed to think about… I'm really sorry about earlier. Your mom didn't mention you." I raise a brow. He blushes. "I mean, she didn't mention you'd be home."

I grab the peanut butter. "I'm sure you said it right the first time. She didn't bother to mention she has a kid, or that said kid lives here." I shake the jar at him, pulling a spoon from the dishwasher. "I'm taking this. If Susan flips out, tell her I promise to replace it."

A soft smile lights his face. "I'm sure she won't mind."

"Then you really don't know her very well."

I move past him and the legs of his chair scratch over the floor. "I've been dating her for a few months so that…what you saw earlier…I wasn't just here doing…"

I slow my pace and take a long, steady breath before turning back to face him. "I'm not Susan's keeper, or yours, so I don't need the details.

Just keep your clothes on while you're outside her bedroom and encourage her to do the same."

He nods, a hand reaching over his head to rub the back of it. "She said you could use a ride to school in the morning. I'll be here and leaving for work about the same time, so I'm happy to take you."

The translation is that Susan complained about me bugging her for a ride. "A friend is picking me up, but thanks anyway." I turn back around and begin to walk, looking back at him over my shoulder. "My name is Dani, not Danielle."

~15~

I'm named after my dad. He's Daniel and goes by Dan, I'm Danielle and prefer to be called Dani. Mainly because Susan hates it. When she was still married to Dad, she'd blow a gasket every time he shortened my name. She wanted a perfect little girl with a proper female name, and her behavior instilled in me a repulsion for all things that even come close to molding me into her idea of what a female is.

Maybe that's why I'm a natural early riser. It's the opposite of what Susan is. But Randall isn't like her—even though I told him I don't need a ride, he's up and waiting for me at the bottom of the stairs with a bagel. "I hope you like cream cheese." He hands it to me. "I wrapped it so you can take it to go if you need to."

"Thanks." I take the food from him. "If I eat this and Susan yells at me for it, I'm saying you forced me."

His nose scrunches. "Why would your mom yell at you for eating a bagel?"

I place my hand on his shoulder. "You really don't know her at all, do you?"

His cheeks redden. "Things between us are getting pretty serious, so what I don't know I'm sure I'll find out soon enough."

"I recommend sooner rather than later."

I take a big bite of the bagel and head out the door. I should tell him to keep his wallet hidden, but he's a grown man dating a grown woman who didn't bother to tell him she had a child at all, let alone one who lives with her, so he'll learn his Susan lesson the hard way.

Making it to the sidewalk, I take another huge bite of the bagel and plop down onto the curb to wait for Madge. I didn't text her to confirm she was still picking me up this morning and for all I know, she texted me to say she wasn't. I pull my backpack around and dig out my phone. Clicking the screen on, I have three missed messages. The first is from Mikey. *Hey, this is Mikey. Are you okay? I'm sorry for upsetting you today. Hit me back so I know you're okay.*

The next message is also from him. It came in two hours after the first. *I'm trying not to read too much into your silence, Dani. I hope you're okay. Let's talk at school tomorrow.*

The next message came in an hour later but it isn't from Mikey. Or Madge. It's from *him.* There's a picture of Madge and me walking into the academy yesterday morning. *You always pick the most beautiful friends.*

I spring off the curb and run into the house. "Randall?" I shout his name, fingers frantic on the keys as I tell Madge not to bother picking me up. "Randall!"

"Yeah, I'm here." He comes trotting down the stairs in his sock feet, rolling down the sleeves of his button-up. "What's going on?"

I catch my breath. "I need a ride to school. My friend isn't going to be able to pick me up."

He smiles. "No problem. I'm sure I can get you there on time. Just give me a couple more minutes and we'll get on our way." He chuckles as he starts back up the stairs. "In my day, we would have been happy to be late for school, but here you are all in a tizzy over it." He winks down at me from the top of the platform. "I promise I'll hurry."

~

The drive to school was awkward. Randall kept attempting to make small talk but I couldn't engage him. I needed the time to think. If Madge gets hurt because of me…

"Dani," Mikey whispers from behind me. He asked the boy who was sitting there to move before calculus class started, but I've been too lost in thought to hear a word Mikey's said since.

"Shh," I hush him.

"You have to talk to me sometime," he mumbles.

I ignore him. A folded piece of paper soars over my shoulder and lands on my desk. I open the message. *Will you eat lunch with me?* He drew two squares next to the question, one labeled yes and the other no. I don't bother to check either box. I crumple the paper, drop it into the floor, and use my foot to push it back to him.

His fingers dig into the length of my ponytail. I spin around. He smiles. "It's as soft as it looks."

I pierce him with a glare and turn back around, feeling eyes on us. I lean forward on my desk to avoid him touching me again. His long legs stretch out on either side of my desk and I feel trapped. Which is probably what he's intending. Trap me here after the bell rings so I'll be forced to speak to him. He has another thing coming.

I throw my hand in the air. "Mr. McKay, I have a question about the assignment."

The willow-framed man approaches my desk, his eyes darting down to Mikey's outstretched legs. I hear the groan as Mikey's forced to pull his feet back and I can't help but smile. He drags his entire desk next to mine, his tattoo pressed tightly along the length of my arm. "I have the same question, Mr. McKay. See if you can explain to Dani and me what's happening here."

As bad as it is to have to make up math questions in a class that I'm acing, it's worse having to hide from Mikey all day, only to see him driving by Sally's bus as if he's checking up on me. The boy has serious issues, and I already have enough of those.

~

According to the person on the legal advice live chat that I just did on one of the library's computers, unless I'm *certain* that the person messaging me is Kira's killer and feel my life is in danger, there isn't much the police can do. They're not going to spend valuable resources, a large one being their time, running down the person on the other end of my phone.

While I'm definitely afraid, I'm not sure that the messages *aren't* hoaxes. I'm also no longer in the right age bracket for Kira's killer. These monsters usually have a range and Kira was pre-pubescent. According to what I've read, that's a very distinct inclination, one that can't be filled via an older female.

The last message I received also came from a different phone number than the first. I've tried everything I know of to trace the numbers, but it appears they *are* burner phones. That doesn't seem like something one of the girls from school would do, especially over comments from a boy I only met once. Zach is yet another reason to never eat ice cream again.

Dani, it's Randall. I just got off work and checked in with your mom. She said you're not home. Do you need me to pick you up someplace?

I stare at my screen. This Susan having a boyfriend thing might work out for me. I look up the address of the supermarket I saw down the street and send it to him. *Pick me up here, and don't tell Susan about the crackers I'm buying to go with my stolen peanut butter.*

~16~

Randall made a show of being ready early this morning, making sure he got me to school well ahead of time. I'm not going to correct his idea that I'm an eager student. Anytime I can be out from under Susan's roof, I'm going to take the opportunity. And being at school is safe. I don't enjoy being around all the people, but no one will come in here and steal me away without at least one person saying something. Hopefully.

Instead of hiding out in the library or what's now become my favorite bathroom stall, I trail a group of kids to the gymnasium where all the early arrivers are hanging out. I'm not as skilled with technology as I'd like to be, and it occurred to me last night that there has to be a tech wiz in this school. The library has a robot that retrieves your books and brings them to you, and the classrooms all have at least one interactive table that teachers utilize in group-think projects. Another reason I'm glad I only have one class with Mikey. His self-proclaimed best bro Angelo has claimed me as his partner twice already. Loudly. And I have no doubt Mikey would be just as bad if he was given a chance.

Scanning the crowd, I look for anyone who seems like they'd know how to pinpoint the location of a sender's message. Or maybe even know how to trace the original purchase point of a burner phone. Randall gave me fifty dollars this morning and as much as I don't want to take his money, I need the cash. I only hope fifty dollars is enough to hire the help I need.

On the back row of the top bleachers, I spot a familiar head dipped low over the thickest book I've ever seen. Lily Beller. A wave of relief floods overtop my anxiety and I move my feet in her direction. I don't relish asking a Beller for help, but Lily is nice, and she's smart. Or else she wouldn't leave here every day to attend college courses.

Unlike her brother, Lily isn't surrounded by an entourage. She's the exact opposite. A wide ring of no one is spread all around her. I wonder if that's her doing or some rule her brother has in place. I hope it's the latter and she tells him that I walked right up to her again because someone has to put the jerk in his place.

"Mind if I sit with you?" I drop my bag beside her and plop down before she has time to answer. "Nice to know I'm not the only girl in this school who understands jeans *are* clothing."

She looks at our nearly matching legs and lifts her eyes to scan the room as if she's just noticing other people are here. "I don't think skirts are practical. Do you?"

I shake my head. "Nope. Because you never know when you might have to climb a tree. Or run."

She laughs. "I haven't climbed a tree since I was five. I fell out of that apple tree and broke Mikey's arm." I glance at her and she shrugs. "I still feel bad about it, but he didn't have to catch me."

"I bet he never tried to again."

She sighs. "He would, no matter the consequences to himself, because he's annoying like that. This is why I now refrain from climbing trees. And from wearing skirts so short that if I drop a pencil, I'd never be able to bend over and pick it up."

I groan. "I'm sure the painted-on minis in this school are all for the benefit of your heroic brother."

She makes a sound similar to mine and closes the anatomy book in her lap. "When he was dating Tanya, he brought her to the house for family game night and my mom had me go to my closet and get Tanya a sweatshirt and sweatpants. Like, didn't ask Tanya if she was cold or anything, just ordered the clothes to be gotten. That's how bad Tanya was at twelve. *Forced* to wear a nine year old's clothes just so she would be allowed to play board games with us."

A stab of pain shoots through my gut and I feel my ears heating up. Mikey has probably dated all the girls in this school and I shouldn't feel any type of way about that, but I do. "I'm sorry you had to witness whatever Tanya was wearing. Nine was a tough age for me, too."

Her head shakes. "Mikey turning sixteen was the worst age for me, and it's still horrible. But I'll be sixteen next year and have my own driver's license so no more getting up early to come here so he can do all his little activities. No one should be awake at this hour, and no one should ever be as chipper as he is in the mornings. It's disgusting."

His voice pops over the loudspeakers, sounding as crisp and cheerful as ever, and we both laugh. "Lily Beller is not a morning person. Noted."

She stuffs her book in her shoulder bag. "I'll be less grumpy in a couple of hours. Everyone pretty much knows not to talk to me until then. Hence the wide berth."

"Yeah, well, sorry to rain on your already gloomy parade but I'm not an *any* time of day person."

Talking to Lily soothes some of the alarm ticking inside my head. "Lily, do you know anyone who's a computer wiz? Someone who can do things like hacking?"

Her face scrunches. "Who are you trying to hack?"

I swallow, tasting the lie on my lips and hating it. "No one. I'm just trying to decide on colleges and noticed that in the criminal justice field there's a big focus on digital forensics. I can barely enter a new contact into my phone so I figured I should brush up on skills in case I decide to go the crime-fighting route."

She holds out her hand. "I'll give you my number and school you on entering a contact. Then probably talk to Gideon Joseph about the rest. He's been in trouble for hacking into the academy's files so maybe he can teach you some things, and after you get out of college you can arrest him for being a criminal."

~

All the tension I released while chatting with Lily returned when Mikey waltzed into calculus class. To my shock, he didn't approach me or even wink. He took his original seat in the back of the class, and I did my best to block him from my mind. I tried to forget Lily's rendition of her heroic brother and the increasing ire I feel over him having dated Tanya. She's the head bunny and reminds me so much of Susan I want to puke.

A tinkling bell marks the end of class and I hesitate, scared to move in case Mikey plans to ambush me. He doesn't even glance at me, his body moving out the door and turning left. If I was faster, I would have hit him in the head with my book.

I leave the classroom and turn right, running straight into a chest. I look up. "I heard you wanted to talk to me?" A boy with ruddy cheeks and red hair smiles down at me.

I step sideways. "I don't think so."

He squints. "Lily said you wanted some tutoring?"

My eyes pop wide. "You're Gideon?" He nods and I clear my throat, looking around at the other students. "Is there somewhere we can talk in private?"

His eyes roam over my face. "Sure. Follow me."

I follow him to the end of the hall and through the door into the stairwell. He points ahead of us down the flight of steps. "The band's storage room is down here. I play the drums and happen to know that no one should be in the storage room right now."

We make it to the room and I stand by the door, leaving it cracked open behind me just in case this kid gets any ideas. "Lily said you're good with computers and things?"

He nods. "I'm mostly a gamer, but coding and stuff like that comes easy so I mess around, give some people some headaches from time to time." A smile tugs at the corner of his mouth. "Ever heard of swatting?"

$$\sim 17 \sim$$

Gideon gives me the laymen's rundown of swatting. For fun, he and his friends swarm targets, hacking their utilities, credit cards, house alarms, and basically any and everything that runs on an internet connection. They hit hard and fast, draining bank accounts and causing general mayhem in the life of unsuspecting marks.

"Sometimes we place fake emergency calls, have police and ambulances show up at a location. Nothing ever gets tracked to us though, because we know how to *cover* our tracks."

"But you got caught breaking into the school's files?"

He laughs. "On purpose. It was a cover for something else, and no, I won't tell you what that something was."

"Good, because I don't care." I pull out my phone. "Can you trace messages that seem to be coming from burner phones? I need to know who bought the phones and where they bought them."

He leans on the shelf behind him. "If I can, it will cost you."

"I'll pay. Half up front and the rest when it's done." My palm grows sweaty. "How much?"

He shrugs. "Won't know until the job is done, but I'll work out a payment plan with you." He holds out his hand. "First, let's see what you're working with."

I hesitate, withholding the phone. "This stays between us, right? You won't tell anyone what you see on my phone?"

"He absolutely will tell." Mikey pulls the door open and leans on the frame, head jerking in a commanding fashion. Gideon takes the order, pulling himself off the shelving and brushing past Mikey on his way out.

"Wait!" I yell after him. Mikey's arm blocks my exit and I glare at him. "I realize your rich boy skull is so thick you have a hard time taking a hint, but I've made myself clear. Stay away from me and out of my life. Got it?"

He snatches my phone, holding it over my head so I can't reach it. "Gideon will clone your phone and if it suits him, he'll use whatever he finds on it against you. The conversation you were just having with him sounded like you don't want what's on here to get out. You're welcome, Dani. No thanks needed. I'm just being a good rich kid with a thick skull."

I step away from him and hold up my palm. "Phone. Now."

He doesn't flinch. "Is someone bullying you?"

My teeth clench. "Yeah. *You.*"

He closes the door behind him and moves toward me. I back up, bumping into the shelf Gideon was leaning on. Mikey reaches for me and my body jerks. His hand falls to his side. "Dani, I'm not trying to scare you, hurt you, or bully you. I'm only trying to talk to you because you walked into my pool party with a chip on your shoulder and it's been growing ever since. Did I do something to you? I've been trying to rack my brain about maybe having met you before but I don't think I have. Is there a party or something that I don't remember?"

Images of him at a party with throngs of half-naked girls all around him make my teeth grind even harder. "I've never been in this state before, and if you were ever in mine, there's absolutely no chance that we ever bumped into each other. Now give me my phone back and go make ice cream dates with Tanya, Madge, and all the other girls who hop around here chasing you."

His arms fold across his chest, my phone tucking under his pit. "You're jealous? That's why you're mad at me all the time?"

I jab my fingers under his armpit and he dances backward, holding my phone back in the air with a grin on his face. I jump but only manage to come down on my ankle, stumbling forward into his hard chest. His arm slides around my waist, steadying me. "Don't hurt yourself. I'm going to give you your phone back, I just want to talk to you first."

I push off of him and press my weight onto my right foot to keep the left ankle from throbbing. "I'm not jealous so stop trying to make yourself relevant in my life. You're not."

He lowers the phone, tapping it in his palm. "I have this thing called compassion. You should try to have some, Dani, because when I look at you a little piece of my heart breaks. You're sad, and yeah, I do think you're all kinds of beautiful but mostly I'm just trying to be your friend because you look like you can use one."

He hands the phone back to me. "If someone is messing with you, I'll stop them. And unlike Gideon, I won't use anything I find out to leverage you. So when you're ready, come find me and show me the messages."

He opens the door, glancing back at me over his shoulder. "Do you still need a job?"

I can't answer him. If I say a word, tears are going rush down my face, and I refuse to cry in front of him. His jaw ticks. "The holiday rush is already starting so my mom does need seasonal help. I'm pretty sure she's planning on calling you in for an interview, and Lily told me you sat with her this morning so I'm hoping I'm the only member of my family you hate. Lily could use a friend, too. And like I said, my mom's store needs help and she's pretty picky with who she allows to work there."

He leaves and I sink to my knees, hot tears running down my face. This would be so much easier if he wasn't nice.

$$\sim 18 \sim$$

The great thing about being a horrible person is that nice people stay away from you, and I'm pretty sure Mikey Beller is a good guy. It's been a week and he hasn't bothered to speak to me. I haven't even caught him looking at me and I even hung out near my locker one day just to see if he would because his mom *did* call me in for an interview.

A part of me knows I shouldn't associate myself with the Beller family because of Susan's infatuation, but I need money and I haven't noticed any other help wanted signs in town. My options are also limited. My employer has to be close to the bus route, and preferably in a high-traffic area. The Carpenter's Boutique fits that criteria so I went for the interview, acted as normally as I could, promised that I understood my employee discount didn't extend to anyone else— especially Susan, and nearly fell out of the chair in Mary's small office when she hired me right there on the spot.

Her husband wasn't shocked, but his piercing eyes told me he would be watching me for the first sign of Susan-like behavior. Personally, I'm going to be watching for the first sign of Susan. I didn't tell her about the job, opting to forge her signature on the necessary paperwork. Then I told Randall that I'm working on a big semester project for school and asked if he could pick me up from the library when I'm out at night. He agreed, and thankfully the library closes an hour after the boutique, so that gives me time to walk there after my shift.

Eventually, someone is bound to mention to Susan that I'm employed at the Carpenter's Boutique but until that day, I'll hide my job. And my food. With the promise of a steady paycheck, I went to the store after the interview and used Randall's fifty for a supply of crackers, bread, peanut butter, and three boxes of granola bars. I'll ration the food the same way I'm rationing my money. Since I can't use Gideon to track who is ramping up their taunting messages, I'll have to save enough to hire a professional. The killer has sent three new messages this week, and this last one is the most disgusting. More photos of me eating the ice cream cone just so I know he was there the *whole* time. *I chose the wrong flavor, but you still look good enough to devour, Dani. I can't wait to taste you.*

Do it. Rage pushes the response through my fingertips. *Come for me. I've been waiting to meet you for a very long time.*

"Dan-ni!" Angelo whoops from the doorway of our chemistry class. "Where were you at lunch? I saved you a seat. Again. And you didn't show up. *Again.*"

I shove my phone into my bag. "You know I eat lunch in the library."

He flips my book closed. "I know all that studying you do is rotting your brain. Give it a rest and come out with us this weekend. We're going up to the cinema to watch a movie."

I place a shaky hand over where my phone is vibrating inside my bag. "I can't go out, I have to work."

"Mikey can fix that. I'll tell him to get your schedule changed and then you can roll with us. There's a sweet party afterward, and you know you want to come dance with me."

Angelo *is* cute, and he and Madge are the only people who talk to me outside of Lily, but as fun as Angelo tries to make everything, he's still Mikey's best friend and I can't be around Mikey. Finding out he works in the woodshop with his dad on occasion was a punch in the gut. When I saw him on the other side of that glass yesterday, I tripped over my own feet.

"Ang, I appreciate you always asking me to hang out but I really need money more than I need a social life. I've already told Mary and Pam both to put me on the schedule as much as possible. Plus, I don't think your other friends want me around anyway."

"Like who?" he questions. "Mikey shut down all that garbage Lauren and Wendy were spouting about your dad."

I turn in my seat. "What were they saying about my dad?"

He rolls his eyes. "Some nonsense about you being crazy like your mom so your dad dumped you here with her and skipped out. I think they talked to your stepbrother or something."

My face flushes. "They talked to William?"

He shrugs. "I wasn't listening that hard. Sounded to me like a whole bunch of cattiness, and Mikey said it was over Zach so he had his little cousin make some calls. Those girls will still be snarky, but I doubt they'll cross Mikey *and* Zach." He nudges me. "Are those girls why you won't come eat lunch with us?"

"No, but they're why you're getting ready to see me get expelled."

~

I wait at my locker after school and right on cue, Mikey strolls down the hall with a gaggle of girls around him. I march up to Lauren. "You look shallow and insecure, but I didn't peg you as desperate. Thanks for correcting my opinion. Now I know exactly how thirsty you are."

She steps away from me. "What are you talking about? Geez, psycho much? Oh wait, I forgot, that's *exactly* what you are."

Mikey steps between us. "Knock it off, both of you."

I glare at her. "Knocking her head off is *exactly* what I intend to do."

"I have a better idea." His arm reaches around my waist and he spins me into the lockers, body pressed against mine as he cages me in and lowers his lips to my ear. "Don't move. This will accomplish what you're trying to do. Punching her will only get you in trouble and possibly fired from the job you just got hired for." His head tilts, nose grazing along my cheek. "They'll buy this better if you run your hand up my back."

My heart is pounding so hard I'm sure he can feel it against him. I meet his eyes. He smiles. "Thank you for not planting your knee in a place that would really hurt." He pushes off the locker and points to where the herd of girls is stomping away. "Mission accomplished. Now they're mad at you for a whole new reason and can't do a single thing about it."

One. Two. Three. I beg my pulse to calm and my lungs to accept the air I'm giving them. *Four. Five. Six.*

His head tilts, hand running along the side of my face. "Are you okay?"

Seven. Eight. Nine.

He leans onto his knees and stares into my eyes. "You look like you're going to hurl. Want me to get a trashcan?"

"I've got to go," I squeak out, tearing away and racing down the hall.

"Want a ride?" he calls after me. I shake my head and continue to count until I'm out of the building. There's a thick wall of shrubs in the landscaping to the right of the steps. I duck behind it, bend over, and lose what remains of my peanut butter sandwich.

~19~

I should be able to make it to work with enough time to sit in the break room and do my homework before my shift starts, but the vomiting made me miss my usual bus so I had to wait for the next one.

"Sorry." I run into the boutique and slide to a stop at the counter beside Pam. "I had a thing after school."

"You're here with plenty of time to spare." She hands me a package from under the counter. "This came for you to today. I'm guessing it's a Christmas present for someone at your house or else you wouldn't be using this address to get packages."

I take the package from her. "I didn't order anything, and I just started here so I don't know what this is."

Her shoulder lifts. "It's here, and it has your name on it, so might as well see what it is. Maybe you have a secret admirer. Who you can also tell to not send packages here."

"Yes, ma'am." I take the package and head into the break room to put my backpack away. The white letter-sized padded envelope is soft in my hand. Outside of my name and the boutique's address, there's no other writing on the envelope. I take a pen from my bag and use the tip to poke a hole through the top of the envelope, pushing the pen through the padding until there's a large enough hole for my fingers to fit inside. I rip the top of the package open and pull out the peach-colored t-shirt.

Shaking it out and holding it up in front of me, my body begins to shake. I drop the shirt and dig my nails into my palms. If there was anything left in my stomach, it would come up right now. This is a Dani-sized version of the shirt Kira was strangled with.

Pam walks up behind me, taking her jacket off the hook near the door before lifting the t-shirt from the table where I dropped it. She holds it up the same way I did. "This is…cute. Where'd it come from?"

"My dad." I utter the first name I can think of, remembering the way the dirty shirt twisted around Kira's neck as he rocked her lifeless body in his arms.

Pam puts the shirt back on the table in front of me. "Don't blame him, honey. He's a man and so few of them have taste. Check the package for the return receipt and you can probably exchange it without him even knowing."

She slips on her jacket and I just stand here, frozen. "I need you to watch the store while I run some errands. I'll be back in about an hour." She waves a hand in front of my face. "Can you handle the place on your own for a little while?"

I nod, throat sore as I fight the emotion down. She smiles, placing a hand on my shoulder. "You picked right up on everything so I know you'll be fine here, but if something comes up, just give me a call and I'll talk you through it. Okay?"

"Yes, ma'am."

I follow her out onto the sales floor and give a reassuring wave as she leaves, but no part of me feels assured of anything. Part of me kept wanting to believe the messages were from girls at school, but this shirt isn't from them. It can't be. One of the things never made public in Kira's case was how her shirt was used to strangle her. We were told that it was critical to withhold particular information, and the specifics of her shirt and how it was used were on that list of never-to-be-divulged information. But the killer knows, and he's making sure I know the messages are from him.

I didn't expect there to be a return label in the envelope but I checked anyway. Then I helped two customers select dresses for the upcoming winter formals that seem to be happening at all the schools around here. We don't have many dresses in the store, but the ones we do have are unique and hand-sewn by a local designer. The dances are all happening in less than two months, and Mary says every dress we get in between now and then will sell, so her designer will be bringing in weekly deliveries.

I stare at the gowns and attempt to force my brain to stay present in this job but I can feel myself crumbling. I'm going to become the crazy person Lauren is already saying I am. Somehow, I thought I could just lay low, graduate, move into a college dorm and then resume my research on Kira's case outside of watchful eyes. But I was right all along—Kira's killer is out there, and he's still hurting people.

Leaving Mary's office door open so I can hear the chime if any customers walk in, I sit down at her desk and click on her computer. It's password protected but I know the password. Davina called it out one day when Pam asked her to check on the date of an invoice. Davina couldn't remember if the "four" in Bellersfourlove was the number four or the word "for". I couldn't unhear what I heard.

Typing in the password, I quickly navigate to the browser and go to a website where I can not only pull up basic information about Kira's case, but I can run a search to find any similar cases in the state of Washington within three years of her death.

Hitting Print on the list of cases, I change my search parameters and look for cases like Kira's in the state of Pennsylvania. Unfortunately, it isn't mandatory for police departments to upload their data, and even if they do, there is no standard of what details they're required to input. Using the victim's own clothing to strangle is a trademark specific to a certain killer, but some departments might only say the victim was strangled, not specifying how or with what.

"What are you doing in here?" Mikey startles me.

I close the tab on his mom's desktop and swivel the chair, snatching the still printing pages from the printer. "I needed to access a few of my files." I jam my finger into the power button but the printer keeps printing.

He stomps around the desk, clicking over the keyboard. "You're not supposed to be in here."

Sweat builds under my arms. He's checking the browser history. "I wasn't snooping. I just needed to print something for school. Research. For a project."

He navigates to the last page I was on. "Whose class? What project?"

I don't answer. He yanks the papers from my hands, staring at the case names. If I make up an answer about a class, he'll check at school and find out I'm lying.

I steady my shaking hands. "Those aren't for a school project, they're for me."

He flips through the pages. "What do you want with these?"

I swallow. "You heard Lauren. I'm unhinged."

"Don't give me that crap." He shoves the papers at me. "You have a real problem with using your voice, but I just caught you breaking into my mom's computer when I know for a fact you've been specifically instructed not to *ever* be in this office alone. So you better find your tongue and tell me what's going on."

I straighten the papers in my hands and fail to hide how badly I'm shaking. "I'll pay for the ink and paper, and I know that doesn't make up for the fact that I broke a rule by coming in here but I really, *really* need this job so please don't get me fired. I swear on my life I'll never come in here again."

He points at my hand. "Explain those."

I don't answer and he folds his arms. "You either tell me, or you tell my parents. Your choice."

I dig my nails into my palm. "My…best friend…" I stare at the floor. I so rarely say this out loud. "She was murdered when we were nine and I'm trying to figure out who killed her."

He steps toward me, hands cupping my shoulders. "I'm so sorry. What's her name?"

"Kira." I sniff, turning away from him and tugging the last page from the printer. I hand it to him so he can see her name for himself.

Tears wet my lashes as he reads not only Kira's name, but the other things written on that page about how that innocent little girl died. I bite my lip. "I'm truly sorry for coming in here. We had a lull in customers and I just…" Tears threaten to drown the words in my throat. "Part of what Lauren said about me is true. I've never been able to get over what happened to Kira and it makes me…this." I point to myself. "My dad *did* leave me here with Susan so he didn't have to deal with me anymore. He got a second chance at a normal kid with his stepson, and he took it."

Mikey pulls a tissue from the box on the desk and dabs at my eyes. "If someone hurt Ang, I'd flip this whole world upside down to find them. So how can I help you, Dani? Eight years is way too long for anyone to get away with killing your friend."

"Almost nine years." I take the tissue from him. "Kira and I share a birthday, and he got to her the day after we turned nine. That anniversary is coming up in two months so I'm just extra emotional about it right now."

He folds me into his arms. "That's normal. Anniversaries of tragic events are hard."

I take my nails out of my palms and rest against him. My dad is the last person who held me, and I can't even remember when that was. "Are you going to tell on me?"

He pulls back, caramel eyes dripping with sorrow. "You can't come in here again, my parents are real paranoid about a lot of things, but no, I'm not going to tell anyone you were in here. And I won't tell anyone about Kira because that's your pain to talk about." His thumb glides under my eye. "Of all the smack the other girls have been talking, they never said anything about this so they must not know. All they were saying was that your stepbrother said you're morbid and really depressed. Outside of that, it's just normal jealous talk, but I see now why you came at Lauren so hard." He hugs me back to his chest. "If people knew what was really going on, they wouldn't be so catty with you."

I push away from him. "No, they'd be worse." His head shakes and I hold up a hand. "Don't you think I've been through this? I've been in seven different schools and most of them between the ages of nine and twelve. Then I finally figured out how to keep it all inside and never tell anyone anything, and that's the *only* reason I managed not to have to switch schools again. Until now. And so far, I've managed to do nothing but gain enemies."

He rubs his hands tentatively over my arms. "I'm not your enemy, and you're not alone. I'm here anytime you need me." I close my eyes and he steps closer. "You have to *let* me be here, Dani." His hands slide around me and the bell on the front door rings. His lips press against the top of my head and then he releases me. "I've got this. Go take a break. And if you need to go home, I'll cover for you."

~20~

There aren't any tags or labels on the peach t-shirt; I checked while I took the break Mikey let me have. Half of it was spent crying in the bathroom and the other half convincing myself that I'll be able to track down where this shirt came from, that it'll be the clue that leads me straight to the monster who snuffed out Kira's life. Not too many places can be selling peach shirts with a white patch across the front that serves as the background for four dancing pieces of fruit with legs, arms, and faces.

Mikey's still at the boutique, only he's on the other side of the glass, the lights of the woodshop bright against the sweat of his tanned skin. His shirt is off and the muscles in his stomach flex as he wraps long fingers around the frame of a chair, hefting the piece onto a bench. The cords of his arms tighten and relax as he smooths stain over the wood, eyes focused on the grain as his hand glides over it in long, smooth strokes.

"Enjoy the show while you can," Pam whispers into my ear. I jump and she shakes her head at me. "As soon as his mom sees his shirt off, she's going to flip. Then no more cute boy in the window."

"I wasn't…" I swallow. I'm not sure how long I've been staring at him or how much of it she saw. "I was just rotating the shoes. We sold two more dresses and two pairs of heels while you were gone."

"Uh-huh." She laughs. "Good job on handling the sales, but now you need to go wipe that drool off your lip before it dribbles all over the floor."

I wipe my lip and she laughs harder. "Before Mikey turned thirteen, the wall was cute. Women didn't much dare come in to stare at John." She lowers her voice. "At least, they pretended not to because where John is, Mary is close by and it only takes crossing her once to find out she protects what's hers."

I shove my hands in my pockets. "And Mikey is hers so you're telling me I'm on thin ice staring at him. Got it. But someone should tell him to put some clothes on because I'm only human."

She follows me to the counter, unwrapping the scarf from her neck. "The Beller men fell straight out of the hunk-of-heaven tree, but I've seen Mary throw out more than one grown woman for ogling her son. Especially when he was younger. She used to get real fired up in his early teen years."

My eyes unintentionally roam to the glass again. Pam pats my shoulder. "Mary doesn't have as big of an issue when the ladies are his own age, but I'm going to need you to keep working while you stare."

I rub my neck. "I wasn't staring so much as happening to notice. There's a difference."

She nods to the door where his parents are walking in. "You might want to stop noticing now."

Pam is right. Mary and John went straight into the woodshop, and though the room over there is soundproof so I couldn't hear what they were saying, the hand gestures said enough. Then Mikey pulled his shirt back on and finished the chair he'd been working on.

I have a feeling that if he worked in this store with any regularity, women would come to know his schedule and flood the store when he was working. As it is, none of the Bellers are here on any form of a schedule I can make out. They come and go as they please, and all of them, including Mikey, like their ability to do so.

Outside of Madge telling me Mikey also works at a car lot, I've never heard it mentioned. And getting Lily to answer a message is nearly impossible. Sometimes she answers days later and other times she'll respond in person, on the rare occasion I bump into her before classes start. Those lackadaisical attitudes are born of wealth and the Bellers seem to be the people around here who have the most of it.

I look up and startle when I find that it's Mikey who is watching me this time. *You okay?* He mouths. I nod and he smiles. *Take a break with me?*

Can't.

He glances at Pam and then back at me. *She'll let you.* I shake my head and he frowns. *Then just stand there and we'll talk like this.* I laugh and he grabs his heart, eyes wide as he pretends to stumble backward. *She smiles.* I force an eye roll at him and then walk away. Still smiling.

~

Saturday mornings are the worst. Since Randall practically moved in, he makes pancakes and has Susan get out of bed so we can all eat together. Every single time the conversation is the same. I place one single pancake on my plate, no butter, no syrup, and Susan still complains.

"Do you know how many carbs are in that pancake, Danielle?"

"No, do you?"

She picks up her morning spirits and sips casually. "Too many for you to eat that and expect to find a boyfriend."

"She's seventeen," Randall says as if that's my only defense against the accusation of daring to be boyfriendless.

Susan stares as I cut the pancake into tiny pieces. "She's nearly eighteen, and as far as I can tell, has no future prospects. Have you even spoken to Michael Beller *once* since you started at the academy?"

I stare at her. "No, I haven't. Because I don't need a boyfriend or a sugar daddy. Now can I eat this *one* pancake and be excused? Or do you prefer me to just be excused?"

She huffs. "Randall went through all this trouble, the least you can do is eat. As thick as your thighs are already, there's not much hope of you fitting into a proper dress for the upcoming dance. Not that you'll have a date anyway. You can't seem to manage even the lowest man on the list, let alone a worthwhile one."

"Susan, that's enough," Randall scolds. "There's nothing wrong with Dani." He moves the platter of pancakes closer to me. "Eat up, honey. You're hardly ever here for dinner and if my opinion counts for anything, you look thin to me. Thinner even than when I first got here so whatever diet you're on, it's working."

Bile rises into the back of my throat. The peanut butter diet I'm on is disgusting. And it's all because of Susan. I grab the plate of pancakes and get up from the table. Susan gasps. "Where do you think you're going with those?"

"To my room so I can stuff them into my face without your commentary."

The doorbell rings and since I'm moving in that direction anyway, I answer it, blood draining from my entire body when I see Mikey standing in front of me. He eyes the pancakes. "Am I interrupting breakfast?"

~21~

I plop the plate of pancakes onto the foyer table and push Mikey away from the door, slamming it closed behind me. "What are you doing here?"

"I'm seeing if you're busy." He holds up a single pink daisy. "Are you?"

The clack of Susan's heels nears the door. I take hold of his shirt sleeve and pull him to the corner of the house so she can't see him if she looks out. I glance to the street. His truck is nowhere in sight. "Where's your truck?"

He peeks around the corner to see what I'm watching for. "It's at my house. My family's property abuts this development just down there." He points to the cul-de-sac. "Why? Are you not allowed to have boys stop by?"

Susan opens the door and steps outside. I shove Mikey against the house and press myself against him, trying to flatten us to the side in case Susan comes down the sidewalk. Mikey's hands rest on my hips. "Now this I like." I slap my hand over his mouth and see the flash of amusement in his eyes. The longer we stand here with his big warm palms holding onto me, the less I'm going to remember why I'm pressed up against him to begin with.

"Stay here," I whisper, sliding off him and peeking around the side of the house. Susan is on the porch, looking down the street. With a huff, she disappears back inside the house. "Let's go." I take a fistful of Mikey's shirt again and dart down the driveway.

We hit the sidewalk and I turn toward the cul-de-sac, where we'll be out of view of the house and he can walk right back to where he came from. His arm slips around my waist and he spins us in the opposite direction. I plant my feet. If he only knew how badly Susan wants him to be here right now. "*Why* are you here?"

He holds up the flower I never took. "I just wanted to see you. Talk to you. Take a chance on making you smile again."

I look over his shoulder to make sure we're hidden from the view of the house. "Now's not really a good time. Susan has a new boyfriend and…things are weird here."

He runs the flower I'm not taking along the side of my face. "How about we go someplace else, then? We can go back to my house or—"

"No." I cut him off. "Aren't you confused on whose door you should be knocking on? Madge lives on the other side of the neighborhood."

His eyes narrow. "Yeah, I know. House with a big blue door. What's that have to do with me coming to see you?"

"You two are doing the whole *undefined* relationship thing and that's fine, but Madge is the closest thing I have to a friend outside of your sister who basically never answers any of my messages." I fold my arms. "All the other girls in your life hate me because your cousin said my name *once*. If Madge finds out you came here…"

He tosses the flower and takes out his phone, stepping closer to me. "Here. Look through all of my messages. I'm not the one in an undefined relationship because I don't operate like that. I'm either with someone or I'm not. And right now, I'm not. Unless you want to change that?"

"You're not funny." I push the phone away.

He stuffs it back in his pocket. "I'm not trying to be. If you haven't noticed, Madge is a little out there. I'm aware that she spouts fantasies about our future from time to time, but mostly because her mom is my mom's best friend. At least, that's the title they use even though Mom keeps some distance between them."

"Kind of a short woman with blonde hair?"

He smiles. "You must have met her at my party?"

I nod and his smile falters. "I call her aunt Kim and her husband uncle Kevin but we're not actually related. I've just known them my whole life, so Madge and I grew up together. Angelo, too. They're all family to me. But Madge's parents have a notion that it would be perfect for her and me to be together, so if she's telling you I'm in an undefined relationship with her, it's because she doesn't want you to connect with me."

My head shakes. "She told me about the two of you on day one, like ten seconds after I met her. She'd have no reason to try to scare me off that early on. It wasn't like I was all over you and carving your name into trees."

His eyes flick to the trees behind me and I already know he's going to do something stupid like carve *our* names into a tree. "Mikey, don't do it."

A grin creeps over his face. "Maybe that's what Madge saw that made her fill your head with lies. Me looking at you in a way that says I'm going to chainsaw your name into a tree."

I turn away to hide the smile but his fingers glide under my chin and he brings my eyes around to face his. "Madge's parents haven't ever been accepting of anyone she likes, so she lies to them about us having feelings for each other. When I date other people, that blows holes in those lies. But I'll talk to her, for the ten thousandth time, because Madge has a knack for making my life much harder than it needs to be."

I turn my chin so his fingers fall away. "You can't be here, Mikey. If you think Madge and her parents are bad, you have another thing coming if Susan sees you out here."

He shuffles around so I'm facing him again. "I'm not concerned about other people and their narratives. I'm concerned about you. And I'm also just trying to get to know you, which is why I came here hoping we could spend some time together today. I want to know all the things that make Dani tick. And for the benefit of full disclosure, only two-thirds of my reasoning has something to do with how smoking hot you are."

Susan's earlier words sting against my heart. I can't let Mikey bait me in. "Your reasoning has to do with the fact that I'm new in town and didn't walk right in and fall on my knees, begging you to date me. That makes you curious. But I'm not a puzzle, and I'm not a conquest. I also don't need the extra headache that comes with Susan, Madge, Tanya, or any other number of females who have a vested interest in you. If any of them saw you come here, especially with a flower in hand…"

He looks away, staring down into the cul-de-sac. "I didn't come here to upset you or ruin your day. And I can't control how other people act, especially if you don't tell me when people say things to you." He focuses back on me. "I'm not going to argue with you about my motivations.

I'm standing right here in front of you being as honest and transparent as I can be. Why you choose to judge me and believe something different, that's all on you."

"I'm not judging you. I'm being a realist."

He laughs, the sound humorless. "If you don't talk to me, ask me questions to figure out how I think and feel, then you're not being real about anything." I don't respond and he runs a hand down the back of his head. "All night, I couldn't stop thinking about your smile. I thought I could keep that going by giving you a fun day that let us get to know each other so we could figure out if there's anything between us other than friendship. But I think I hear you saying you don't even want to be my friend."

My eyes fill with tears. "It's so much more complicated than that."

His eyes drop to my lips and then lift back up. "If you ever want to talk about why you think it's complicated, let me know. Until then, I guess I'll leave you alone." He takes a step away from me. "I know things are rough for you right now, but you should try to smile more, because you're even more beautiful when you do."

Ever since the panic attacks started back with regularity, I've been emotional. So close to breaking every single moment. Few of those moments worse than this one, having to stand in place while the sound of Mikey's heavy footfall fades away.

I turn in the opposite direction and walk past Susan's house, the wounds of loss etched deeply into my soul. Kira. Dad. And now Mikey.

Meandering along the sidewalk, I hear the profanities being shouted before I register the passing car. It's Wendy and Tanya, windows rolled down and mouths working overtime. Maybe I should message Mikey and tattle on them since he's so keen on knowing if anyone is being mean to me.

~

The house is quiet, which probably means Susan is *entertaining* Randall. I quietly top the stairs, ready to retreat into my room. Randall is standing in front of my door. "Hi, honey. Are you okay?"

"Fine," I lie.

He moves aside so I can pass and then follows me inside the bedroom. "Your mom is sorry for the way she behaved this morning."

"No, she isn't."

"She is," he insists. "She puts pressure on you because she loves you and wants to see you succeed."

I stare at the package on my bed. Same type of envelope in which Kira's Dani-sized shirt was delivered. "Susan wants money, and she's willing to pimp me out to get it. There's no love in that."

"You shouldn't say things like that about your mother." His tone is gruff, something I've not heard from him before.

I face him. "Where did this envelope come from?"

He glances at the bed. "It was delivered while you were gone. Where were you anyway? I was just getting ready to come look for you. I would have been out earlier but Susan was upset after you stormed off like that, and I just got her to lie down for a nap."

"I'm here now so if you don't mind…" I wave my fingers at the door. "Shut it behind you, please."

He walks out of the room and I wait until I hear his footsteps move away from the door before going to the bathroom and grabbing a tissue. The only good thing about this house is that every single bedroom has its own private bath.

Pulling on a pair of fleece winter gloves, I carefully rip open the top of the envelope, tipping the contents onto my comforter. I feel my arms begin to quiver as I use the edge of the envelope to move the silky white ribbon around, scooting each bow over my bedding until the long tail of a kite stretches across it. A replica of the tail from the kite I was flying when I found Kira's body.

Chest hollow as my heart pounds, I remove a plastic baggie from the box I bought for my sandwiches and carefully coil the ribbon inside, sealing the bag. "Gotcha, sucker." Whatever the reason might be as to why I'm suddenly on the killer's radar, I intend to capitalize on the attention. Since I'm not his demographic, he may never attack. This might all just be a game to him, but I'm not going to miss an opportunity to provide law enforcement with potential DNA.

Tucking the baggie inside the envelope the kite tail was delivered in, I roll the package up and place it inside an empty cracker carton. With any luck, this killer was stupid enough to believe I'd just throw this all away and never think to use it for DNA.

The only thing I need to be careful about is handing it over to law enforcement only to have them place it in a box of their own and never actually do the testing. Before I let them table it forever, I'll keep eating peanut butter until I can afford to hire a private lab.

~22~

I'm suffocating. I'm in the living room of our house at the lake, nine years old again and soaking wet. Dad is beside me, wailing. His screams make it harder to breathe. I run outside. Kira is on the inflatable in the lake, giggling before she jumps off. Her head goes under the water and now it's me screaming because her tiny arms are thrashing but her head isn't surfacing.

Kira! I reach the shore and the water stills, flat as glass as it mirrors the sky above.

Cupcake? It's time to eat, Dad calls from behind me. I spin toward him, the sights and sounds of my ninth birthday party growing so vivid I cover my mouth. I can smell the cake, the thick white icing too sweet and the pink polka dots too red.

I study the faces of the people, landing on the sallow cheeks of the baker as he carries the cake from the house to the squealing delight of everyone but me. The snap of butterfly wings draws my attention up. My rainbow kite soars across the sky. Kira screams and I look down again, but the party is gone. My legs are trapped in briars and Kira is fighting for her life. *Kira!* I scream for her, skin and blood dousing the briars as I fight to get free. *Daddy! Help!*

"Danielle!" Something hits my face, my body plucked from the briars and thrown onto a bed. I scream but I can't move. "Wake up, honey. Wake up. You're having a bad dream."

I push my feet into the mattress, backing away from the figure hovering over me. "It's me," Randall soothes. "You were screaming."

I blink, tears sliding down my face as I gasp for air. Randall gets off the bed and opens the window. "I'll go get your mom."

"No," I wheeze.

"Do you need a doctor? You're covered in sweat."

I focus on my shirt, it's soaked through. *One. Two. Three.* Having Randall staring at me rapidly decelerates my heart. *Four. Five. Six.* I take a gulp of air and steady my voice. "I'm fine now."

He sits back on the bed. "You were…melancholy when you came home earlier. Did something happen? Is that what caused your bad dream?"

I tug the comforter around me. It's wet, too. "Nothing happened."

He folds his hands in his lap. "It isn't good to keep things inside. Especially when they're bothering you this badly. I'd like to help you but I can't unless you open up and tell me what's happening."

I sit silently, controlling my breathing and continuing to count. He swallows. "Can you at least tell your mom what's going on?"

"*Nothing* is going on."

He frowns. "Did a boy do something to you? I was one so I know how they can be, and if one of them has threatened you or made you do something you didn't want to do, you can tell me."

"Leave. Please."

He slowly pushes to his feet, looking down at me one last time before slipping out the door and closing it behind him. I let my tears out, silently crying while my pulse continues to regain a normal rhythm. If there is any such thing as normal. Where I'm concerned, I don't think there is.

~

Another week has passed and I'm realizing now what a coward I am. Every time I muster the courage to speak to Mikey, I chicken out just as fast. He's caught me looking at him a few times, but all he ever does is give a half-smile, and then he looks away.

Kira's killer can't decide what he wants to do either. He's been silent since the kite string arrived. I'm not stupid enough to believe he's gone, but it could be that he's lost interest. And if he's lost interest in toying with me, then he may have found another victim. A possibility that had my stomach churning all through Susan's mandatory country club lunch. I worked early yesterday so I managed to get out of Randall's Saturday pancake breakfast, but Susan pitched a fit. This afternoon I didn't fight her. I went to the lunch, endured her disapproval of my inability to bring home a cash prize, and held my tongue while she fake laughed at every single thing Randall said. Most of which was answers to my thirty-seven questions about his job. I still don't understand what type of *acquisitions* he makes. Probably because Susan kept laughing.

I get out of Randall's car and slip next door to the neighbor's house. "Hi, would you like me to walk Benny for you?"

"Absolutely." Teresa pulls a leash off the hook she keeps by the door. "This dog is going to be the death of me if I don't get him regular exercise. He broke out of the backyard twice yesterday."

"I'm sorry I wasn't here or I would have helped you get him."

A broad smile crosses her face. "I know, which is why I came looking for you. Benny took right up with you so now you're my secret weapon. And anytime you want to walk him, come on over and get him. I'll pay you to do it. My knees just hurt too bad to walk him anymore."

"I'll come over anytime I'm free," I promise, scratching Benny's head as I clip the leash onto his collar. No one told me she came looking for me and since there's money in this for me, I'm even more annoyed that I had to sit through that stupid lunch.

"This way, Benny." I lead him away from his house and walk deeper into the community. One thing I need to do is figure out which homes have men living in them and make a file with their descriptions and addresses so I can trace who they are and if they've ever lived in Washington state. It's a long shot, but it's also a starting point.

It's doubtful Kira's murderer followed me here. It's more likely that I stumbled into his new hunting grounds. Except I haven't found any records of missing children from this neighborhood or any of the more upscale ones around here. And I'm not sure if I should cross-reference Kira's case with the usual target demographic of low-income neighborhoods, minority populations, and children with drug-addicted parents.

Kira's parents were devastated after her death. That devastation led to divorce, and while I didn't know what was happening at the time, I realize now that her mom turned to alcohol to cope with the loss. The last time I called her, I couldn't understand anything she said. And that makes my sorrow even worse. Had I been taken instead, no lives would have been destroyed. Susan wouldn't have cared unless crying about it earned her a dollar, and I now know that Dad would have bounced back fast, and definitely better than he's fared by having to deal with post-Kira Dani.

Dad *has* been texting me some, and he's called a few times, but he does so when he knows I'm in school so that alone proves he doesn't really want to talk to me. He's placating me. So I'm ignoring him.

I stand at an intersection, eyeing the stately houses lining the streets around me. *Anything* could be going on behind the ornate walls and no one would know. "Cute dog for a cute girl!" Angelo's voice slams into me seconds before I register him running down the driveway of the house across from me.

I wait for him to reach me, smiling when he drops to his knees to play with the excited poodle. "He's not mine, I walk him for a couple who work a lot and have bad knees."

He stands. "From what I hear, *you* work a lot. When are you going to ask the Bellers for some time off so you can come see a movie with me?"

"Never," I reply. "I'd rather work."

"Ouch." His eyes narrow. "You just going to come right out and dismiss me like that?"

"Yep," I answer.

He folds his arms, the corners of his lips curling into a grin despite his posture. "If you hang with me now, I'll forgive you."

I glance at the house he came out of. Mikey is walking out the door, Tanya not far behind him. "Is this where Tanya lives?"

Angelo nods. "She invited some people over for brunch. There's still food left if you're hungry."

"I wasn't invited, and I wouldn't go in there even if I was. Plus, I have to finish walking the dog."

Mikey ambles up beside Ang and leans over to pet Benny. "Hey, big fella. You're a good boy."

Tanya shivers as if the dog is gross. "Is that thing yours?"

I stare at her full face of makeup, her smooth and styled golden-brown hair. Angelo slings an arm around my shoulders. "Nope, not her dog. Mikey, you coming with us?"

He looks up, clocking Angelo's arm around me before leaving off his admiration of Benny and straightening his shoulders. "Nah, I'm going to head home. Hit me up when you're finished and I'll swing back and get you."

He holds out his hand and Angelo tosses what I assume are his car keys into Mikey's palm. Disappointment trickles through me as Mikey walks away, and my gut twists when instead of getting in the car, he leans on it and starts talking to Tanya.

Turning away before I see them kiss, I lead both Angelo and Benny down the sidewalk. "Is that your car, Ang?"

"Yeah, the dealership I work for hooked me up. I got a sweet deal, and they take the payment out of my check so that I don't have to worry about financing. Things have been tight with my mom and me, so having the extra car without a big payment helps a lot."

"You must be an outstanding employee."

His shoulders shimmy. "I'm outstanding at everything I do. But Mikey's aunt and uncle own the dealership, and their daughter Sophie runs it, so I have an inside lane. I could try to get them to hook you up, but you have to be extra nice to me."

"Trust me, not even the friends and family discount will fit my budget."

"I feel that pain." He sighs, pointing to a big house that's across from us. "Up until about two years ago, I lived there. Then my dad went to jail for embezzlement, and Mom and I got booted. We moved into my grandma's old house and let me tell you, you haven't seen small until you walk into a square box with seven-foot ceilings. Dang near take my head off every time I walk under a light."

Mikey and Angelo are both well over six feet so I can't imagine how giant they look in a small house, let alone an old house with low ceilings. "At least you didn't get booted from the academy."

"Thanks to my swimming scholarship. And thanks to Mikey being too Mikey to join the team. He helps coach and he runs extra practices, but there's no one in this state, and probably the country, who could beat him if he competed. He's one of those freaks of nature." He kicks a pebble off the sidewalk. "I've been swimming with him practically my whole life and get a bunch of private lessons, but I'm still low man on our team. Good enough to be on it, but let one more kid join who can put up a better time and I'm toast."

"Hmm, so you're *not* outstanding at everything."

He bumps me and we both laugh. I glance at him. "So Mikey doesn't compete because he's giving you a spot on the team?"

He stares at his old house for a beat longer and then turns away. "Mikey doesn't compete. Full stop. He's just not into *winning* anything. Titles, awards…none of it means anything to him." He wets his lips. "But if it came down to him giving up a dream to make mine happen, he'd do it without thinking. And that's why I had to get out of Tanya's house. Mikey's been in a mood and didn't want to go, but I begged him and he can't ever say no to me. So we got there, and *then* I realized my boy was two seconds from exploding. He doesn't usually get worked up over anything, so I'm glad you walked by when you did. It gave me an excuse to get out of there because everyone else in there is female, meaning if he detonated, it was *my* head getting clocked."

"It didn't look like Mikey was mad to me, or in a hurry to get away from Tanya."

Angelo's tongue clicks. "He's always eager to get away from her. Everyone knows Tanya's particular flavor of hot is equal to how crazy she is. You're familiar with that." He grins. "We all saw your mom's *hot* hanging out at Mikey's pool party. And I'm going to call Mikey back here and convince him you're a man so he can *show* you how mad he is if you don't agree to come out with us this weekend." I open my mouth and he waves a hand in my face. "Yes, Dani. Yes is the right answer."

~23~

It's Friday night and I sit on my bed listening to fifty-thinking-she's-still-twenty-five remind me that she's disappointed in my general existence. "*Another* Friday night and you're sitting at home, alone." The ice in her glass tinkles against the sides. "What's it like to be you, Danielle? No friends, no life, just you and those books of yours. *All* the time."

Randall's hand cups her elbow. "Dani's been out almost every night for weeks. Let her be, honey. She needs to rest."

"Ha!" Susan staggers as she steps backward, managing not to spill her drink. "This one hasn't been out. She's been at the *library*. When I was her age, we wouldn't be caught dead at the library, let alone spend *all* our time there."

I glare at her. "And look what that got you. Fifty and still peddling your body for a buck."

"You ungrateful brat!" She throws her glass at me, feet propelling her body forward.

Randall grabs her arms from behind, holding her back. "Both of you need to stop provoking one another."

She gets one arm free, shoving a hand in my direction. "*She* needs to go out and find someone who wants to put up with her because *I've* had enough of her attitude. No wonder your dad begged me to take you!"

I relax my face. I won't give her the satisfaction of knowing she hurt me. "The day I turn eighteen, neither of you will have to worry about who has to put up with me. I'm moving out, and you're *never* going to see me again."

"Who do you think is going to pay for you to have a new place to live?" she snarls. "Not me. I'm tired of taking care of a lazy, self-righteous daughter. Not your father, he got tired of you before I did."

I get off the bed and face her. "*I'm* going to take care of me, because despite the resemblance I have to you, I am *nothing* like you. What I get in this life, I'll *earn*. On my feet, not lying on my back!"

Her lip curls. "What kind of job is a high school dropout going to have? I can't wait to see."

My teeth clench. "My high school tuition is paid. I'm not dropping out of school."

She leans into my face. "If you leave this house, you're completely on your own. No tuition, no free car rides from Randall, no nothing. So before you threaten me again, you better weigh your options, little girl."

Saying I'm leaving isn't a threat. The only way she'd take it as such is if there's a financial reward coming her way for me being in her house. "How much?" I ask. "How much is your ex-husband paying you to house me every month? And does he know that not a single dime of it is used for my benefit except for the monthly tuition, and that's only because you want me to rope some rich kid into dating me." She doesn't respond. I fold my arms. "I think it's about time I answered one of Dad's calls."

Her hand lands across my face, the sting of the slap shocking Randall as much as it does me. He drags Susan from the room, her mouth gaping open without a single sound coming out. I place a hand over my cheek. No one has ever hit me before.

Randall stomps back into the room. "You two have *got* to stop this constant fighting!"

Tears threaten my eyes. "Tell that to your unrepentant, self-centered narcissist because it's *her* who starts fights with me. Not the other way around."

"Because she wants what's best for you," he snaps. "She's worried about you. We both are. You were sent here to see if your mother could help you and you won't let her even try."

"I'm here because she knows this is her last shot at getting rich via me. Once I'm eighteen, she can't control me anymore."

He pinches the bridge of his nose. "She isn't trying to control you. And she isn't the one who cooked up this scheme for you to come live here." He meets my eyes. "She told me everything, Dani. Your dad begged her. He said you didn't turn out…normal."

My body stills. He stares at me and then looks around the room before bringing his eyes back to mine. "I work with a young man who is twenty-three, and I know that's a little old for you, but you *are* almost eighteen and I know Susan would approve of him. I can arrange a date. That will get her off your back for a little while. All you have to do is make her think that you're following her advice and attempting to make connections."

"I am *not* going to pimp myself out just to make all of you *feel* better about who I am as a person. I'd rather leave now and live on the streets."

He throws up his hands. "Yeah, you do that and then see what kind of *dates* you end up going on." He turns toward the door. "I have to go back and check on your mom. And until you learn to speak to her with respect, you're grounded."

I stand where I am until I hear the click of Susan's bedroom door. Grounding me while also complaining about me being home too much is a contradiction that would be *disrespectful* of me to point out.

Slipping on my shoes, I carefully tiptoe out of my room and down the stairs. I need fresh air. It's as if all the oxygen in this house is filled with tiny shards of metal.

I hesitate at the door but the house is quiet, so I slowly open it and walk out into the night. I step onto the sidewalk and move beyond the reach of the streetlights, lurking in the shadows of the trees lining the side of Susan's house closest to the cul-de-sac. The moon is full and bright, giving me a good view of my surroundings as I pull air through my nose and exhale out my mouth.

My phone beeps, the screen illuminating my pocket. I glance back at the house. The interior is dark, the landscape lights reflecting off the glass of the windows. I tug out my phone. *I loved you at this age. So…succulent. Just like Kira.* My lungs constrict. Of the three childhood photos attached to the message, I only recognize one. It's the picture I kept on my nightstand until Dad said having the memory of my ninth birthday was part of the reason I had nightmares. He threw away the photo of Kira and me blowing out our birthday candles.

The other two pictures could be from anytime that year. Before Kira died. Because I'm smiling in these pictures, and after her death, there was never any reason to smile.

Trembling, my fingers slowly move over the keyboard. *You'll like me more now. So tell me where you are, and I'll come to you.*

~24~

I wait for Kira's monster to respond but he doesn't. The floodlight on the corner of Susan's house comes on and I retreat farther into the cul-de-sac. "Dani?" Randall's voice rings out. I don't answer. "Danielle?" He's closer now. I can't go back into that house. Not yet.

Turning deeper into the cul-de-sac, I run, pushing my legs as hard as they'll go while hot tears spill down my cheeks. I reach the end of the sidewalk and keep going, branches slapping at my face as I break through the trees and crash into the woods.

"Dani!" An arm slams around my waist, the force of it doubling me over as I come to an abrupt stop. I scream, arms and legs flailing out as the arm drags me backward, trapping me against a hard chest. "It's me. Mikey. Dani, it's Mikey. I've got you, you're okay." His voice is soft against my ear. "You're okay, I've got you."

I collapse, sobs jerking out of my body. His arms tighten around me and he settles us on the ground, shifting me onto his lap and tucking me against his chest. Despite his soft words and calm exterior, his heart is pounding. I suck in a gulp of air and close my eyes, counting the beats of his heart.

He sits quietly while I cry, lightly rubbing my back with one hand while his other arm holds me against him. Until his entire body convulses and he nearly dumps me off his lap. "Shoot." He scrambles to reposition me. "Sorry. Are you okay?"

I meet his eyes. "Are *you* okay?"

He blows out his breath. "A spider was on me. I hate those eight-legged demons."

Instead of heartache, laughter bubbles up. I cover my mouth but it's no use. He scoots me off his lap and places a kiss on my forehead, dimples popping into his cheeks. "I'd appreciate it if you could keep the whole me being scared of spiders thing to yourself, but it sounds like that's going to be tough for you."

I rein in my laughter. "Your secret is safe with me."

His hand reaches out, cradling the whole side of my face as his thumb gently glides underneath my eye. "And yours are safe with me, so tell me what's going on. Why were you running like that? And crying?"

I move my face from his hand and look away. His fingers slide under my chin and bring my gaze to rest on his. "You were running too hard for this to be a little thing. What made you run into the woods and scratch your pretty face all up in the trees?"

My hand jumps to my throbbing cheek, tracing over two big welts where a branch caught me. Mikey slides around to the side of me, draping his arm around my back and lowering his already soft voice. "Is this about your friend Kira? Or did something happen with your mom? Because if she did something to cause this reaction in you, I'm going to your house right now to have a chat with her."

I pull my knees into my chest and pick at my sleeve. "You knocking on Susan's door is exactly what she wants. It wouldn't matter what you said, she'd only register the fact that she managed to get you there."

"I bet I could make her register more than that."

"Doubtful," I grumble. "All she ever talks about is you. She wants to know if I saw you, if I talked to you, if I dragged you into a janitor's closet and jumped you."

He groans. "Well, that just shows you how out of touch she is. All of the janitors' closets are locked. You'd have to take me to the band closet where you met with Gideon."

I elbow him in the stomach and he chuckles. "So she told you to force yourself on me and you ran out of the house crying? Am I that bad?"

I focus on the tiny snag in my sleeve. "There's a lot more happening than just her obsession with you, and today's been…extra terrible. I couldn't take another second of being stuck in that house."

He rests his forehead on my temple. "Then it's not the thought of being near me that made you flip out?"

I shrug him off of me. "Would you stop? Even if you did actually like me for some inexplicable reason, Susan is legitimately out of her mind. Your parents hate her, they barely tolerate me, and I can't afford to lose my job because they think I'm only working in the boutique to carry out some Susan-ordained plan to snag you."

"They don't think that."

I get up from the ground and dust myself off. "What about you? Why are you out here in the middle of the night?"

He stands, looking away before meeting my eyes. "I'm on my way to Madge's house."

I turn and walk away. He grabs my arm. "Wait, Dani. I'm not going there to see her. I don't even know if she's home. My uncle Kevin asked me to pick up his car and take it into the dealership tomorrow." He steps to my side and urges me around to face him. "My *real* uncle, Avery, owns a chain of car lots. His oldest daughter runs them, and Ang works there. I go in and help out sometimes. And I'm picking up Kevin's car this late because I don't want to hear his Madge sales pitch. Her parents sort of treat her the way it sounds like your mom treats you." He tugs a set of keys from his pocket. "They think I'm coming in the morning but I have a spare set of keys, so I'm sneaking over there in the cover of darkness and stealing the car."

I swallow, feeling the prick inside my gut for always being so apt to think the worst of him. "It's none of my business what you're out here doing and who you're doing it with. It's just frustrating when you kind of flirt with me and then…"

"Kind of?" He huffs. "I went to the library today and picked up a few relationship books because damn if I know what women want—when their name is Dani Madison."

I fold my arms and he mimics the posture. "I'm not *kind of* flirting with you, Dani. I gave you all I've got and none of it worked. If I ever meet someone else who makes me want to jump through hoops just to get one tiny little smile out of them, I need to be better prepared."

I cover my mouth to hide the current smile and turn away. His hand circles my wrist and tugs my fingers away. "See why I need the books? I have no idea why you're smiling right now. All I know is it's a heck of a lot better than seeing you cry." He steps closer. "If Susan is the reason you're always so upset, she needs to be dealt with."

I shake my head. "I'm almost eighteen. After that, she isn't my problem anymore, so just drop it. And those relationship books will tell you that sometimes females just need to cry. Hopefully they tell you that men need to cry sometimes, too. It's…healthy."

He lifts a brow. "I know. My dad's a sap. He cries almost as much as my mom and sister combined."

I laugh, picturing big and burly John Beller crying. Mikey smiles. "It's true. The Beller men are very in touch with their feelings. Our camping trips are big blubberfests. Especially when my uncle Avery gets going about how much he's *blessed*." Mikey's eyes roll and a groan slips from his throat. "Don't ever ask him about the day he married my aunt Sheila. Not unless you have two boxes of tissues on you."

"Noted." I step away from Mikey's warm body, heat rushing up my neck and into my face when he grabs my hand and curls his fingers through mine.

"Go to the movies with me tomorrow night, Dani." His eyes tilt to the sky and then back to me. "Tonight, rather. Please?"

~25~

My body's reaction to Mikey is one I can't ignore. Even though his fingers are no longer laced through mine, I can still feel them there. When he touches my back or lets his shoulder rub mine as we carefully pick our way out of the woods, gooseflesh breaks over my skin and heat rushes underneath my surface. It's taking all I have to not throw my arms around his neck and discover what his lips feel like.

"The Cineplex has six huge screens," he explains. "They're positioned atop an outlet mall so it's basically a drive-in movie theater with the added perk of shopping. We just choose which movie we want to see, find places to park near that particular screen, and then spread blankets over the nearby grass and just hang out while we watch the movie."

"But how do you hear anything with six screens and tons of people?"

He holds the last tree branch out of the way and follows me as I pass into the open. "There's an app that you use to tune in to the movie. We just have a car or two hook us up with audio, and it's loud enough. And the stores in the outlet close at nine so we usually go for the movies that start then. The parking is set up around grassy areas, and there are picnic tables, so it isn't like a standard mall parking lot where it's all asphalt and noise. It's more like a park that just happens to have a mall sitting in the middle of it."

Angelo has described this place to me, but not in such detail. "It sounds really cool."

"So you'll go with me?" Mikey asks.

"No." I huff. "I'm not going to sit on a blanket in the middle of all of your friends, pretending to watch a movie while what I'm really doing is keeping an eye on your buddies Tanya and Wendy. And let's not forget Lauren. If Zach is there and he even says hi to me, she's probably going to dump a bucket of blood over my head. Said blood being my own."

He shoves his hands in his pockets as we step onto the sidewalk. "Zach just got back together with his girlfriend, so Lauren and anyone *else* who happens to like him are out of luck. He loves Celia and I don't see that ever changing. As for Tanya, Wendy and the rest of them, I've told them to lay off of you so if they're not, just say so and I'll deal with them."

"Ugh," I groan. "You *really* don't know anything about girls. The whole reason they're messing with me is *because* you told them to leave me alone. They would have picked on me, saw it got them no reaction from me, and then moved on if it weren't for you interfering."

He slows his pace as we get closer to Susan's. "I'm sorry I made things worse for you. I underestimated how those girls were going to react and overestimated how I thought you'd react."

"Which is the whole reason you're standing here right now." I stop before we reach a place that's visible from the house, noting that the floodlight is off now. "I treat you differently than they do, so you're trying to figure out why. But that doesn't mean that you like *me*, it only means that you're curious. And we know that's true because I haven't been nice to you. At all."

He removes his hands from his pockets and presses them to each side of my shoulders. "I haven't been nice to you either. You're dealing with a lot, and here I am throwing myself at you and trying to figure out how to get those janitors' closets unlocked." I shake my head at him but can't help smiling. He steps closer. "How about we start over? I'll stop hitting on you, you'll stop being mean to me, and we'll be friends. Friends who hang out sometimes, talk to each other all the time, and occasionally go to the movies together. The windows on my truck are tinted dark, so we can go to the movies and sit inside the whole time. Just the two of us."

~

Mikey's hugs are like being wrapped in a warm blanket. They almost make me want to let him get to know me the way he says he wants to. But the little my parents know about me has them detesting me, and I don't think I could handle Mikey looking at me the way Susan does.

Last night was rough. Embarrassing. And one of the welts on my cheek is still raised and red. As the minutes of my shift tick down, I check my phone. I messaged Mikey this morning, asking if he managed to pull off the grand theft of his uncle's automobile. *I did. And I drove it like I stole it, but I think for that to be fun I need a sexy co-pilot.*

I'm sure Ang will ride your shotgun.

He is sexy. But I was thinking more along the lines of blonde hair, a ponytail, and a nice fitting pair of blue jeans. Which isn't me flirting, you just happen to resemble the girl in my dreams lately.

I didn't respond back to that, and he didn't say anything else. But I want to.

Despite the confrontation I had with Randall last night *and* this morning, I'm not grounded. He doesn't have that authority and as far as I'm concerned, neither does Susan.

Madge, are you going to the movies with everyone tonight? If so, can I tag along?

~

Mikey described The Cineplex perfectly. It's movie heaven, right outside under the open sky. What he failed to mention is the sheer size of the place. I stand in front of the last shop Madge disappeared into and survey the acres around me, a dizzying display of people, cars, picnic tables, and more green space than I would have imagined possible.

In the haze of too much contact with Mikey, I nearly forgot that a man I suspect is a serial killer somehow has photos of me as a child. He either got them from someone or took them himself, and neither of those options is better than the other. They both mean he was close to me.

I scan the crowd for any face that takes me back to my childhood. "I'm going to find you," I mutter. "I promise I *will* find you."

"Find who?" Angelo's head pops over my shoulder.

I grab my heart and spin around. "You nearly gave me a heart attack."

"I meant to." He winks, adjusting the stack of pizza boxes in his arms. "You coming to eat with us?"

My pulse quickens. "Us?"

He nods to the far right of where we stand and I see Mikey's truck. On the grass beside where he's parked is a garden of colorful blankets. I don't have to go over there to know who all the girls are. I turn back to Angelo and point at the store behind him. "I'm here with Madge. She's shopping and I don't know what we're doing after."

He adjusts the boxes again, balancing them on one muscled arm and slinging his other around my shoulders. "Madge isn't going to be done shopping until the place closes and kicks her out. Come eat with us while you wait on her."

I walk with him, heart pounding faster with each step. I dressed warm. A hoodie pulled over a long-sleeved fleece. The other girls are dressed in cute tops and skinny jeans, with pretty boots and feminine jackets. I plant my tennis shoe-clad feet. "I really think I should wait for Madge. If you guys are watching a movie later, I might see you then." When it's dark and I'm less noticeable.

He cocks a brow at me and practically lifts me off the ground with his one strong arm. "First we eat, and then we watch a movie. Because I don't want your pizza lips smacking in my ear when I'm trying to hear what's happening on the screen."

I groan and go with him willingly because doing so is better than making a scene. I just spotted Wendy spotting *me* and now she's in the process of alerting her friends. "Do you guys always do this? Eat here and then watch the movie? Because Madge said no one would be here until later."

"When you ladies are here, we're here." He picks up our pace. "Yo, people! Look who I found wandering around all lost and sexy."

I find Mikey in the sea of faces. He smiles and walks toward me and I suddenly wish Angelo didn't let go of me. He's dropping pizza boxes on the closest table, and I'm just standing here. Mikey stops in front of me. "You came."

I clear my throat. "I'm here with Madge. She wanted to do some shopping."

He nods. "She'll come find us after the stores close. Until then, where do you want to sit?"

I tuck my hands into the back pockets of my jeans. "Inside Madge's car. Alone. Away from here."

He groans, looking over his shoulder. "Ang! Come help me move the cooler."

Angelo stuffs an entire slice of pizza in his mouth, offering me the second napkin-wrapped slice. I take it as he talks around his mouthful of food. "Where we moving the cooler to?"

"Over to the table," Mikey answers. "Dani wants to sit in the bed of the truck tonight."

Before I can object, he hops onto the tailgate of his truck and lowers the oversized white cooler to Angelo. The two of them are wearing t-shirts and the way Mikey's muscles ripple, bringing his swirling tattoo to life, overloads my brain. I avert my stare to Angelo and his equally impressive muscles as he walks the cooler to the table. He doesn't give me goosebumps the way Mikey does so it's safe to stare at him.

Mikey bumps my shoulder on his way past and I spin around enough to see him pull blankets out of the crew cab of his truck. He hops back into the bed, spreading one large fluffy blanket over the bed near the back glass and then he piles the others on top of it. He looks at me. "It's ready, come on up."

I stay where I am. He jumps over the side of the truck and lands directly in front of me. "You can either get up there of your own free will, or I'm going to pick you up and place you in my truck." He leans toward me. "And I'm going to be very, very gentle about it. Some might say downright tender."

"Fine." I hide my grin and climb onto his tailgate much less gracefully than he did.

He folds his arms on the side of the bed and watches me as I situate myself against the side farthest away from everyone and pull a blanket over my legs. "What kind of popcorn do you like, Dani? Extra butter? Plain? Super salty?"

"You're not buying me popcorn."

His brows furrow. "Of course not. I'm buying *myself* popcorn, but I never finish a whole box so I'm going to share with you." He pushes off the truck with a click of his tongue. "Geez, what do you think this is? A date?"

~26~

I fold my arms and face forward, ignoring Mikey's chuckle as he waltzes off to get the popcorn I didn't ask for. Angelo jumps into the back of the truck with a pizza box and two bottles of soda. "Here you go, pretty lady." He slides under the blanket with me. "This is nice. Why didn't I think of this instead of always sitting down there on the cold ground?"

"You're warmer down there with all the girls."

He laughs. "Some of them are freaks, that's for sure."

I look around us. Dusk is setting and there's more than one couple already making out. Mikey jumps into the bed like some kind of agile panther and motions for Ang to slide over. He does. Taking me with him and away from the safety of the side of the truck.

Mikey drops down beside me, sandwiching me between the two of them. "Popcorn?" He holds the box out to me. I glare at him. He lifts a piece to my lips. "I got extra butter and extra salt, but I need a second opinion on whether or not it's good."

Angelo's head juts across me and bites the popcorn out of Mikey's fingers, his lips dangerously close to mine. "Too salty."

Mikey slaps him in the head. "*Dani's* popcorn."

Angelo shrugs, stuffing only half a slice of pizza in his mouth this time. "Dude, why haven't we been doing this all along? Up here in the high seats where we don't have people up in our business all night?"

Mikey rolls his eyes. "The high seats still have *some* people in our business. And what's with you talking with your mouth full? Geez, man. There's a lady present."

"Sorry, Dani." Angelo laughs, mouth still full. "I'll make it up to you."

Placing the popcorn in my lap, Mikey adjusts himself under the blanket that's over my legs and slides his arm around my back, leaning over as if he has to be this close to eat the popcorn. I look off to the side and catch three sets of eyes staring at us. "See that?" I whisper to him.

He glances at them and shrugs. "Their attitudes aren't our problem."

My teeth clench. "I'd rather not have *all* of your exes gunning for me every single day."

His head rolls to the side, eyes locked on mine. "I'll cop to dating Tanya for thirteen whole days. But I was twelve and only kissed her once, without tongue, so I'm going to say that doesn't really count. As for the others, never so much as a single non-date at the movies sitting in the back of my truck begging them to give me just one little smile." He holds another piece of popcorn up to my lips. "I'm going to need to see that smile."

"If someone sees me sitting next to you and tells Susan, she'll have our wedding invitations printed before the sun comes up again," I hiss.

He looks off in the distance. "I see the problem."

"Good." I adjust but his hand clamps around my waist, holding me in place next to him.

His gaze falls over my face. "We should at least wait until after we graduate to explore our wedding date."

"Mikey!" I yelp.

He laughs, letting go of my waist and shrugging his shoulders at Angelo while ignoring all the other stares my outburst garnered us. Madge's perfect red head bounces around the side of the truck. "Help me up," she orders. Mikey stands, jumping down and lifting her onto the tailgate. I take this opportunity to push Angelo over to the other side of the truck so that Madge has no place to sit other than in between Mikey and me. He jumps back into the truck just as Madge takes her seat, jaw ticking when he sees what I've done. With a huff, he plops down beside Madge.

Tension presses against my lungs as Madge attempts to nestle against him. He's not under the blanket anymore. He's sitting with his knees bent up, his arms plopped over them so that his elbows poke out toward her. He looks cold, and Madge thinks so too because she's tossing a blanket over him. He swats it off. She sits back with a frustrated exhale. "Fine.

Freeze to death so you can sit there showing off your tattoo. Who are you trying to impress anyway? I think Tanya got the memo by now and—"

"Madge!" Angelo snaps. "Movie. Watch. *Quietly.*"

"*O*-kay," she nips, pulling her phone from her purse. "I have better people to talk to than any of you anyway." Her nails click over her screen and I nudge her. She rolls her eyes. "Not you, *them*. The moody boys who haven't learned that brooding hasn't been a good look for the last decade."

"Madge!" both of them snap, and she makes faces at them, putting her attention back on her phone. I meet Mikey's eyes. They trail to where Angelo's arm is around me and then he faces forward again. I sit up but that doesn't help, Angelo's hand only falls to my back, absently rubbing circles as he watches the movie.

~

The credits begin to roll and I have no idea what this movie was about. I spent the whole time thinking about Mikey's perception of what was happening on this side of the truck bed. "Ready?" Ang stands up and holds his hand out to me.

I avoid his palm and stand of my own accord. We jump down from the tailgate and Madge follows while Mikey scoops up all the blankets, not bothering to fold them.

"Do you have a curfew?" Madge asks. "My friend is at a party and he said we should stop by."

I glance at Mikey. He jumps over the side of the truck, avoiding the tailgate altogether. I swallow. "I should probably just go home."

"Why?" Ang questions. "I know the party she's talking about. I was planning on stopping by there myself. Come with us."

Mikey starts his truck and Ang taps on his window. "We're going to drop by the party. Madge and Dani are coming."

"Whatever," Mikey mutters. "Tell them to get in and I'll drive them to Madge's car."

Ang opens the back door for us and Madge slides in ahead of me. Ang runs to the passenger door and hops into the shotgun seat. Madge leans up over the console between him and Mikey. "Turn left."

Mikey sighs. "I know where you're parked."

She kisses his cheek. "How sweet of you to make sure you know where I am at all times."

He punches the gas and she falls backward. "You're such a jerk."

He doesn't respond but I see Angelo grinning, and he doesn't lose the grin until we reach Madge's car and he jumps out to open her door. "I'll see you two *fine* ladies here in a bit."

I slide part of the way across the seat toward the open door and catch Mikey watching me in the rearview. Before I mouth that I'm sorry, he looks away.

Inside Madge's car, I stare at Mikey's taillights and wonder if there's any way to mend what I broke, and if I really even should. It's better if he thinks the worst of me, then he won't pursue me and we can just go our separate ways and not deal with any of the pain that will come if we let our teenage hormones drive decisions that aren't good for us.

Madge pulls into a vacant lot and parks beside Mikey's truck. The lot is full of other vehicles and the house next to it has people sprawled all over the lawn. Madge jumps out of the car and I open my door, pulling it back closed when I almost bump into Mikey's. He gets out and meets Madge at the front his truck.

I shiver as the night air hits my face. The temperature is dropping fast. Angelo heads toward the sound of the music, bumping fists with other partygoers as he approaches the door. I trudge along behind Madge and Mikey. The two of them seem to know plenty of people here as well, but I don't recognize any of them. These aren't our classmates and most of them look too old to still be in high school anyway.

Mikey stops abruptly and I slam into his back. He glances over his shoulder. I tug at the strings of my bulky hoodie. "Sorry." He reaches ahead of him and opens the door for Madge and then pivots to the side, holding it open for me. I walk by him and offer a weak, "Thanks," but he focuses on something or *someone* in the house.

Two steps inside the door, a wave of heat mixed with the smell of sweat and perfume assaults me. I look around. All the furniture is pushed to the outskirts of the living room and in the middle, bodies writhe and grind, everyone dancing to the overly loud music. Then my eyes land on the *someone*. An ebony goddess is stomping toward us, her green eyes ablaze. Mikey steps around me and she digs the pointy end of her nail into his chest. "I thought I told you not to bring her here."

My eyes go wide. I open my mouth then close it again when Mikey laughs and pulls her red-polished dagger from his chest, gripping her hand in his. "Madge brought herself here, and only after Geoff asked her to come."

She whips her head around and I follow her glare to where Madge is cuddled on some boy's lap, his thick arms around her and their lips working overtime. I gasp but the goddess in front of me burns with rage. "I'm going to rip those extensions out and make her eat them!"

Mikey pulls her back against his chest and Angelo strolls up behind us, clicking his tongue. "Arabella, I thought you said you were locking your man down? Looks to me like Geoff's locked, but not with you."

"Not helping, Ang," Mikey bites.

Angelo moves around me and rests a hand on Arabella's jaw. "There's plenty of love to go around. No need to fight." She lunges for him and Mikey holds her tighter, shaking his head as Ang moonwalks away, spinning around with perfect timing and fitting himself right in the middle of a gyrating trio of women.

Keeping his grip on Arabella, Mikey ticks his head for me to follow him. He practically carries Arabella to a couch and plops down, tucking her into the crook of his arm while she shoots death daggers at Madge, who is still obliviously sucking face with who I assume is Geoff.

I sit on the far end of the couch and tuck my feet against the bottom. Every female here dressed to prioritize fashion over warmth. Especially Arabella. Her hair and makeup are on point, and her tight-fitted fuchsia dress showcases each of her perfect curves. And it looks good lying against Mikey's black t-shirt, his bicep around her shoulder. Susan is right. I'm never going to end up with anyone unless I try, and until this very moment I've never understood that one day I would *want* to try.

I touch my dry lips. I don't even have a tube of ChapStick, let alone lip gloss. And no one else at this party has anything close to a basic ponytail. I run a hand down mine just to confirm how ridiculous I look. If I could have changed the way Dad told me to, the way Susan has spent her life telling me to, I could be like these other girls. Then I wouldn't have to deny how much I want to be the one tucked under Mikey's arm.

~27~

I'm failing miserably at not eavesdropping on Mikey's conversation with Arabella.

"Why didn't you say hi when you were at the house the other day?" he asks her.

She groans. "Thirty-five dresses. *Thirty-five.* Your mom has me working so hard my fingers are raw. But I got the new place."

"You got the house?" Excitement tinges his voice and I turn back his way, sadness crawling through me. His complete attention is fixed on her face. He's enraptured.

She, on the other hand, isn't. Her eyes are still trained on Madge. "I closed on the house yesterday. Geoff is supposed to be helping me move tomorrow, so you better take your little tart of a friend and get out of here before I strangle her with his tongue."

He lets go of her and tucks against the cushiony fabric of the armrest. "I'm not getting in the middle of that drama, but I will help you move tomorrow. I'm crashing at Ang's tonight so I'll be around."

Her shoulders slump. "You know that girl isn't going to take Geoff anywhere, not even to that dance. What's he want with a kitten when he can have this cat?"

Mikey scrubs his face. "All I know is that she really likes him, and you really like him, so he's doing a heck of a lot better than me."

She throws her head back and laughs. "What's wrong? Those snobby academy girls not giving you any love?" She glances at me, as unimpressed with me as I am. She points around the room. "Boy, you know you can have your pick. And you better pick quick because I need to finish your suit for the dance, and you have to know what color your girl's dress is going to be before I can make the vest."

113

He sits forward. "I'm not going to the dance."

Arabella's name clicks in my brain and I gasp, drawing both their eyes to me. "Sorry. It's just, you're *the* Arabella. The designer. I've been hanging up your gowns for weeks and it's… You're amazing. All of your clothes are so, so pretty."

A smile tugs at the corner of her mouth and Mikey leans around her. "Arabella started out in your job, then Mom found out she could sew and now she's a fancy designer."

"Trying to be." She softens. "You're the new girl? I heard Mary finally filled my spot."

I blush. "I heard the person I was replacing left big shoes. Pam said she'll let me know if I ever fill them."

She laughs again, the sound turning to venom as Madge approaches—her hand tucked into Geoff's. "Skank," Arabella spits.

"Thanks." Madge smiles at her. "See you!"

Mikey's arms shoot around Arabella, holding her in her seat. "You don't want someone who doesn't want you. Trust me."

"I don't want *her* to have him either," she bites.

"Dance with me." He lifts her into his arms and deposits her on the floor in front of him, his hands circling her waist so she can't get away. It only takes her a second to succumb to his movements, their bodies winding together until I'm sure she can't remember there even is a Madge. Or a Geoff. At least, if I was her, I wouldn't be able to think of anyone else while Mikey touched me the way he's touching her.

He looks so good with Arabella it physically hurts. Like each part of them was molded for the other. I break my eyes from them and search for Angelo. He's still in the middle of the three girls he was with earlier, dancing with two of them and kissing the third. I look away, eyes landing on couple after couple. People are either dancing or making out. My palms sweat and my pulse thuds. I get off the couch and walk toward the door, training my focus on nothing but that handle because if I glance in Mikey's direction and see him kissing Arabella, the cyclone inside me is going to spin out of control.

The night air jars my senses, the cold contrasting with my sweat to make me shiver. I tuck my arms around me and walk toward Madge's car.

Rounding the front of Mikey's truck, I'm greeted with an empty spot. Madge is gone. I look around. No one is outside anymore except for three men standing at the back corner of the house with cigarettes in their mouths. I walk out to the street. There aren't any sidewalks on this side but there's one on the other. Instead of crossing over, I take out my phone and dial. "Daddy," I whisper, not sure why I called him and knowing exactly the reason all at the same time. "I want to come live with you. Please? I'll be different, I promise. I'll do everything you say. I just want to leave this place."

His voicemail cuts off and I stare at my screen, wiping my eyes and then tucking my hands under my armpits to warm them while I wait to see if he'll call me back. I shouldn't have ignored his handful of calls. I should have figured out sooner that the advice he gave me was right. I'm not okay. And unless I make changes in my life, I'm never going to be okay.

"Need a ride somewhere?" a gravely voice asks.

I turn around, straight into a massive chest. A muscled arm steadies me as I step backward and stumble into the street. His brow lifts. "Bad night?"

I swallow. "Very."

"Here." He extends a single-serve orange juice bottle, pointing at the shivering my legs are doing despite me trying to stop them. "There's vodka in here. It'll warm you up."

I study him. He's around my age, maybe a little older, and way cuter than the guy I hooked up with so I could get rid of my virginity. I didn't like the label so I ditched it, and I didn't have to be drunk to do it. "No, thanks. I'm going back inside soon. But did you happen to see where the car went that was parked right there?"

He glances behind him. "Madge's car?" I nod and he shrugs. "She went home with Geoff."

I shove my phone in my pocket. Dad isn't going to call me. "Do you know where Geoff's house is? Or if they plan on coming back?"

He taps his chest. "I imagine you won't see her again tonight, but this right here will warm you up if that's what you're looking for."

He bounces his pecs and flexes the biceps hugged in the tight fabric of his shirt, but it would take me chugging that whole bottle of *juice* to fall into his arms. "If you happen to see Madge, tell her Dani is looking for her."

"If you came here with Madge, you must be one of those fancy academy kids?"

I nod. "I know my looks are deceiving, but that's where I come from."

He shrugs at Mikey's truck as we pass by it. "That means you know this fool. Hopefully, your fancy education has you too smart to hang with him, though."

"I came to a party in a place I've never been and am now stranded and standing out in the freezing cold with a complete stranger who is trying to get me to drink from an open container. Yep, I'm super smart."

His laugh is warm. He screws the lid back on the container and holds out his hand. "I'm Nick. So now I'm not a stranger. And my house isn't far from here. My house is where my car is, and I've barely sipped from this bottle so I'm sober enough to drive you anywhere you want to go. So you're not stranded, and I know where Geoff's place is if that's where you want to go."

I glance at Mikey's truck. I'll hedge my bets with him. Even if I have to sit in the cab and watch him make out with Arabella the whole way back to Susan's. "Thanks, but I'm just going to go back inside. And I can't shake your hand because my fingers are currently frozen to my sides."

Shivering my way into the house, I'm hit with an even thicker wall of heat and sweat than before and I welcome the sickening combination. Avoiding letting my eyes wander, I walk toward the couch. It's full. I change my trajectory and head for a recliner that's pushed into a lonely corner by itself. I claim the seat and lean onto my knees to conserve my body heat. Doing so puts me in the position to see the one person I didn't want to see. Mikey isn't dancing with Arabella anymore. There's a whole different slice of beautiful spinning in his arms, her leopard-print dress displaying all her goodies. My body flushes and I sit up, scooting as far back into the recliner as I can go. I don't want to be here.

Scanning the room, I find Angelo. He's still with those three girls but now his lips are on a different one and the four of them are disappearing through a doorway. My eyes automatically snap back to Mikey. Madge and Angelo both hooked up with people straight away and I wonder if that's why they come here. I wonder if this is what all parties are like. The only one I've ever been to is when I walked into that frat house at sixteen to find a guy to ditch the remaining label on my body with. It was a risk, but I had mace and a small knife. When a blonde kid made eyes at me in the first thirty seconds, I gave him an encouraging smile and things happened fast from there. I was back out the door within ten minutes.

I stare at the floor, more uncomfortable now than I was before. The corner of a magazine is sticking out from under the chair. I tug it free. While everyone around me succumbs to their urges, I get to sit here alone and learn about car engines.

~28~

"There you are." Mikey plops down on the cushioned arm of the recliner, wiping sweat off his forehead with his shirt. "I was getting ready to come looking for you."

Sure he was. Right after he finished *looking* at all his dance partner had to show. "I was outside." I ignore the inches of flesh showing below his shirt as he tugs it up to wipe his face again. "With Nick."

I don't know why I felt compelled to add that last part, and now I wish I didn't. Mikey's shirt slides down his abs, his body still as stone. I look up. His eyes are narrow little slits. I swallow. "I was looking for Madge, and Nick told me she left."

Mikey's jaw ticks. "I'm surprised he isn't passed out by now."

I stare back at the magazine and flip a page. "I think he's working on it. And from your reaction to his name, he wasn't lying about you two not being tight."

He flips the magazine closed. "You were outside hanging with Nick and talking trash about me?"

I meet his glare. "I was outside looking for *Madge* and because she ditched me here, he introduced himself and offered to give me a ride home, which I declined. He then *mentioned* that he wasn't fond of you because he deduced that if I came here with Madge, I must also know you." I jerk my magazine open again. "I didn't respond to his comment because I don't care what he thinks about anyone. All I need is for him to tell Madge I'm still here if he happens to see her come back. I'd appreciate it if you did the same. And pass the message to Angelo if he ever frees himself from the multiple women he's doing who knows what with."

I stare at the pages in my lap, pretending to read. Mikey's hand slides across the page, plucking up one hand and then the other. "You're freezing, Dani."

"Yeah. It's cold outside. That happens in winter."

He sighs. "I'm sorry about Ang. He's my best friend but that doesn't mean I agree with everything he does. In the truck on the way here, I told him to watch out for you and he said he would. It's just, there's someone here he didn't expect to see tonight, and when she's around, he's…different."

I look up. "Why would you ask Angelo to look out for me?"

He lets go of my hands. "You two seemed pretty cozy during the movie and I knew if he came here and got rowdy, you'd be upset. When I saw you gone from the couch, I clocked Ang's position and realized why."

I sit forward. "Wait, you think I'm jealous that Angelo is with other girls?" The sadness in his eyes is heartbreaking. "Mikey," I place my hand on his arm, "I only had Madge sit between us at the movie because you don't understand how easily a whisper in Susan's ear will set her off."

He swallows. "So you ditched me for my best friend to protect me?"

I plop back into the recliner. "I didn't ditch you. There is no *us* to ditch. Just go dance with all your concubines."

"That's harsh, Dani." He stands, pulling me to my feet. "I wouldn't call you a concubine. More like—" I swat him and he chuckles, eyes drinking me in as his fingers tighten around mine. "Dance with me, Dani."

Time stops. Restarts. My breath catches in my chest as he holds me against him. "I don't dance."

His hands slide onto my hips. "Just move with me. Like this." His longer fingers flex, pulling, pushing, guiding my body into the sway of his. "There you go." He smiles. "See? You *can* dance."

"Not like you."

"Because you're thinking about it." His lips fall to my ear. "Don't think. Just feel what the music makes you feel, and move with me."

What I feel is more than just the allure of the music. It's the spark of his body brushing against mine. The burn of wanting more as my arms drape around his neck, and the ache inside as his forehead rests on mine. I want to kiss him.

His neck tenses under my soft stroke. He spins me away, bringing my back against his chest, his mouth lowering to my ear, hot breath rolling over my neck. "You're a *great* dancer." The hair on my neck flutters with his exhale and his hands burn a trail across my stomach, his fingers pulling me against him tighter. I close my eyes and let the feel of him sink into my soul. Mikey isn't of this world; he's a world all his own.

I don't remember my hoodie coming off. All I remember are Mikey's hands. Long, strong fingers sliding against me as he rescued me from the suffocating fabric.

In our corner of the room, my chest pressed against his and my arms around his neck, my mouth rushes toward his. He dodges the collision and removes my arms from his neck. "I'm danced out. Let me go find Ang."

My face burns, the room spinning back into focus. I clutch my hands together and avert my eyes from the lips I nearly attached myself to like a succubus. "Yeah, it's getting late. I'm going to go see if Madge is back yet."

His fingers stroke across my cheek. "Madge won't pop up again tonight. Not unless Arabella raids Geoff's house and kicks Madge out."

"Mikey!" The girl in the leopard-print dress calls his name. He glances back at her and holds up a finger, fishing his key fob out of his pocket and pressing it to my palm. "Hop in the truck. I'm going to check on Ang and then I'll be right out to drive you home."

My feet stay stuck to the floor as he moves to the part of the dance floor where the girl who called his name is. She latches onto his shirt and I pluck my feet from the hardwood, forcing them out the door and away from this house. Mikey wants me tucked away in his truck because he's also trying to hook up with multiple girls, and he's embarrassed that he had to almost be seen kissing *me*.

Checking the corner of the house where I presume Nick came from earlier, I find it empty. There are a lot fewer cars here now, too. Too bad I didn't take Nick up on his original offer. I walk toward the street, pulling out my phone as the cold rapidly reduces my body temperature. My dad hasn't called me back but that's not going to stop me from using his credit card to call for a car again.

Dashing across the street to the sidewalk, I start walking toward the nearest intersection. There has to be a street sign or a mailbox around here somewhere. Commotion erupts on the porch of the house I just came out of and I instinctively turn toward the noise. Among a tide of people spilling out of the house is Mikey, my hoodie thrown over the same shoulder the girl in the leopard-print dress is tucked under. Her petite frame forces him to bend over when he places a kiss on top of her head. I turn away and tuck my hands against my body as I walk.

"Dani!" Mikey's voice booms. I keep walking toward the intersection. Feet pound over the sidewalk behind me and an arm catches me around the waist, spinning me into the same chest I was much too close to only minutes ago. Mikey's eyes squint. "Did you forget where I parked? My truck is the one towering above everybody else's."

I push away from him and hand him the key fob. "I wasn't running off with your property. I'm just looking for a house number or a street sign."

It occurs to me to use the map on my phone and I open the app. Mikey plucks the phone out of my hands and stuffs it into his pocket, hoisting me over his shoulder and jogging back to his truck while I kick and scream.

Managing to control my wiggling body with one arm, he opens his truck door and deposits me on the seat, reaching around me to lift the console and jumping in the truck faster than I can scramble away. His hands latch onto my hips and he pulls me to him until we're tucked against one another. "I don't know why you're suddenly running away from me, but I'll take you home and I'm not going to stand out in the street letting you freeze to death while you argue with me about that for some inexplicable reason."

He slips the hoodie over my head, hands working underneath to feed my arms through the sleeves. "Why didn't you come out here and get in the truck?" I don't answer and his fingers hesitate underneath my hoodie, hands sliding down to my waist. "What happened in the last two minutes to bring on such a change, because I have no idea why you're upset. Please tell me so we can talk about it."

I scoot away, pulling the fabric of the hoodie down until he removes his hands and no part of us is touching. "We're not together. I don't need you to drive me home, I'll find my own way."

His dark lashes fall over his cheeks. "Are you acting this way because you tried to kiss me and I pulled away?"

"No," I snap.

He leans against his door, body angled to mine. "I didn't let you kiss me because of what you just said. I need to know you *want* to be with *me*, and I thought we'd nail that down as soon as I got out here. Instead, I find you halfway down the street, shivering like a leaf in a windstorm and with this look right here on your face." He motions to me. "You're really doing your best to confuse the heck out of me and it's working. I have absolutely no idea what's happening between us."

I fold my arms. "Nothing is happening. I had a momentary lapse in judgment, and you corrected it before it got out of hand. Now it's over and I won't ever try to kiss you again."

"*Why?*" He groans. "You say a lot of words, Dani, but you never answer my questions. Outside of all the made-up obstacles in your head about why your mom is the whole reason we can't be together, *why* are you dancing with me like that one minute and running away from me the next? This should be a pretty simple conversation to have. You either like me or you don't. Pick one and stick with it."

I narrow my eyes at him. "Don't you dare try to blame this on me. The obstacles I told you about are very real, and whether you choose to believe them or not isn't my problem. And I only danced with you like that because *you* put your hands on me and *made* me move that way. Just like you did with all the *other* girls you danced with tonight. Girls you didn't pull away from. Girls you *wouldn't* pull away from. I'm the only one who gets left by herself on a couch in a house where I don't know anyone…" I let my words trail off, the cyclone that's always under my surface wanting to whirl up out of me. I press my nails into my palms and bite away the tears in my eyes. "Do you know the address here? I'll wait inside until a car comes."

~29~

My phone is still in Mikey's pocket and he's not giving me the house's address. He's only looking at me. I can feel his stare boring into the side of my face as I do my best to keep my eyes trained straight ahead and breathe.

The passenger door opens and cold air rushes into the cab. Angelo hops onto the seat, the whole truck shaking as he shoves himself right up against me. "Now *this* is my lucky night." He smacks a wet kiss on my cheek. "You staying at my place with us, Dani?"

I attempt to clear my throat of the emotion knotting inside it. Angelo leans into my face, a wide grin stretched across his lips. "You can have my room all to yourself. Unless you want my company."

"Ang," Mikey growls.

Angelo raises his hands into the air with a chuckle. "Just kidding. She's got the whole room to herself tonight. I'll even buy us some pizzas on the way because this party worked up my appetite."

My skin heats under the intensity of Mikey's stare. "It's your choice on where you want to go, Dani. You can stay with us at Ang's, where you *will* have a room all to yourself, or I'll drive you home. Either works for me. Think about it while I drive us down to grab the beast over there his food, and then just let me know."

~

Pulling up to a tidy one-level brick home with a chain-link fence around it, I'm hit with yearning. The house is small but cute, and it's all I need. It's *more* than I need. "This is where you live, Ang?"

He nods. "You're a long way from your neighborhood, Dani."

I follow him out his door, closing it behind us since he has five pizza boxes in hand, and because I'm still ignoring Mikey even though being

123

near him is the only reason I'm stupidly choosing to stay at Angelo's house. "How much does a place like this rent for?"

He side-eyes me as he unlocks the door, glancing up at Mikey, who is holding open the screen door. "We own this house, Dani. Remember me telling you it was Grandma's place?"

I sigh, my breath coming out in a cloud of smoke and my hands already frigid. "I wasn't implying anything, I was only asking a question."

He shuffles through the door and I move to follow him, but Mikey tips the screen door into my path. "I'm sorry I left you sitting on the couch alone. I didn't consider how uncomfortable you might be. I was upset, and so was Arabella. Dancing was a good distraction for both of us. But Arabella and Janelle, the only two girls I danced with tonight besides you, are only friends."

I shiver. "You don't have to say that. I'm over it anyway."

He hands me my phone. "At least one of us can forget how hot that dance was because I can't. Dancing with you was unlike anything else, and the *only* reason I pulled away from your lips is because of how I was feeling in that moment. I desperately needed to get us out of that house because I didn't want our first kiss to be in front of an audience. I wanted it to be where we could work out our feelings, and I'm sorry my actions sent you the wrong message. If I knew that you liked me, Dani, I wouldn't have ever left your side tonight."

"You heating the whole outdoors?" Angelo calls from the kitchen.

Mikey opens the screen door wide and motions for me to go inside. "I'm just reassuring Dani that you *will* keep your paws off her tonight."

Angelo winks at me as I cross the threshold. "He said paws, not hands, so we're still good."

I sit on a stool at the counter, a hollowness inside my chest. "I think he referred to your hands as paws because after seeing you with that trio of goodies, I think you classify as a dog."

He acts hurt, giving me puppy dog eyes. Mikey leans on the wall. "She's got you pegged, Ang, and it only took one party."

Angelo shrugs. "Every man needs love, and I like to find mine in multiple locations. Can't help it if all those locations come at once."

I tug a napkin from the stack and add a greasy slice of pizza to the top, handing it to Mikey and quickly looking away when his fingers slide over mine. "Are your friends coming here for pizza, Ang?"

He lets out a howl. "Not if I want to keep my head attached to my shoulders. You two saw what went down in there. I was just dancing and minding my own business, and then wham, those girls were all over me. I didn't do anything wrong."

I glance at Mikey and he puts down his half-eaten slice of pizza, jerking his thumb to the right. "Ang's room is over here. The only way to get away from his veiled bragging is to hide out in here." He glances over his shoulder to where Angelo is following behind us. "This is the only place we know for *sure* he won't be tonight."

Mikey flips on the light and Angelo moves toward the bed, kicking laundry into a pile in the corner. Surprisingly, the bed is made. "Are your sheets clean?"

Angelo grins. "Mostly. And after you're in them, I'm never going to wash them again."

Mikey swats him in the head. Angelo makes a face at him. "I'm using my manners and paying her a *compliment*. Would you wash your sheets if she slept in your bed?"

Mikey tugs off his shirt. "Here, Dani. I got a little sweaty when we were dancing tonight, but you can sleep in this if you want to change."

Angelo grabs one of his shirts from the pile of laundry on the floor. "Don't wear his dirty clothes. All of these are clean, so wear my shirt, and I won't wash it either."

Mikey puts Angelo in a headlock and drags him from the room, winking at me before he closes the door. I sit on the bed and laugh as I hear them continue to pretend scuffle, though Mikey might not actually be playing as much as Angelo is.

There's no contest on whose shirt I'm wearing. Cocooned in Mikey's, his scent all around me, I climb under the sheets and check my phone in case Madge is looking for me. She isn't, but someone else is.

I bolt upright, stomach roiling as I scroll through the photos. I'm twelve years old in these, and standing in front of a mirror in nothing but white lace underwear, one arm awkwardly covering my newly forming chest. I took these pictures in order to trap a predator but I never had the guts to use them. They sat on my phone for a while, and then I deleted them.

Getting out of bed, I pace the floor. *One. Two. Three.* How did he get deleted photos? *Four. Five. Six.* My pulse continues to accelerate. A crashing pot and banter from two boys draws my attention to the door. I shouldn't have come here. I can't have a panic attack in front of Mikey.

I sit on the bed and drop my head between my knees, starting my loop of counting over and focusing on the distant sound of Mikey's voice as he and Angelo transition into what sounds like video game playing. *Henry.* No, I shake the thought from my mind. I know him. I *love* him, almost as if he's my grandfather.

A tear slides down my face, dropping onto the long black fabric of Mikey's shirt. I can't do this right now. I can't melt down in Angelo's room, half dressed in only Mikey's shirt, while considering whether or not the person who murdered Kira was living under the same roof as me. For them to know I took those pictures, they had to be.

~30~

I wake with a start. I don't even remember falling asleep. It was all I could do to hold on to enough oxygen not to have to scream for help. Last night's panic attack was close to needing a trip to the emergency room.

Sitting up, I pull my knees to my chest and press my face into the fabric of Mikey's shirt. It's a good thing I don't wear makeup or else I'd have to explain all the smudges. As it is, all my tears have already dried, and because of them I never got a chance to fully enjoy being wrapped in his scent.

The sun is up but the house is quiet. I take one last inhale of Mikey's shirt and crawl from the warm sheets. I slip on the jeans I wore last night, make the bed, and then tug Mikey's shirt over my head and lay it neatly overtop the comforter.

Putting my long-sleeved shirt and hoodie on, I make my way to the bedroom door. Angelo's room is in the back of the house. The kitchen is straight ahead and there's an archway off to the side of that with two doors. One is the bathroom, and I assume the other is his mom's room. I never saw her last night and I'm hoping to get out of here without seeing her this morning.

Walking softly, I tiptoe through the kitchen and slip into the bathroom. As expected, last night shows on my face in the absolute worst way. I pull my hair back into its ponytail and wash my face before using the tube of toothpaste on the sink to brush my teeth with my finger. I still have no idea where I am, but once I make it by the boys and out to the street, I'll consult my map while walking as far and fast as I can.

With my breath as minty fresh as it's going to get, I sneak back out into the little hallway and stretch my neck to peek into the living room.

Angelo is asleep on the couch but I don't see Mikey. I take a step out of the hallway and feel him behind me before I hear him ask. "Are you hungry, Dani? I can fry a mean egg."

"No, you can't either." A woman shuffles out of the door that I assumed correctly was Angelo's mom's. "I saw the mess you made in here last night, and don't blame it on Angelo either. All he ever cooks is a bowl of cereal."

She brushes past me with a head-to-toe look-over and I step backward into Mikey's bare chest. I jerk away from him and he smiles at me just before turning to follow the woman into the kitchen. "The pizza we ate last night was terrible. I had to make me something else, but I cleaned up afterward, so what mess are you talking about?"

She points at the sink, the sleeve of her floral robe wiggling with her fingers. "There's *your* clean, then there's *my* clean. Just because you washed them doesn't mean they're back where they belong. Your fingers aren't any more broke than mine."

"Told you." Angelo staggers in, tussling my hair before hugging his mom. "Late night last night?"

"Don't start with me," she warns him, eyes turning on me. "You must be Dani."

"Yes, ma'am."

"Ma'am. Uh-huh." She frowns at the boys. "I assume they treated you right."

"I gave her my bed," Angelo says in agony.

"I gave Angelo my couch." Mikey pops toast out of the toaster, bouncing the hot bread on his fingers. She takes a plate off the drying rack and shoves it at him. He grins. "See? That's why I left the dishes out. Easy access."

She pushes him aside. "I'll make the eggs. You go sit down."

"No time." He shoves half a slice of toast in his mouth. "I have to go see Mammaw."

She swats a dishtowel at him. "Go on if you're going. And put on a shirt!"

"Yes, ma'am."

She swats him again. "Don't ma'am me. And stay away from Nym! You hear?"

He lifts innocent shoulders, a grin tugging at his lips. "I'm going to Mammaw's."

"Going to Mammaw's and making sure you walk by Nym's house." Her head shakes. "I'm telling you now, women like that are trouble. One look at those claws she calls nails tells you that."

Angelo comes out of his room with a fresh shirt and tosses one at Mikey. "Nym's just trying to give Mikey a good back scratch with those nice pointy nails. He needs it, Mom. It's been a while since my boy—"

She stomps toward him. Both boys take off running. "Dani?" Mikey yells. "You good for a minute?"

With him gone, I can make my escape. "Yeah." I wave from the edge of the kitchen, laughing as he shoves Angelo out the door and raises a hand to the angry woman in the robe.

"We're not going to see Nym. Scout's honor."

Her pace picks up and Mikey dashes off the porch. "Boy!" she yells. "You're no scout so put your hand down. And you better stay on this side of the road!"

She stomps back into the house and watches them from the window. I watch, too. Mikey stuffs his muscled arms into the same t-shirt I wore last night and lifts it to his nose. I know what he's doing and if he knew how much of a wreck I am, he wouldn't try to find my scent on his shirt, he'd take it off and burn it.

He'll probably end up trashing it at the very least because other than body odor, I don't have a scent. I don't use lotions and pretty-smelling shampoos. I'm just plain, lives-with-murderers, Dani.

"No sons of mine are going to mix up with the likes of Nym," the woman mutters, turning to look at me. "That painted-up doll rolls from one man to the next, and Mikey is the biggest fish walking these streets. Angelo is second. And like I've always told *both* of my sons, it's better to have girls who are *friends* than *girlfriends*. You feel me?"

I nod. "I've never had a boyfriend so I guess I'm living that advice."

She treks back to the kitchen and opens the refrigerator. "But you're here. So which of my boys are you trying to sink your claws into?"

I tug at my hoodie strings. "Neither."

"Good." She holds out a carton of eggs. "Now get in here and help me make breakfast. I'm not running a free boarding house. You stay here, you work."

I can run as fast as the guys so I could just turn and rush out the door, but I have no doubt that this woman talks to Mikey's parents. My employers. At the job I can't afford to lose, especially over spending the night in the same house as their son and then running off when asked to help out.

Lumbering back into the kitchen, I take the carton of eggs from her. "I didn't want to hurt Mikey's feelings, but *I'm* the one who makes a mean egg."

Her eyebrows raise. "You cook, little one?"

I shrug. "Only a few things but I heard eggs were the hardest so I started there. I figured if I could master an over-easy egg, everything else would be simple."

She looks me over once more. "Mary said you were something. I think maybe she's right."

~31~

Mikey and Angelo were back before breakfast was finished cooking, forcing me to once again choose between running as fast as my legs can carry me or sitting down to breakfast with the three of them.

I thought I'd be okay eating with them but the second the platter of sausage was passed to me, panic welled up and pushed tears to my eyes. I had to excuse myself and stay in the bathroom until I could tamp down the sudden fear of stuffing my face like a fool in front of Mikey. When I hit the embarrassing mark on how long I was in the bathroom, I went back to the table and took just one link of sausage to go with my one egg and one slice of toast. When everyone else was finished eating, I scraped the food from my plate into the trash and helped Mikey wash the dishes.

He tugs my ponytail, announcing, "Val, before I run Dani home, you should talk her into taking dance lessons with you. She's a natural."

I glare at him. "Dance lessons?"

He nods. "Val's a dance instructor. Ang and I both took lessons for years."

I point between them. "And that's why you're both such good dancers. Not that just *feel* the music crap you told me last night."

Val laughs. "Well, unless you can feel the music and let it touch you, you'll never have an easy rhythm, but it does sound like he was unloading a whole mouthful of junk on you."

Mikey's eyes go wide. "How is what I told her any different than what you just said?"

She pats his cheek. "Because you're a boy, and I bet you made it sound sleazy."

He sighs. "Val teaches down at the community center and they have female-only classes if you want to avoid us sleazy guys who were raised by

Val." She pinches him and he chuckles. "Dani, I'm going to jump in the shower and then I'll take you home. Make Val be nice while I'm gone."

~

Awkwardly, I sit in Mikey's shotgun seat while he tells Arabella that he'll be back around noon to help her move. He clicks off the phone and I swallow. "It sounds like Arabella needs you, so I can just call a car."

He lowers his console and glances at me. "I don't have to pull into your driveway. I just want to make sure you actually make it back to Susan's. And I want to use this drive to talk to you."

I sink down into the seat, the console lowering feeling like a way to tell me to back off—as if I'm going to crawl across the bench seat and force him to snuggle against me. "You don't have to explain Nym. But Val's pretty set against her so you might want to talk to her about that."

"Val's a little judgmental when it comes to Nym, but outside of that being wrong, I don't need to discuss anything about Nym with anyone because I'm not interested in her."

I fiddle with the hem of my hoodie. "Why? Is Nym's mom as crazy as mine?"

"No. The problem with Nym is that she's our age, but looks like she's ripped straight out of a magazine. A centerfold kind of magazine. She dresses to give the impression that she's ready for her close-up, so Val has a chip on her shoulder when it comes to all things Nym. But I imagine all moms would."

"Mother's intuition."

"More like Nym is a hotrod and mothers think all fast cars are dangerous."

And all boys want one, I think to myself as I stare out the passenger window.

After a few minutes, Mikey says my name, his voice stiff. "Dani, has anything ever…*happened* to you?"

I look his way. His knuckles are white as he grips the steering wheel. "Like what?"

His Adam's apple bobs. "Have you been *hurt* by someone? Physically. Like…how Kira was hurt but only you're still alive?"

Pain traces the edges of my heart. "After what happened to Kira, Dad kept me pretty sheltered. Until now."

He glances at me. "Is someone bothering you now?"

I scratch my forehead. "No, that's not what I was meaning."

His grip on the steering wheel loosens. "Is your mom doing things that are worse than what you've told me? I mean, I know that's all psychological and it's painful, but physically, is she hurting you?"

I stare at him. "No, she's not the reason I'm a terrible person. I'm broken all on my own."

He meets my eyes. "You're not broken, Dani. You're hurting, and I really wish I knew how to help you."

My eyes get cloudy and I look away, thinking about the photos on my phone of a naive twelve-year-old who thought she was going to make a difference in the world. I contrast her stupidity with that of my current self. I'm still stacking the odds against me.

Mikey turns onto the highway. "Sorry if I brought up stuff you don't want to talk about, Dani. I just want to make sure you're okay and that you have someone to talk to if you need it because, well, Lily hardly talks to anyone and Madge is Madge, so I'm guessing you haven't confided in either of them."

"I don't have anything I need to confide."

He sighs. "I understand that it's hard for girls to tell guys certain things, so if you need me to help find a female—"

"I said I'm fine!" I cut him off. "If you think I'm so sad and lonely and miserable and that bothers you, then stop trying to drive me everywhere. Stop trying to talk to me. Stop pretending that you like me for any other reason than I'm a charity case for you, and *stop* trying to change me when this is who I am." I tuck myself back against the door. "*This* is who I am. I told you that, and it's not my fault that you talked yourself out of believing it."

~32~

Mikey drives slowly through my neighborhood and it feels crummy to sit next to him in such heavy silence. He parks at the patch of trees just before Susan's driveway. "You don't have to tell me everything that's going on with you, Dani, but at some point, you're going to have to be straight with me about some of it. Especially the parts that have to do with me. I don't feel the way you're accusing me of feeling, and yesterday was an intense roller coaster of emotions. I want to understand what all of that was about."

"Which part?" I face him, not able to keep the tears at bay any longer. "The part where I told you not to cuddle up next to me at the movie but you did it anyway? Or the part where I tried to kiss you and you practically ran away and then gave me a line about wanting this big special first kiss when I literally saw you kiss another girl before you ran across the street and threw me over your shoulder like you had a right to."

His face is steady, voice calm. "I agree that I shouldn't have manhandled you, I had no right. As for me sitting next to you at the movie, I guess I see your point, but I'm not in the business of letting outside parties decide who I can and can't date. If I like you, and you like me, I have a hard time believing there's any reason not to sit where we want to sit. And I absolutely did *not* kiss anyone at that party last night. You must have been looking at someone else."

"It was you. With the little leopard-print dress under your arm and my stupid hoodie on your shoulder. Not to mention all the times you kiss girls at school. It's like you're running a booth at a carnival."

His body shifts, back leaning against his door and his arm sliding across the back of the seat. "While I do like this jealous side of you because it gives me hope that I'm not crazy in thinking that last night's

134

dance was anything less than two people hot for each other, we need to work on your definition of what a kiss is because if I peck a cheek or press my lips to the top of a head, that's no different than what I do with my mom or sister. If I *kiss* you, Dani, you'll know the difference."

Heat flushes up my neck. "Whatever your definitions, you show everyone affection and from what I saw, *hot* is the only way you dance. That's not me being jealous, that's me knowing the difference between words someone says and actions they take. Like Madge telling me the two of you have an understanding and that in the end, you're having a big wedding and lots of babies. And how you didn't seem to care at all that she ran off with another man last night, let alone a much older one."

His jaw ticks. "Geoff is twenty-two. Yeah, too old say the laws, but he and Madge have been hooking up on and off for years, and mostly because she pursues him. He's a decent guy and he's talked to me about the situation. He loves her, but…" Mikey rubs his face. "It's complicated for them because even without the age gap, Madge's parents won't be open to her dating Geoff. He's not what they have in mind. So you and Madge aren't so different in that regard. I mean, I'm not sure any of us are. Our parents have ideas of what they want for us and some of them are more vocal about it than others."

His parents have an idea for him to never look at someone related to Susan. "Do you think Madge loves Geoff?"

He nods. "I'm positive she does."

"And that doesn't bother you? You watch her sucking face with him right in front of you and feel nothing?"

He leans forward. "We're going to cover this one more time because both my words *and* actions regarding Madge are the same. She says things about dating me to appease her parents, sometimes she gets carried away and starts believing her tales, she's in a secret relationship with an older guy that her parents would hate because of his overall situation in life, and the only thing that would have set me off last night would have been seeing *you* kiss someone else. In fact, if I even saw you *talking* to Nick, I would have been more hurt than I already was by just hearing his dirtbag name come out of your mouth. Because he isn't a good person, *and* because I'm jealous."

I jump out of the truck and slam the door behind me. Mikey's engine starts and before I make it to the front door, I hear the crunch of the tires as he backs into Benny's driveway and pulls back out. The sound of his truck moves away from me until the roar of the engine dies off in the distance. My stomach aches. To be as vulnerable with him as he is with me would mean revealing too much. He'd find out I'm not hurting, I'm gashed open and bleeding out.

Susan opens the door. "What was that? Did I hear a truck drop you off?"

I push past her and she grabs my arm. "Danielle, *who* brought you here? And where have you been all night?"

I yank free. "I'm surprised you noticed I didn't come home."

Randall steps out of the living room. "Don't speak to your mother that way. We both called and texted, but you didn't answer. You're still a minor and that means we're responsible for you, so answer your mother's questions without the attitude."

I spin to position myself where I can see both of them. "I'm *barely* a minor, and you can both take your fake concern and sell it to someone who thinks it's worth the breath you're wasting because before too long, Mommy here stops making money off of pretending to clothe and shelter me."

~33~

I'm angry. More so than I've ever been. The closer I get to eighteen, the harder Susan, and now Randall, come at me with rules and insults disguised as guidance. I know I'm wrong, that if I'd been listening to everyone around me my whole life I'd be a different person right now, but I didn't. And it's too late to start now. It's too late because Kira's killer is closer than he's ever been, or at least closer than I ever knew he was. I can't abandon her now all because I'm in love with Michael Beller.

It's hard to admit to myself that I care so much about him. And with the way I treat him there's no way he could guess, but in the darkest part of night when my mind is too tired to scribble down information that may lead to an angle on the identity of Kira's killer, I replay images of Mikey until the curve of his lips and the caramel of his eyes lull me to sleep. And when he's sitting next to me like he is now, it's nearly impossible to think of anything but our dance. Tomorrow night will be one week since that heated exchange took place, and I wish I could go back in time and erase myself from ever having gone to that party.

With Madge's insistence and Angelo practically dragging me from the library, I've started eating lunch at their table. Monday, Mikey spoke to me but sat on the other side of the table between Tanya and Wendy. The next day he sat between Jackie and Opal and slowly made his way around the table each day until he was next to me. That day was yesterday, when he was on my right. Today he's on my left with Madge on my right and Angelo on hers.

Mikey slides a crinkly white bag toward me. "This is from Zach. He said there's more of these where this one came from if you feel like stopping by his place."

I look up at him. He sighs. "He's asking you to come to Scoopz, not his house."

"I know that," I whisper. "And you could have given me this cookie at any point throughout the day but you chose to do it now? Just so all of *them* will see and get themselves fired up all over again."

He swivels on the bench, mouth dropping to my ear as his hand runs down my ponytail. "*If* I wanted to orchestrate a girl fight, I'd do something like this." He runs his nose over my earlobe. "Then I'd get up and walk away because as long as I'm sitting here, none of them are going to say anything to you."

His hand runs down my back, mouth still on my ear. "I'm giving you Zach's gift now because it's food, and lunchtime is when you eat food. I thought a chocolate chip cookie would go good with your peanut butter sandwich. Which is what I told Zach when I asked him to bag that up for you. When he heard your name, he gave me the cookie for free. Which I decided was perfect because if *I* give you a cookie, there's no telling what you'll do."

He gives my ponytail a tug and straightens. "You've managed to sit next to me for two whole days without running away, so we're making positive progress."

I push to my feet and slide out from under the table. "Dani," he groans, but I don't stop. I walk out and head to the nearest restroom, pulse slamming against my ears.

I duck into the first stall and wait, seconds feeling like hours as I try to calm myself down. I can't engage with Mikey on a personal level. I only stayed next to him yesterday and endured the torture of wanting to feel his hand slip over to my knee because he barely talked directly to me. He and Ang were doing their own thing and mixing in the general table conversation while I just sat there like a lump of coal. When he puts his attention on me, I begin to splinter. Desire breaking through the walls I keep trying to rebuild until I'm flooded with anger and panic.

Noise picks up in the hallway, signaling the end of lunch. Shoes click over the bathroom floor and I remain silent. I recognize Opal's voice first. "What is up with Dani this time? That girl is legit weird."

"She's pathetic," Tanya nips. Their voices are coming from the area by the row of mirrors; they're probably putting on their post-lunch lip gloss.

"Desperate," Lauren adds with a laughing lilt to her voice. "Do you think she even notices how obvious she is?"

Wendy makes a disgusted sound. "She knows. Her problem is that she doesn't realize Mikey and Angelo feel sorry for her. I think she thinks they actually like her."

"If she only knew that Mikey is basically forcing people to be nice to her." Tanya giggles. "Can you imagine being her? Sitting around thinking you're somebody when really, all you are is a pet project of the hottest boy in school."

They walk by again and I quickly lift my feet as Lauren remarks, "Everyone here knows Mikey is yours, Tanya. That's why he's never dated a single other girl in this school. Ever. Dani is wasting her pathetic little existence going after our men. Just wait until I shove that cookie back in Zach's face."

~

The house was too quiet last night. Randall took Susan away for the weekend and after the car service dropped me off, I wish I'd stayed at the boutique and found a way to sleep in the break room instead of being in this house with every pop and crack wreaking havoc on my nerves.

As silly as I felt, I was too scared to sleep in my bed. I barricaded my bedroom door and curled up in a ball in the closet while I checked Henry's daughter's social media again. It doesn't appear that he's the killer. She has photographs of him in her shop during times that I've received pictures of my current self, so unless Henry has an accomplice, or *was* the accomplice of the murderer, Henry isn't my suspect. Neither is my dad, though logically I know he's the only other person who lived in our house during the time I took those provocative photos.

Before leaving the closet, I flip on the light and press my ear to the door, listening for movement in my room or elsewhere. I don't hear anything but I stay a beat longer, letting my eyes roam over the clothes that Susan hung in here. The racks and shelves are filled with slinky dresses, short skirts, string bikinis, and high-heeled shoes. If I wore any of it, I'd look like Mikey's description of Nym.

There are a few tops that are scoop necks instead of low-cut, and one draws my eye. It's red, with bell sleeves that cinch at the wrists. I take it off its hanger and slowly open the closet door. My dresser is still flush against the other door.

Leaving the barricade in place, I run to the bathroom and lock myself inside. I don't have to work today so I'm going to take an extra-long hot shower and enjoy being alone in this creepy house as much as I possibly can.

Squeaky clean and finally managing to get my mass of thick hair blown dry, I tug the red scoop neck over my head and check my appearance in the full-length mirror on the back of my closet door. The top doesn't look bad with my jeans. I tie a thin brown belt around the waist and think Mary would be proud of the choice. She's been teaching me how to accessorize so I can help customers pull a look together. Pam teaches me, too, and Davina, but everyone admits that Mary has the eye for what will look best together, even when her choices are unexpected.

It takes an hour to curl my hair with the big round curling iron Susan gave me, saying I'd look better with my hair down and having some wave to it. Of course, she's right. It looks much better, but who has time to do this every day? And am I only proving Lauren right by trying this out? Am I being desperate? If I am, I might as well go all in.

Putting on makeup is new to me. Susan provided a whole kit of the stuff and I try to mimic what I've seen on other girls, but the result is clownish. The blue eye shadow is too dark and the red lipstick makes my lips look two sizes too big for my face. I reach for a washcloth. The doorbell rings and I freeze. Despite Susan's aptitude for being seen, she rarely has company. I'm not sure if that's because of Randall or her preference is to go out to meet people, not have them in her home. Either way, I can count on one hand the number of times I've heard her doorbell ring.

Tiptoeing to my bedroom door, I push the dresser out of the way and walk into the hall. I doubt I'm going to open the main door, but I can at least go look out the window to see who it is. It could be the killer, after all.

I'm almost at the top of the stairs when I hear the footfall. Someone is coming up the stairs. My heart pounds. There's a small knife in my backpack. My backpack is in the closet. I turn back to my room. "Dani? Good, you're home."

I clench my teeth, willing my heart to stop breaking my ribs. "Randall, what are you doing here? I thought you were with Susan."

"I was," he answers as I turn toward him. "She's having a spa day today and I'm going to set up a little romantic dinner for us while she's being pampered." He makes a show of the flower bouquet cradled in his arms. "I rang the bell so you'd know I was here. Didn't want to scare you."

I swallow. "Next time, probably just shoot me a text."

He frowns. "You're not great at responding to messages, Dani. Your dad called your mother again because he says you still haven't answered one of his calls."

I fold my arms. "Same as he's never answered one of mine. Oh, and he also discarded me to a woman who has zero interest in me unless I can add dollars to her bank account."

He walks toward me. "You know that's not true. Which is another reason I came back early today. I'm going to make us some lunch and then we're going to have a long talk. Now, if you don't mind, go to the kitchen and pour me a cold beer while I put these flowers and a few other things in your mom's room."

I walk past him. I absolutely mind pouring his alcohol but I also don't want him coming into my room while we're alone in the house. If he wants to talk to me, he can do it downstairs. Better yet, I might just pour his beer and then go hide in the woods until dark.

~34~

Yanking open the freezer door, I take out one of the frosty plastic mugs lined up on the second shelf. Susan bought these after Randall basically started living here, and she told me they were for his beer. Her implication being that they weren't here for me to use. Just like everything else in this house. Unless she specifically bought it for me, I'm not to touch it.

Taking a bottle of beer from the refrigerator, I tip the contents into the icy mug. Randall prances in and takes the mug from me. "Thanks. And you look nice. Just as pretty as your mom."

I fold my arms. "I'm sure you think that's a compliment."

He pulls an envelope from his back pocket. "This was on the front porch for you. And if you're dressed up because you thought you were going to have some boy come over today, think again. Until things change around here, starting with your attitude, your mom and I are forced to take action. I'll drive you to school, pick you up, and that's it. Because we know you've been lying to us about all this supposed time you spend at the library. And where are you getting the money to pay for the car service you've been using? We asked your dad about it and he said there are some charges on his credit card, but not to the tune of how often you pay for a ride."

I hear his words but even if I could respond, I wouldn't tell him that Mikey has been my recent driver. As it is, I can't respond. Because this letter *is* addressed to me, but the address written under my name isn't mine. It's Kira's. While Randall drones on, I slide the tip of my nail underneath the butterfly sticker that's sealing the envelope and slowly lift the letter out. On the single folded sheet of paper is a photo collage. In the center there is a heart with the words *Dani Madison's Greatest Hits.*

When I was thirteen, I mustered the courage to once again attempt trapping a predator using my own photos. This time, I intentionally took them in a position where my head was never in the photographs. I also decided not to cover my chest. I kept these photos saved on my phone for a long time. Whenever I was chatting on some app with a predator, I'd consider sending one of these when he inevitably asked for a picture. Sometimes predators are specific in what body parts they want sent, others pretend they only want what you're comfortable sending, and they'll send their own to coax you into believing it's okay to send back the exact same part of your body that they so bravely sent to you. I never fell for any of that, and I never hit send on any of my pictures. All I ever did was state my age over and over, have the predator acknowledge he understood I was a kid, and then I turned all the information I had over to a tip line.

"Dani." Randall shakes my shoulder. "You're not listening to me at all, are you?"

I crumple the paper in my hand and look up, unable to speak. His brows knit together. "Here." He presses the beer into my hand. "Sit down and drink this. I'm going to go see who is at the door and then we'll finish this conversation after both of us have had something to take the edge off. The stress of this situation is getting to all of us."

He walks away and I close my eyes, numb even to the sound of the doorbell gong. My chest tightens. *One. Two. Three.* I open my eyes, plop the beer onto the counter and head for the safety of my room.

"Danielle isn't only sick, she's grounded. She isn't allowed company." Randall's voice breaks through my surging panic. I keep my path angled for the stairs.

"Isn't she a little old to be grounded?" Mikey's deep voice drowns out Randall's.

I shuffle toward the sound of his voice. Randall's back is to me but Mikey's tall frame towers over him in the open doorway. His eyes land on me and he smiles. "She doesn't look sick or grounded to me."

Randall's stiff shoulders jerk around. "Go back into the kitchen, Dani. I'll handle this."

Mikey ignores him, lifting his chin at me. "Come take a walk with me."

Randall shoves Mikey back from the door and Mikey regains his ground, coming in fast. I run toward them, pushing around Randall and yanking free of his grip when he grabs at me. "Your beer is on the counter. Go drink it before you decide to assault any more of my friends."

I have to tug Mikey's arm twice to get him to step away from Randall. We reach the end of the sidewalk and Randall yells for me to stop. "I'm going to have to call your mother if you leave this property!"

I throw up a hand. "Tell her I'm with Mikey Beller. She'll be thrilled!"

Mikey growls. "Hopefully she'll be just as thrilled when I shove her boyfriend's arm down his throat. That's who that guy is, right? Your mom's boyfriend?"

I stop at the trash bin and throw in the photo collage that's still crumpled in my palm. "Yeah, that's Randall. He used to be fairly decent. He'd make excuses for Susan, sometimes give me money or gifts after one of her outstanding tear-down sessions, but now he's basically her twin." I face Mikey. "What's your excuse? Why are you here picking fights on my doorstep?"

He presses his hand against my shoulder and moves us out of sight of the front door, his eyes staying on Randall until the trees block the view. "I didn't pick that fight, he copped an attitude after he said you were sick and I asked if I could go check on you. I figured that wasn't your dad, but asked just to be sure, which made his attitude worse. Then he started with the whole grounded spiel and," Mikey rubs my arms. "That's when you came around the corner looking the complete opposite of sick, and grounded by anyone in that house over my dead body."

"And what was your plan if Susan was there? Just felt like being adored today so you decided to knock on her door?"

He takes off his button-down flannel and wraps it around my shoulders. "I didn't knock on her door, I knocked on yours. And what I feel like is spending time with you on your day off. I want to show you something."

I shrug. "Show it, then."

He rubs the back of his neck and clocks my shoes. Strappy leather sandals. I thought I'd at least try them on since they don't have heels. "To see it, you have to take a walk with me." His eyes drag up my body, lingering at the top of my scoop neck before lifting to my face. "You're going to need to put on more clothes. Because it's cold out here." He clears his throat and wipes a hand down his face. "Why are you so dressed up anyway?"

I remove his flannel from my shoulders and shove it at him, spinning toward the cul-de-sac as it drops to the ground. "Is this where the thing you want to show me is?"

I keep walking even when he grabs my arm. He slides in front of me. "I'm serious, it's too cold for you to not at least have a hoodie or something on. And you need your normal shoes." He glances at my feet again. "Why are you even wearing those? It's practically winter already and I've literally never seen you in anything other than tennis shoes."

"And today I'm wearing these," I bite. "If you want to show me something, show it. If my clothes are a deal-breaker for you, fine, I don't want to see whatever this is anyway." I cross my arms. "Despite what you and your friends think, I'm not desperate to be in your little clique, and I don't need anyone's advice on how to dress."

He backs up, hands in the air. "I'm not complaining about your clothes. I'm just trying to take you somewhere and I would have brought my truck over and taken you there a different way if I'd known today was a dress-up day. But if you're good, I'm good." He steps to the side and motions for me to continue toward the cul-de-sac. "Will you at least put my flannel on?"

I don't respond and he slips the shirt back over his arms with a groan, glancing at me as we walk but not saying anything. We reach the end of the sidewalk and he motions to the woods where I ran into him that night. I walk ahead of him, humiliation scorching my face. I can't believe I'm wearing this stupid shirt. My hair catches on a branch and I yank it free, leaving a clump on the branch.

"Hey." Mikey's hands are as soft as his voice. He smooths my hair and cups my face. "What's going on? Why are you so angry? And what was the quip about a clique?"

I pull his hands from my face, forcing myself to let them go. "You showing up at my door saying you want to show me something, then immediately backpedaling so you don't have to show it to me, is going on."

He sighs. "I didn't backpedal. It's just, you never look like this."

"Are my sandals that much of a problem for you?"

He shoves his hands into his pockets. "Not even your attitude is problem for me. But I am having a hard time stringing words together with you standing here looking like you just stepped out of a magazine."

I glare at him. "Ha ha. Now can we go?"

He shrugs. "That's up to you. We can stick to my original plan or do it a different day. Until you decide, I'm just going to stand here and stare because I'm not teasing you. You're always beautiful, but today? Wow, Dani."

"Don't get used to it. Tomorrow I turn back into a dud."

He moves forward. "Like I said, you're always beautiful to me. So I don't know what all that junk was that you unloaded on me. What I do know is it's clear that *I'm* the one knocking on *your* door and trying my hardest to blow down your walls and I'm not doing that because you're a dud, desperate, or any of the other asinine things I've heard you say. I'm not even doing it because you're a whole serving of beautiful. It's more than that, and maybe if you would spend time with me, we'd be able to figure out how much more."

He moves away from me and runs his hands through his hair. "Every time I think I'm done begging for your time, I find myself walking over here. Today isn't the first time, but what I have to show you is important enough that I went ahead and knocked on your door." His eyes fall on mine. "If you want to run away from me again because I'm being honest with you, be careful because those sandals aren't made for running like your normal shoes are."

~35~

Two hundred yards into the woods, we come to a fence. It's ten feet high and stretches as far as the eye can see. Mikey opens a panel, fingers running over a keypad. He closes the panel and there's a snap, then he pushes a section of the fence open. I inspect the hidden hinges as we pass through. I could have stood here all day and never noticed them.

"This is the back end of my family's property," he explains as we enter the dense woods. "My parents used to be crazy paranoid so there was razor wire on top of this fence for years. When Lily was about five, Dad had us all out riding around in his UTV. Lily saw a bird sitting on top of the wire and was convinced that it would die. She cried all day. Dad took the razor wire down the very next day."

"I bet your mom was relieved to not feel like her family was living inside a prison."

He laughs. "That wire coming down was the only time I've ever seen my dad buck my mom. She wanted it left up, but he couldn't handle Lily's tears. Everyone thinks he's a big brute and when it comes to his family he can be, but my mom is worse."

"Your mom Mary, or are we talking about Val?"

He grins. "Val is loud, but she's got nothing on Mary. Even Val knows better than to get on my mom's bad side."

My eyes go wide. "And now I'm much more afraid of losing my job. Thanks."

He chuckles as we trudge deeper into the woods. A stick jams under my toes. I yank it out and wait for his rebuke but he doesn't say he told me this would happen. Instead, he begins scraping his foot along the forest floor, clearing the path for me. His kindness always makes me feel worse. "You don't have to do that. And I'm sorry I'm in such a bad mood today. And every day."

He smiles. "No problem. The only thing you do that really bothers me is accuse me of things. I'm hoping we can one day move past all that, and this is the only way I know how to speed us toward that day. Lock you behind a gate and force you to spend time with me."

"As long as your mom doesn't find out, I guess I'm safe enough."

He slides his hand along the sleeve of my shirt, letting his palm fall down into mine. "If she finds out that I made you walk out here, in sandals, *I'll* be the one in trouble."

I don't pull away or even attempt to stop myself from closing my fingers tightly over his. His grip matches mine as he continues to watch the ground, kicking larger sticks and rocks off the overgrown path. A lump lodges in my throat. Of all the people in the world, why does this one have to be my first love? And why meet him now, when between Susan and Kira's killer, I can't explore a relationship with him.

We stop at the edge of a ravine and Mikey whistles. "It's a long haul down there, and even longer getting back up the other side. You think you can handle this?"

I glance to the steep climb on the other side. "These sandals aren't going to make it easy."

He shrugs. "Too bad. There's no backing out now."

I take a step forward. "I didn't say I wasn't going, only that you were right. I should have changed my shoes."

He tugs me away from the edge with a chuckle. "Even if you weren't wearing sandals, I wouldn't make you walk down there."

He moves us farther along the ravine, stopping where an ATV is parked alongside saplings. He drops my hand and plucks a helmet from the seat. "Ever been on one of these?"

I nod. "Yeah, my dad used to have quads and we'd ride sometimes."

Mikey fixes the helmet on my head and then puts on his own, straddling the back of the seat. "Want to drive?"

I grin. "*This* is what you brought me out here to do?"

He takes off his flannel and holds it in front of him. "My surprise is farther out, and now I have to insist that you cover up that pretty shirt."

I sit in front of him and he slips the flannel over my arms, hands coming around my waist to work the lower buttons into place. I stop him from moving higher. "It's been a while since I've driven *anything,* so you better hold on."

~

As fun as it is to be in control of this powerful machine, I'm more enamored with the feel of Mikey's long arm circled around my waist and his hand resting on my opposite hip. When he's not using the other hand to point out the route, he lets those fingers settle on my stomach.

Well beyond the far side of the ravine, Mikey points ahead of us, motioning to a stone-sided house nearly swallowed by the woods. I maneuver through the trees and park near the structure. "Whose house is this?"

He tugs off his helmet. "My sister's. Her little playhouse."

"*This* is a playhouse?"

He slides off the back and loosens my helmet. "Lily asked for a place where she could have tea with her dolls. My dad, who has issues doing anything small when it comes to the women in his life, decided to interpret Lily's request as meaning she needed her very own fairy-tale cottage in the woods."

He points in the direction we'd been heading before we veered left toward the cottage. "My house sits at the base of that next hill over. Far enough away that Lily really felt like this place was magical, but close enough that we could bring her up here daily." He takes my helmet and sets both of them to the side. "She outgrew this place and no one has been up here in a couple of years. I cleaned it up some this morning and there's still a lot more to do, but the generator works so we have power, and the well hasn't dried up so we have water."

I kick my leg over the seat so I'm facing him, feet dangling. "This is what you wanted to show me?"

He clears his throat. "Not exactly. What I want to show you is inside, but before we go in there, I need to tell you something."

I twist my fingers together. "Nothing good ever follows those words."

He picks up my hands, pulling my fingers apart and lacing his through them. "When I was thirteen, my parents told me about some things that my mom went through before I was born. What they told me changed my outlook on people. I think that's part of the reason I stick so close to the people I know. Maybe that's what you meant by calling my friends and me a clique. But the truth is, I'm tight with Angelo, then Madge, and everyone else is more of an acquaintance."

"Tell that to Tanya."

He nods. "This is what I like about you, Dani. You make me think. About everything. I've never had to consider my actions so heavily before, but now I'm taking a whole week to decide if I should give you a cookie and still getting it wrong."

I look away and he lets go of my hands, bringing his fingers to my face and turning me back to him. "After you stormed away, I replayed what happened for hours. I don't think being affectionate with you in public is an issue, you do. I don't care about your mom, but Susan bothers you. And those two issues are at the root of you not giving me a chance to even be your friend. My approach has been to *show* you that I don't care about those issues, but now I realize that whether I agree that they're obstacles or not, I *have* to care, simply because you do."

"Mikey—"

He slides two fingers to my lips. "I trapped you out here so I could tell you with my words how I feel, and show you with my actions. So let me say this, Dani, because you're always looking for a reason to ax me and I want to cover all my bases."

I roll my eyes at him and he winks. "After you told me about Kira, I thought I understood what you were going through because although it wasn't what my mom went through, it seemed similar enough. I think I was pretty wrong about that. So before I inadvertently do more damage to you, I need you to explain to me what happened at Ang's the other night because you scared the living hell out of me and the next morning you acted like…nothing even happened. And then you were mad at me again."

My body goes rigid. "What do you mean? You heard me crying?"

His head shakes. "I was there, Dani. I saw you. You were…screaming. I was playing a video game with Ang and then we heard this sound that wasn't coming from the game. I practically tore the bedroom door off the hinges to get to you."

I pull his hands from my face and get off the four-wheeler, breath growing shallow. "I didn't scream. I kept my panic attack under control."

He paces beside me. "You were halfway on the floor, Dani. And that wasn't a panic attack. You were clawing at the bed and making horrible sounds. I definitely made out Kira's name a few times and I tried to wake you but Ang said I shouldn't, that it was some kind of night terror and that he'd heard if you woke people up from one of those, it would do major damage. So I just let it play out. Was that the right thing to do?"

My throat constricts. "You two sat and watched me?"

"No," he whispers. "I sent Ang out of the room. I stayed with you, mostly just sitting on the floor beside the bed, and I did hold your hand once you were calm enough for me to touch you. But that next morning, part of why Ang and I left was so we could have a chat about how to handle what happened. I didn't want him bringing it up and embarrassing you, so I told him I'd talk to you on the way home."

My head spins. "That's why you were so weird in the truck, asking me all those questions about someone hurting me?"

He swallows. "I was a little worried that the way I treated you at the party triggered some kind of memory that made you have that reaction."

"No." I shake my head and let my hands rest along his cheeks. "Mikey, you didn't do anything. And then I yelled at you for doing nothing. So what did you tell Angelo?"

His lip ticks up. "That you're super jealous and it turns me on."

~36~

My face burns and Mikey laughs, admitting that he only told Angelo that I'd had a bad dream and was embarrassed about it so Angelo shouldn't bring it up. As thankful as I am not to have to *also* have this conversation with Angelo, I'm still mortified.

I move away from Mikey so he can't feel me shaking. "I used to have episodes like you described when I was a kid. But I've had lots of therapy and now if I have a nightmare, I usually wake up. I have panic attacks, too. Lately, they've been ramping up and I'm having a hard time controlling them. I guess the one I had that night didn't go away like I thought it did. I'm so sorry, I had no idea that I put you through that."

He moves close to me. "There's nothing to be sorry about. I'm just worried about you, and I'm no therapist but I want to try to help you." His fingers glide through my hair and tuck it behind my ear. "Watching you go all woman-possessed didn't make me like you any less, either. And then you walk out of your house today looking like my own personal magazine cover."

I sink my fist into his gut and he laughs, slipping his arm around my waist and leading me to the cottage. This door has a keypad, too, and his fingers quickly enter the code. He tugs me through the door with him, the temperature change making me shiver. It's cooler in here than outside. And dusty.

I sneeze as a cloud of dust passes through the beam of light from the open door. He frowns. "Sorry. If you like what I set up and want to come back, I'll finish getting the place cleaned up."

He leads me through the living room where several beanbag chairs flank a long, low table that seems the perfect height for kids to play board games on, and then he walks us into the kitchen. Unlike the living room, the kitchen is pristine. There's even a fresh tablecloth on the table. He points to the frilly white chairs surrounding it. "That's where Lily used to have tea with her seven thousand dolls. You should have seen this place before she gave them all away."

I smile. "I can imagine it was very little girlish despite being a whole house. Are the appliances real?"

He nods. "Everything works, I checked it all out this morning to make sure. But it's well water only out here so I stocked some bottles of water in the refrigerator. Are you thirsty? I added some soda and sweet tea in there, too."

I tilt my head. "All I am is confused. Why am I here? Other than you trying your best to convince me that you like how I mistreat you."

"I'm getting there." He winks, leading us back out of the kitchen and down a hallway. "This door is the bathroom, and that one is the bedroom. There's an air mattress in the closet but no actual furniture." He opens the door as if to prove to me that he's being honest, closing it when I nod that I can see he's telling the truth.

He walks us back to the living room. "My aunt and uncle have eight kids, so with Ang and me in the mix, Lily had a full house when everyone came to a sleepover. Sometimes even Val and my grandma showed up. The older the boys got, the more we'd camp outside instead of being in here with the girls, but like I said, the era of this place being used is gone. I think security stops by whenever they run patrols to check the property's borders, but they don't come inside. They only make sure the doors are locked and the windows aren't broken."

I stop in the middle of the living room. "That's great. I'm glad you're nice and protected in your fortress of however many acres. But what does any of this have to do with me?"

His head ticks to a whiteboard propped against the wall beside two large tote bags. "I'm giving you the history of the place so you understand that no one uses the cottage anymore. And I'm telling you about security because they're the only people you should ever encounter out here, but they won't bother you. I'll tell them to steer clear of the place if you decide to take me up on my offer."

I squint at him. "Which is?"

"Would you like to use this place as your war room?"

"War room?"

He chuckles. "My Aunt Sheila has a temper. When someone crosses her, she's been known to orchestrate a nuclear event." His expression turns serious. "I want to help you find who murdered your friend. One of my cousins is dating an FBI agent, and I have all kinds of other resources we can tap into if you're ready to let other people get involved. If you're not ready, you can still use this place as your home base because it doesn't seem like you have anyone in your corner." He waves his arm around. "This is my way of showing you you're not alone. Yes, I'm attracted to you, but I can separate my attraction from the work. When we're here, it can be all business. I'll shoot my shots elsewhere."

He leads me to the tote bags, holding open the top of one to reach in and pull out various items. Pens and pencils, highlighters, notebooks, tape, and even a stapler. "You can make a list of what you need and I'll get it, I just picked up some things to get us started."

I drop to my knees and sort through the second tote. File folders, sticky tabs, and even a laptop. I look up at him. "You got all of this for me?"

He hesitates. "That's another one of those things I really had to think about because I didn't want to subconsciously have strings attached to you being here. In the end, my decision came down to the worst-case scenario being that one or both of us ends up truly and completely despising the other. But there's no way we don't make headway on Kira's case. Even if you're never comfortable letting me bring in other people, the two of us together *have* to be able to capitalize on what you've already put together. So I'm doing this for Kira. Not either of us."

Tears flood my eyes and he kneels beside me, rubbing a strand of my hair between his fingers. "We haven't started working yet so I do have something that *is* just for you. Wait here while I go get it because I need to shoot just one more shot before I can put kissing you out of my mind for the day."

~

I unpack the totes, spreading the contents over the long table in the center of the living room. Mikey even bought graph paper. "What do you think?" he asks, walking across the room with a plate in his hand. "Can I plan on bringing you out here more often?"

I climb to my feet and look into his face. "If you're serious about this, yes, I can come anytime I'm not at school or work. Just let me know when your schedule is clear and I'll meet you at the gate."

He holds the plate out to me. "If your schedule is clear, so is mine."

The ceramic plate is covered in tiny sandwiches cut into the shapes of flowers and arranged like a bouquet, with thin red candy strings tied in a bow at the bottom. "What is this?"

He lifts a delicate sandwich from the plate. "Lily showed me how to use cookie cutters to cut the bread. She used to do stuff like this when she was young and had tea with her dolls." He puts the sandwich to my lips. "I made your favorite. Plain peanut butter, no jelly."

I slap a hand over my mouth to stop the sobs but it's too late, they're heaving from my body. Mikey's eyes go wide and he drops the plate. "Dani, what's wrong?"

I can't answer. I can barely breathe. He hoists me into his arms and plops down into a beanbag, settling me on his lap while holding me tightly to his chest. I bury my face in his neck. He rubs my back, offering soft words while I cry.

His hand stills mid-stroke, and then I feel it. The slight tilt of his body as he slips off the beanbag in a slow-motion slide that's both lazy and yet too fast to stop. His body pitches sideways and we topple over, his arm shooting up my back and his hand cupping the back of my head to keep it from hitting the floor. Nose to nose, he just stares at me, eyes wide with worry. My sobs turn to laughter.

Slowly, he smiles. "Sorry about that. I guess my next order of business is getting us some grown-up furniture in here."

I rake the back of my hand across my eyes. "I'd much rather fall off a beanbag than keep crying like a lunatic."

He sits up, bringing me with him. "As much as I wish those were happy tears, they weren't. What did I do wrong?"

I press my knuckles into my mouth because I can't stop laughing now. "I hate peanut butter."

His eyes bug out. "But that's literally all I ever see you eat anymore. Even at work when I drop by to stalk you in the breakroom, you always have peanut butter crackers or a peanut butter sandwich."

When I'm eating, he does always come into the breakroom for water when he's around. "You're stalking me?"

He shrugs. "I keep tabs on your schedule. When I think you're not going to yell at me, I dip in and see if forced proximity makes a difference in how you feel about me."

I tug my knees up and bury my face. He scoots to my side and wraps an arm around my shoulder. "I'm sorry about the sandwiches. But now I need you to explain this peanut butter situation to me because nothing like this was in any of those books."

I tilt my face sideways so I can see him. "You seriously read relationship books?"

He nods. "I'm currently on number seven. Not a word about the double meaning of peanut butter."

I lift from my knees and play with the hem of his flannel that I'm still wearing, my thoughts jumping from the mail that came today to the smell of the peanut butter to *his* smell. "I'm not crying over the sandwiches." I glance to where the delicate bread he took so much time to cut is now spilled across the floor. "You're really sweet and thoughtful, and you're being this way to someone like me. It's uncomfortable."

"Someone like you?" He strokes my cheek. "Beautiful, smart, independent, hard-working, loyal, and so dedicated to your friend that you go through the motions but you won't truly live until you catch who killed her."

My head snaps up and he smiles. "I see you, Dani. You're the one who is sweet and thoughtful, I'm just a guy who is trying to force you to live just a little so that I can experience all of you. And I'm sorry that me being selfish makes you cry. I'm trying so hard to do the opposite of upsetting you."

"You don't upset me." I sniff. "You do the opposite, and *that* upsets me. It hurts to like you so much. I don't fit in anywhere so people usually just leave me alone, but you don't. And when you do, I hate it. So I default to just being angry because I don't know how to deal with this. I'm one meltdown away from shattering into a million pieces."

His eyes trace the trail his fingers make along my face. "This is how you deal with it. You talk to me, and let me be the glue when you're feeling overwhelmed because even when you're infuriating, I still can't help falling all over every chance to talk to you for even one single second."

~37~

All I've wanted since first putting on makeup was to wash it off. My face feels better now and I know I look better. My funny clown face transitioned into horror film clown with all the tears I shed today.

Mikey's fear was palpable when I came back from the bathroom and he motioned to the table where he'd set two places, our ham sandwiches cut in half and a bag of chips nestled between our two plates. He was afraid these sandwiches would trigger me, too.

I glance into the living room where the dainty spilled sandwiches were. "I would have cleaned up the peanut butter sandwiches. I'm the one who made you drop them anyway."

He chugs a bottle of water, washing down his food. "I've removed all peanut butter from the premises, so don't look too closely at the box outside because I might have bought peanut butter-flavored toaster treats, granola bars, cereal, crackers, cookies, and something called YumBuns? They kind of looked gross to me but it said it was peanut butter and I was still under the impression that my girl loved peanut butter."

My mouth gapes and he shrugs. "It's a curse, Dani. Lily asks for a playhouse and Dad builds her an actual house. I see you eat a few peanut butter sandwiches and go buy stock in the worldwide production of peanut butter." He runs a hand down his face. "I don't want to upset you again, and I know your tears were about all the things you keep inside rather than about the peanut butter, but can you please explain to me *why* you eat peanut butter if you hate it?"

I pull a chip from the bag and proceed to break it half, and then break that half in half before dropping it onto my plate. If Mikey has proven anything to me, it's that I can trust him. "I used to not mind peanut butter, but almost since the day I moved here, it's all I've been eating. Breakfast, lunch, and dinner are usually the same. The only variation is whether I eat my peanut butter with bread or with crackers. Occasionally, a meal is something different. Like when I had pizza with you and Ang, and breakfast with you the next day. But mostly my diet is peanut butter. Which I shouldn't complain about because Susan says I need to lose weight and I am, just not quite fast enough for her."

He scoots his chair around and kicks the bottom of mine so the legs spin out and I'm facing him. "At breakfast, you only ate a little of what was on your plate and you never put much on it to begin with. And right now, you're picking at that sandwich while mine is long gone. Are you telling me that *you* don't want to eat? Or are you telling me that *Susan* won't let you eat?"

I pick at a spot on my jeans. "Depends on your definition of *want* and *let*."

He flattens my hand to my knee, forcing my eyes to his. "You *wanting* to eat is what I saw at my pool party, where a really hot girl piled her plate full of food and the first thing she ate from that mountain was a dessert that I happened to make. Susan not *letting* you was her coming over and ripping that plate out of your hand. She got what she deserved that day, and you put up such a fight that I just assumed you didn't let her bully you." He moves forward, his hands on my waist. "You are *perfect*, Dani. Please tell me you aren't starving yourself or doing some crazy diet just because Susan has too much filler in her face to see out of her eyes correctly."

Just last week, I overhead Susan telling Randall that *I* needed injections to *fix* my face. She said I needed to get rid of my wrinkles and have fuller lips. "If I eat at Susan's house, she's pretty snotty about it. And not only because I'm overweight already, but because she says I'm basically freeloading. To avoid having to hear her mouth about it, I provide my own food. Peanut butter is cheap and shelf-stable, so I can keep it under my bed, and she doesn't clean or anything so she has no idea it's there. Buying food is part of the reason I needed a job so badly. I'm also trying to save up to get a car, and if I get a car there's gas and insurance. So I just stomach the peanut butter and the weight loss is an added perk." I tentatively place my arms around his neck. "Susan is certain that for me to properly seduce you, I have to look exactly like her, with all my bones sticking out, but a girl can only do so much."

Anger flashes in his eyes. "This isn't funny, Dani. Don't make jokes about your health. Susan is going to force you into an eating disorder, if she hasn't already."

I push away from him and get out of the chair. "It isn't like I chose any of this, Mikey. I'm doing the best I can but that's not good enough for anyone. And if I do what *I* want to do, that *disturbs* everyone. Then you bring me here and act like this is a safe space, that *you're* a safe space, and now you want lecture me too? Should I eat what and how you tell me to when I'm here? And what and how Susan tells me to when I'm with her? Then explain to you why I'm not still the chunky girl you're apparently attracted to while simultaneously explaining to the psychotic wench I'm being forced to live with why I'm not thin and beautiful the way every other girl in our school is?"

He stands and strides toward me slowly. "Option three. Take me home with you and I'll explain to that wench why your hips are perfect." He moves closer. "Why your waist is perfect." His hand rests along my jaw. "And why your face is so darn beautiful I stopped going to swim practices because I can't listen to one more guy talk about how hot you are without wanting to punch every one of them in the mouth. I don't have a right to stop anyone from asking you out, so I haven't done that. But since Angelo doesn't make you as angry as I do, I *have* asked him to basically hang out with you constantly because no one is going to step to you at school when one of us is around. And you don't go out, so that's not been a problem. Though having you come to that party with Madge and not me was stressful as hell."

His hands grip my waist and his forehead rests on mine. "Let's go to your house right now and I'll tell Susan why that night had me so worked up, because this jealousy thing is what's new to me, but I can explain it real well. I want to date you, I want to find out who took your friend from you and end them, and I want to help you deal with all the trauma because when you smile, my world shifts on its axis. And when you laugh, Dani, it's like my skin is on fire. Anyone who takes that smile from your lips and the breath from your laugh is my enemy, and that includes any guy who steals my chance to be the one you direct all that energy at."

My palms sweat, the intensity in his eyes burning through me. "If you go to Susan's, she'll probably knock you over the head and tie you up in the basement."

His chest heaves. "I can handle her. And I can handle taking this real slow, because first and foremost, I *am* here to be your safe space. Whenever you're ready to date me, I'm here for it. If you're never ready, I'll deal with that. If I have to watch you date someone else, I'm going to need a minute, and then I'll begrudgingly suck it up and deal with it. But what I refuse to be a part of is you hurting yourself because of some foolish talk you're hearing from Susan or *anyone* else." His hands slide from my hips to my back. "Let me be your glue, because you're not the only one who is breaking into a million pieces."

My lips crash into his and he doesn't pull away. He devours me, mouth and body moving with mine as we walk back into the living room. My fingers trail over his back, down to the hem of his shirt and underneath the fabric. I want to feel his skin under my palms. His muscles pop as his hands drop to my hips and hoist me up. I wrap my legs around him and he detaches from my lips long enough to lean back, tug his shirt off with one hand and drop to his knees, gently balling the shirt under my head as he lays me down. "Now do you see why I didn't want an audience for our first kiss?"

~38~

Mikey is more than my first love, he's my forever. I feel it inside my soul when he kisses me. I sit up on my knees while he tugs his shirt back on, thankful that he's the only one of us that shed any clothes. "So what happens now?"

He wraps his arms around me and tugs me to his lap. "I'm a pretty patient guy, and normally not a lot gets under my skin, so I meant what I said earlier, slow is good. I'll follow your lead on what, when, and how. *But* I do have some non-negotiables because this jealousy thing I've got happening is going to explode on someone's head if you don't at least sit next to me in class, and at lunch, and with Angelo in all the classes you have with him. You also have to walk with one of us to and from all of your classes."

I raise a brow. "Are you being serious or am I supposed to laugh now?"

His lips press into a thin line. "However serious you think I look, it's worse. And Rory keeps saying he's going to take you to the winter dance. Since I obviously can't take you because of the obstacles you think are important and therefore so do I, I need you to do this effortless thing where you're either beside Ang or me, at all times. Or some guy is going to say something stupid, and I'm going to punch him in the throat."

"You do realize that no one at school talks to me, right?"

"You spent Monday's entire lunch talking to Rory. And by Wednesday, he was *right* beside you, practically feeding you that peanut butter sandwich you apparently didn't want to eat."

I fail to hide my grin. "Is that why you sat next to me on Thursday?"

He kisses the smile on my lips. "My sudden bend toward violence isn't your fault but while I work out my issues, I need to be next to you because Rory isn't going to speak to anyone I'm near."

I cross my legs in front of me. "So that's the reason you keep yourself nestled in the middle of all the hottest girls in school? To make sure all your options stay open and dateless?"

He folds a hand over my knee. "I don't date girls I go to school with. I've had that rule since the brief nightmare with Tanya in middle school. All the girls at school know that, and they also all know that I'm not remotely interested in them so I'm not cramping their style. They're the ones who come to me anyway, so it isn't like I'm doing to them what I'm getting ready to do to you. Don't worry, though. While I'm at school pretending that we're not together in any way, I won't hang on you or do anything stupid like I did with the cookie. I'll play it totally cool. Unless Rory decides he's slick enough to pick up a girl who is right next to me. If he does that, I'm going to work out all the reasons this jealousy thing is new to me on Rory's face."

I lace my fingers through his. "I didn't even know that kid's name until you said it, and it was him and Madge who talked while I pretty much just sat there. But this violent streak of yours is disturbing so I'm going to need to speak to Angelo because he lied to me. He told me you weren't competitive. Over anything. Not even girls."

He drags a hand through his hair. "Which is why I haven't told Ang how flipping nuts I'm going over you. I can barely talk about you at all without showing that I'm feeling some sort of way, and Ang definitely wouldn't keep it on the down-low. He'd have too much fun at my expense, because he wouldn't realize how teasing me would affect you." He presses a kiss to my lips. "It should all be fine now, though. Until you're ready to go public, we'll spend time together privately, and while we're growing our bond and getting to know each other better, we'll find the man who hurt Kira. Ready to get started on that?"

~

It's difficult to openly talk about theories regarding Kira's case with someone else. And those theories become complicated to explain when I leave out the contact I've had with the killer. Whether the man intends to actually come after me or he's only enjoying tormenting me, getting Mikey involved could make him a target, too. That's why, every night we spend at the cottage, I decline his offers to get anyone else involved. I don't want a digital trail left behind that leads to Mikey in any way.

And the more I think about the photos that were stolen from my phone when I was twelve and thirteen, the more I think the killer is a hacker like Gideon Joseph.

"Done," Mikey announces when he finishes highlighting cases similar to Kira's that are within a two-hour radius of where her family used to live. The stapled sheets of paper I handed him earlier are from what I last printed at the library. I told him that my dad trashed all of my previous work and that I had to start fresh. "Only one case mentioned strangulation, so I highlighted it in orange. The blue ones are cases where the assault was similar, but without the child being strangled." He passes the pages to me. "There are five altogether. Were you expecting more or fewer?"

I flip through the paperwork to see what he highlighted. "The fewer the better from a human standpoint, I just wish there was a glaring connection between all of these kids. A common teacher or scout leader, youth pastor, coach, camp counselor." I hand the pages back to him. "I wish the reports included all the activities that the child was involved in and the name of their schools, churches, any camps they attended. I don't understand why law enforcement doesn't do that."

He adjusts a blanket across my lap. The second time I came here, he had piles of pillows and blankets waiting for us, folding chairs, and a space heater so the room isn't cold anymore. We've been using the pillows and blankets and sitting on the floor at the low table in the living room. "You said most kids know the person who attacked them, so it does seem obvious that every case should include that information. I assume it's in the original files but just doesn't get loaded onto the websites we can access. If you let me call my cousin Sophie, her boyfriend can probably get us copies of those original files."

I cup my hand around his knee. "Soon. I just want to get the work I lost back and go through the data again because a true stranger abduction is rare and I *know* it's a near impossibility in Kira's case. She was too well guarded. I'm certain she knew the person, which means I knew them, too. Maybe not well, but there's a likelihood that I even interacted with him after the murder." *And he's currently reliving the event but tormenting me.* "I was the easier target, so there's something about *why* he chose Kira that's important. I think she must have interacted with him before, because otherwise she wouldn't have gone with him, and I don't see how it's possible that he could have taken her from her home unless he lured her away after having built trust with her."

He scratches his jaw. "You said her dad couldn't have been involved? Or..."

I raise a brow. "My dad? No. Neither of them are capable of what happened to her, and Kira's dad treated her like a princess. If he had your dad's money, he would have been building her cottages and calling them playhouses."

His hand drifts to where his phone is resting on the table. "Are you still leaving your dad's messages unanswered?"

My head suddenly feels as heavy as my heart. I rest it on Mikey's shoulder. "I guess he's calling when it's convenient for him or sending a three-word text, but no, I don't see why I should respond to him when he never took any of my calls. I've wanted to leave here so badly, and he knows that and hasn't left one message that even acknowledges how I'm feeling. He can be like you and tell me I'm overreacting, but he should at least acknowledge that I'm having a reaction."

Mikey tilts my chin up to his. "I've never said you overreacted to anything. We simply have different reactions to the same stimuli. It's like how you got jealous when I *formerly* hung out with who Madge refers to as bunnies, and I get jealous when guys breathe in the same room as you." His shoulders bob. "We're just different. And I hope you're feeling a little better about being here because I'm torn between hating how your dad uprooted your life and being glad that he did. It feels like being happy that your journey led you here is condoning the journey, which I don't."

I press my lips to his nose. "I know. And I feel the same. I never thought I'd have anyone I could talk to about Kira and when I'm with you, it's easy to forget about the rest. Then I go into Susan's house and start planning for the day I move into what I hope is a clean rental room in some nice old lady's house, transferring to public school, and buying a bicycle for transportation since I'll never be able to afford to put gas in a car even *if* I could afford the actual car."

His hand cups the back of my head and he reclines us until my back is resting against the pillows and his face is hovering above me. "I can help with some of the issues you're having. Without being allowed to come over, I'm not sure what I can do about Susan, but the financial stuff isn't a problem. It would be my pleasure to provide for every need and want my girlfriend has. And Ang and I have been talking about renting an apartment after graduation. He's going to a local college to stay close to Val and take a salesman position at the car dealership. I'm undecided on if I even want to go to college because I haven't found that *thing* that I'm passionate about. Except for you. And I wouldn't mind having you as my third roommate."

"Did you just ask me to move in with you?"

His hand runs the length of my ponytail, fingers sliding through the ends as his mouth moves closer. "I just called you my girlfriend. Because that's what you feel like to me, Dani. By graduation, hopefully that won't be a secret anymore. But if it is or if you don't want to share a room with me, we'll get a three-bedroom. Or you can live with an old lady and her cats, and I'll come over there to kiss you like this."

~39~

An owl hoots in the distance. I open my eyes, the weight of an arm draped around my middle freezing me until I remember where I am. I'm in the cottage with Mikey. *Still.*

Sliding from under his arm, leaving the warmth of the blankets behind, I fish my phone out of my backpack. We normally leave here no later than eleven but it's three in the morning.

"Mikey." I shake his bare shoulder. I have a bad habit of wanting to touch him and the moment my hands start roaming underneath his shirt, he sheds it. No doubt if I was more handsy, he'd shed the rest of his clothes also. "Mikey, we fell asleep." I nudge him harder.

His hand snakes out and tugs me down to him. "Go back to sleep."

"It's three already."

"We don't have to be up for hours," he mumbles.

I attempt to pull his hand free but he holds on tight. "Where do you tell your parents you are when we come here?"

He rolls onto his back and rubs his face. "I don't tell them anything. The time I'm here is my free time, and I'm not technically breaking any of their rules."

"What do you mean by *technically?*"

He groans. "It's three in the morning. Do you really want to have this talk right now?"

"They don't want you to date me, do they? So your technicality is that we're not officially dating."

He sits up, finding his shirt and pulling it over his head with a muffled curse. "My dad dated your mom in his early twenties. She was apparently the same then as she is now, and when that wealth-obsessed attitude broke them up, she faked a pregnancy to try to force him to

166

marry her." I gasp and he nods. "Totally sick. But it's old news. And yes, they did ask me to stay away from you. Which was easy since you told me the same thing. Then I decided I don't care what any of you think."

He grabs me by the hips and tugs me to him. "Now, can we go back to sleep? Because I'm not the one who has an issue telling my parents who I'm dating. This down-low thing is all you. And if Susan has an issue with you staying out all night, we can just tell her about us and according to you, she'll be thrilled. So sleep, Dani. I'll get us to school on time."

~

Mikey stands at the edge of the manicured trees on the far side of Susan's lawn, where he's hidden just out of view of the reach of the lights. We've worked out a system where he waits for me on the edge of the woods in the cul-de-sac when we're going to the cottage, and on the way back I allow him to come as close as he is now. Only because it's full dark and he insists, and I secretly feel much better knowing that I don't have far to go on my own.

There's always guilt festering inside me because there's a possibility that the murderer will see Mikey walking with me, and I have no idea if the man's twisted mind would decide that harming Mikey is the best way to torture me. Looking to the dark place where I know Mikey is, I blow a kiss in his direction and then slip inside Susan's house. We didn't exactly fight, but we both ended this night agitated.

Mikey's absolutely right about us having different reactions to things. His default reaction is that nothing is a big deal. Mine is that the life he's carving out for us at the cottage isn't a real-world scenario. He's playing house, always having food for us and sometimes cooking that food himself. At school, he leaves bagged lunches in my locker because somehow he knows the combination and thinks he's being slick feeding me without anyone knowing the food came from him. Then there are the stolen kisses and secret touches, his leg rubbing up against mine and the way he sits behind me in class and braids my ponytail. I love all of it, but the instant I'm away from him, the weight of the *real* world rushes back in and all I see is how the house he's building comes crumbling down if his parents, Susan, or even Kira's killer finds out about us.

Trudging up the stairs, I'm grateful that my backpack is lighter. Being able to leave my notebooks in the cottage instead of lugging them around with me everywhere is saving my shoulder. I don't know if Susan would ever go through the things in my room, the peanut butter and empty cracker box under my bed haven't been touched, but I worried that she'd come in looking for a diary and stumble upon the notebooks pertaining to Kira's case so I kept them with me. Dad always had an issue with finding the notebooks in which I'd write down descriptions of people I remembered, particularly men he did business with and occasionally brought home for dinner.

Dumping my backpack on the floor beside my bed, I'm startled when the bedroom light flips on. I spin around. Randall is in the doorway with his arms crossed. "Where have you been?"

"Out."

He shuts the door behind him and walks toward me. "You've been out with that boy again. I've told you repeatedly that there *will* be consequences if you keep seeing him."

"And I told you to kill the *dad* vibes. I already have one of those."

"Does he know about this?" Randall pulls a folded paper from his back pocket and shoves it at me. "Is *this* what that Beller boy has you out doing at all hours of the night?"

With a groan, I unfold the creased paper, the crinkly feel of it under my fingertips making sense now that it's fully unfurled. My breath dies in my chest. "You dug this out of the trash?"

Randall paces to my left and back again. "I had a bad feeling about that boy and I've been trusting you to be smarter than all of this, but I can't turn a blind eye any longer. You can *not* and you will *not* see that boy again."

My pulse accelerates with the rising anger. "You *dug* this out of the *trash*?"

He stands in front of me. "The one time your mom and I tell you we're going away for the weekend, I come home to find you gussied up, and that boy just conveniently happens to show up? You're not fooling anyone and neither is he, and *that's* why I had no choice but to find whatever it was that you stuffed into that trash bin." He snatches the photo collage of me out of my hands, shaking it. "What else are you out there doing with that boy?"

I tear the paper from his grip. "What have you been doing with *this* for over a week?"

My vision tilts, all my days stringing together as I try to remember exactly when I threw this collage away. Randall tugs on his earlobe. "Once I realized what that was, I folded it up and put it away. I've been debating whether or not to show it to your mom, but I was hoping you'd figure out for yourself that boys, especially arrogant punks like that Beller kid, will say and do anything to convince a girl to do what they want. He doesn't care about you, Danielle. Think of what it would do to you if those pictures got out."

My chest heaves. I walk toward him. "These pictures have nothing to do with Michael Beller and the *only* reason you didn't tell Susan he was here is the same reason you didn't mention *grounding* me. Because you know if Susan finds out I've been with Mikey, she'll beg me to stay out all night with him and encourage me to do a heck of a lot more than take nude photos for him. Now get out of my room and don't you *ever* go through my trash again."

~40~

I stand by the sinks in one of the academy bathrooms, staring at my reflection in the mirror. I look pale, and my eyes are red, both from waking up at three this morning and from spending over an hour crying in my bathroom at Susan's before summoning enough courage to face Randall in the light of day. He's seen me naked. The fact that he thought the photos were current suggests he really didn't look at them, but him even glancing at my naked body for even a fraction of a second is humiliating.

Madge struts into the room and pushes her perfectly painted face in front of the mirror next to mine, touching a tube of gloss to her lips. "No offense, Dani, but you look terrible."

"It's still offensive even when you say it's not."

She puts her gloss in her bag and takes hold of my shoulders, turning me to her. "I get your whole no-makeup ambiance and it's cute, really, but you should consider a little eyeliner. And probably some blush and lipstick to break up the whole walking dead feel."

I glare at her. "Your insults are cute. Really."

She grins. "Did you see how *yum* Mikey looks this morning? I was just by your locker and," she smacks her lips, "my man is on fire this morning."

I turn back to my reflection. "What about Geoff? You know, the guy you abandoned me for?"

She laughs. "He's a whole different kind of *yum*. More like a *Yes, please!*"

I adjust the strap of my backpack, hitching it higher on my shoulder. "Geoff seems to think you're just as yummy, so maybe you should stick with him and leave Mikey alone."

170

She leans on the sink, still facing me. "Why? Because you like Mikey and want him all to yourself?"

My neck heats. "No. Because you shouldn't throw yourself at someone who doesn't have any intention of reciprocating your feelings, and especially not while dating someone else."

She lifts her hand, a smug look on her face. "May the best woman win. Pinky swear to still being friends after? No hard feelings when Mikey bends his knee and begs me to marry him?"

I barge out of the bathroom and straight into Mikey. He's leaning on the wall outside and snakes his hand out to grab my wrist as I move past. "Good morning. It's been a while since I've seen you. Let's go catch up. In the band closet."

Madge waltzes out of the bathroom and looks at his outstretched arm. I tug away and he lets his hand drop with a sigh. "Hey, Madge."

She cozies up to his shoulder. "Hey, yourself. Did you miss me so much that you had to follow me to the ladies' room?"

He pushes off the wall. "Actually, I needed to ask Dani about a chemistry problem we have. Do you mind?"

Her shiny hair moves like pretty waves of crimson as she shakes her head. "Not at all, go right ahead."

He swallows. "It's a private question. Right, Dani?" He grips my elbow. "We'll see you later, Madge."

I go three steps and glance over my shoulder. She pushes off the wall with a grin, winking at me and holding up her pinky before turning away and walking off with a swing in her hips. I pull away from Mikey and look up at him. "She *knows*."

He looks down the hall behind us. "Who? Madge?"

I don't respond. I walk. He comes after me but I throw up a hand and shake my head. "I told you this wouldn't work. Now girlfriend number *one* knows and it won't be long before the others do. You can't hover over me anymore."

~

"Dani!" Angelo yells directly into my ear.

"Ouch!" I press a palm over my aching drum. "What's wrong with you? Geez!"

He pulls out a chair at my library table and straddles it. "I whispered, but you didn't hear me because your nose is always stuck in a book."

He flips my notebook closed. I've been scribbling down descriptions of boats that I remember from my days on the lake. Kira's mom had been making breakfast and didn't realize Kira wasn't in her room until shortly before Dad and I discovered the body. Kira's time of death was six hours before we found her. Our backyards abutted the lake and we were just at that age where we'd get up early and run down to the shore at first light. It's possible Kira went before the sun came up and her abductor was there, his boat close enough that he was able to grab her and get to the isolated side of the lake before anyone else stirred. The boat would also explain the lack of physical evidence around the body. The attack didn't take place there. It happened on his boat or at a different section of the shore, and then he discarded her where we found her.

I glare at Angelo. "I'm studying. You should try it sometime."

He snakes an arm around my shoulders and drops a sleek blue cooler bag on top of my book. "Mikey was borrowing your chemistry notes and saw that you left your lunch in your locker. I told him I'd bring it to you, but I didn't realize doing that would make me miss my own lunch. Why are you back to sitting in here by yourself again?"

I look down at my unpainted nails and remember the scent of Madge's perfume. She smelled good enough this morning that *I* wanted to bury my face in her neck, so I can see the appeal for Mikey. And Tanya always smells like a pillow of cotton candy so I can see him wanting to taste every inch of her. "The girls at your table already outnumber the boys four-to-one so you don't need me there. And I also prefer studying over hearing about how many calories are in a handful of raisins."

Angelo grins, plopping a kiss on my temple before unpacking the lunch bag. "These raisins?" He jiggles the bag of yogurt-covered dried fruit that Mikey figured out I like. "How about I just eat all of these and then you don't have to worry?" He pulls out half of a submarine sandwich that's piled high with ham and pepperoni, diced banana peppers, tomato, and gobs of mayo. "This is all you though because it's disgusting."

I can't help but smile. Mikey said the same thing when I put this combination together a few days ago. He picked up cold subs to take to the cottage for us and had me look over a menu and text him what I wanted on mine. "I bet if you take a bite, you'll love it."

Ang pats my knee. "Nope. But I am going to sit right here and watch you eat it because maybe this is the secret to how you got these meaty thighs."

My face falls, a whole new level of uncomfortable snaking through me. "I happen to like my *meaty* legs just fine."

"So do I." He chuckles. "Why do you think I want to sit here and eat these raisins while staring at you?"

I shove the sandwich away. "Shouldn't you be somewhere attached to Mikey's hip?"

He pops a handful of raisins into his mouth. "That boy is in a *mood* today. Something is up with him lately and between school, work, and swimming, I haven't been keeping up like I should. I'm going to have to take him out for some man-to-man time, though. And you and your meaty thighs are going to have to come watch me swim. I have a meet coming up soon. You in?"

~41~

Sitting in the break room before my shift starts at the boutique, I finish scribbling every little detail I can remember about boats I saw on the lake as a child. If I was still living with my dad, I'd be able to sift through the boxes of old photos that he packed away. He erased all memories of Kira from our house, and in essence, erased my childhood.

I was such a wreck those first few years after the murder, he decided that never speaking of our time at the lake house was best. He thought the complete break from that life helped me, but I didn't stop having violent nightmares until I started taking action to solve not only Kira's case, but to catch other offenders along the way.

"A funny thing happened to me today." Mikey's voice sounds behind me, crawling over my flesh like a livewire. "I was sitting outside the school waiting for my *only* girlfriend, when it hit me that despite her knowing I was waiting for her because we planned to stop by Scoopz before coming to work today, my girlfriend wasn't coming. She also didn't answer my call or respond to my text, so therefore I had to drive the long way around to get here just in case she never made it to the public bus stop and was lying on the side of the road somewhere."

He pulls my chair away from the table and spins me to face him. "Nice to see that you made it here safely, Dani."

All the hairs on my body stand on end with his proximity. "Keep your voice down. Pam is right down the hall."

He leans closer. "Don't. Care."

I shove out of the seat and away from him. "What happened to you caring about things that I care about?"

He moves forward. I take a step backward. He reclaims the closeness of that one step, his big arms folding on either side of me, my ponytail

174

trapping itself between the wall and my back. "What happened to you caring enough about me to have a conversation with me?"

I wiggle my palm between us and push on his chest. "You knew from the start we couldn't actually be together. Your parents would flip out if they even suspected you were standing this close to me. So *move*, before someone sees us."

He clenches his chiseled jaw, staying exactly where he is. "You're not the first girl my parents have asked me to stay away from. You *are* the first one I'm ignoring them over. And at this point, they probably don't even care."

I shove him again and this time he moves. An inch. "Probably, my foot! I still don't know why they hired me, it feels like some kind of a test and right now you're putting me in a position to fail it. I told you we couldn't have personal contact here. I *can't* lose this job. Not unless I have something else lined up, which I don't, because I spend all of my free time with you instead of out looking for an employer who isn't going to fire me because I like their son."

He leans against me. "I spend all my free time with you, too. I also do absolutely everything we agreed to. Then this morning, you just flip a switch and won't even let me get near you? Sorry that *this* part of our relationship actually likes being near the person he's dating."

He pushes off the wall and runs his hands down his face. "You're driving me absolutely insane, Dani. You *left* today while I was sitting outside patiently waiting for the few minutes we were finally going to get to spend together." His eyes lower to mine. "I need to feel like you care about me just a smidge if we're going to keep this up. Otherwise, it feels like you're only making excuses. My parents aren't going to fire you or try to stop us from dating. They wouldn't do that. To either of us."

I stay against the wall, folding my arms and fighting the tears nipping at the back of my lids. "I'm a minor. To even accept this job I had to get consent, and the look on your parents' faces when they gave me the forms to have filled out, along with them directly saying that I couldn't have people in here loitering while I'm working—with special stress on *even my family*—made it clear that Susan wasn't allowed to come in here. So I *forged* her signature. If Susan or your parents find out about that, I'm toast. If they find out we're dating, I'm toast. Gone. Done. So what am I supposed to do with the feelings I have for you when simply *having* those feelings is me throwing rocks in my own glass house?"

"Dani," he whispers.

"Hey, kids," Mary addresses us. "How was school today?"

I freeze, eyes locked in battle with Mikey. He's too close to me, his back to his parents, and if he doesn't move away soon, this moment is my last one working here. He gives me an eye roll and turns around. "Today was horrible. How was your day, parents?"

His tone is flat. Both John and Mary flick their eyes to where I'm still pressed against the wall. John's head tilts. "Are you okay, Dani?"

I nod but Mikey glances at me and shoots off another eye roll. "She's lying." My mouth gapes open and he moves forward, leaning his hands on the table so he can shift closer to his parents. "The new hire paperwork that minors have to have filled out by parents, Dani forged her mom's signature."

Mary's eyebrow raises and she looks up at her now smiling husband. "That explains why Susan hasn't been in here using Dani as an excuse to irritate us."

John nods, kissing Mary's nose. "Told you Susan didn't change her spots, you're just too optimistic about humankind."

Mary pulls a chair out from the table. "One of these days I might decide to be bitterly hopeless." She jerks her head at Mikey. "Give us a minute alone with Dani."

He glances at me. I can't speak. He drags in a breath and lifts his hands from the table. "Dani thinks you're going to fire her and won't believe me when I tell her you're not. Hopefully you two can convince her that everyone here likes her. I'll be in the woodshop hammering the heck out of something if anyone needs me."

His long strides take him out of the room and I'm left choking on the thickening silence, John and Mary staring at me with matching expressions. I stand as still as they're sitting. John gets out of his seat, rounds the table, and pulls a chair out. "Have a seat, Dani. We know your shift is about to start and we won't keep you from it."

I move into the seat and he slides the chair back to the table. Mary smiles at me, reaching her hand across the table to where mine are piled. "Oh, sweetheart, you're trembling. We're not firing you, we just need to have a talk so we're all on the same page about the situation if anything should arise."

John retakes the seat next to his wife. "We have excellent lawyers so we're not worried about being sued over you forging paperwork. It's just better that we understand everything so we know what to possibly expect and how to counter it."

Mary nods, her hand squeezing my fingers. "I take it that your mom doesn't even know you're working here?"

I lick my dry lips. "Um, I thought it was best if she didn't. I know it's only a matter of time before someone in the community happens to mention it to her, but I figured since I'm new and most people don't even know she has a daughter, I could make it until I was eighteen. Then, if she found out, it wouldn't be a problem. I mean, from the forgery standpoint."

Mary sits back. "How much do you know about our history with your mother?"

I pick at my sleeve, pulling the ends of the Henley down toward my still shaking fingers. I look up at John. "Mikey told me what Susan did to you and I'm sorry. I didn't know, or I would have refused to get in the car the day of the pool party. She was insisting and saying it was a school thing, and I was honestly just tired and wanted her to shut up."

He chuckles, dimples in his cheeks reminiscent of Mikey's. My heart pangs as John reaches his own hand across the table and pats mine. "I'm as much to blame for what happened between your mom and me as she is. And I know from experience what's it like to just want her to shut up."

"And I know from experience what it's like to truly despise someone." Mary folds her hands neatly in front of her. "There will never be a time when I'll be friends with your mother. There will never be a time when I'll be fine with her being near my business or my family. But in the spirit of not being bitter and holding grudges, we hired you. Not because I'm extending an olive branch to Susan, but because you truly seemed rattled the day you half-applied for the job and then ran out."

"Because Mikey was being obnoxious," John mutters.

She eyes him. "Like father, like son."

He shrugs and Mary winks at me. "Pam and Davina tell me you're a great help to them and when I'm here I see how eager you are to learn.

That's why you're no longer on probation. We do need you to stop committing crimes, though. No more forgery, and if you still choose to work here after you turn eighteen, we'll redo the paperwork. Deal?"

I smile. "Yes, ma'am. And my birthday is almost here. December sixth."

Her eyes go wide. "That's right. I do remember seeing that your birthday is the day after the big dance. Do you have a date yet?"

I clear my throat. "I'm not going to the dance. Dancing isn't really my thing."

~42~

If Mary isn't in the store, a revolving list of girls are always asking the rest of us to pass messages to her letting her know that they stopped in. It's all a ploy to get to Mikey via his mom. They think that if she favors them, she'll push for him to favor them also.

On days like today, when Mary is physically present, those girls hover around and suck up to her. It's disgusting. Especially when it's Tanya, Wendy, Opal, and Lauren.

Willing myself to completely ignore their presence, I find that I keep looking up to that stupid glass wall where Mikey and his dad are visible as they work. After the way Mikey put me on the spot with his parents earlier, I'm going to waltz over there and punch him in the face if he takes his shirt off.

Glancing up from the jewelry I'm straightening after the Bunny Clique messed up the display, I catch Mikey watching me. I make a gagging face and nod to where his *friends* are monopolizing his mom's time. He mouths *breakroom* and tilts his head that way.

Mouthing *no* back to him, I tug on my shirt. *Surprised you're keeping it on.*

He slides his hand up the bottom of his t-shirt, bunching it so a tiny bit of his abs are exposed. *For you.* He jerks his head in the direction of the breakroom again.

I try not to, but a smile snaps to my lips. He grins. *Breakroom. Please, Dani?*

I take a breath, shaking my head with less vigor this time. *Can't.*

He waves. At someone behind me. I hear the toe of her shoe clicking on the floor. Mikey turns away from the glass and I swallow before facing Pam. "Having fun?" she asks.

I scratch my cheek. "Not really. Can we make a new rule that certain people aren't allowed to touch the jewelry?"

She lowers her voice. "Customers messing up our work is par for the course in retail. More importantly, whatever you're doing with that boy in the window, I advise you to stop it."

"I'm trying," I mutter, turning back to the jewelry with an attempt to not see what Mikey is doing now. I fail. But he isn't even in the room with his dad anymore.

~

Grabbing my backpack and contemplating whether or not I should call for a car since Mikey apparently left and I'm not entirely sure how things are between us, I shuffle toward the door. He steps over the threshold, a grin on his lips. "Are we going to our spot tonight?"

I lift a shoulder, letting the silence pile up around us. He takes a step forward. "Thanksgiving break is here, Dani. I'm going to have to go spend time with my family at our Potomac estate and since you won't come with me, I want to spend time with you now."

I've been dreading this upcoming week. No school. I was allotted more work hours but it still leaves too much time at Susan's. "Whether or not we go to our place, we do need to talk about everything that happened today."

He looks around as if checking to be sure no one is listening. "Am I allowed to walk beside you out to the truck? And what's the verdict on opening your door? Don't want to do anything that gives the impression that I like you or that you actually like me back."

I stare at him and he stares back, our wills locked in battle. He smiles. "I'll drop how badly my feelings are hurt if you come out to the cottage with me. I have something for you, and I want to give it to you before I leave."

~

Mikey parks in the cul-de-sac and we walk together through the woods. I tug at his hand. "Wait. What about the four-wheeler? Are we walking all the way to the cottage?"

He smiles. "That's my surprise."

"Walking? In the dark?"

He moves the light from his flashlight over the ground. "I've never made you walk in the dark, and I'd never let you go down into that ravine on foot. No matter what shoes you're wearing."

We near the ravine and he shines his light toward a group of trees. A four-wheeler is parked there but not the one he's been riding out here. He pulls a keychain from his pocket and places the golden D encrusted with crystals into my hand. "This is for you, so you can come in and out of here while I'm gone visiting family."

I press the pretty keychain back into his palm. "I'm not going to come in here unless you're with me."

He runs a hand over my shoulder. "I want you to. The cottage is yours whenever you need a place to go, so please take the keys, Dani, because I don't want to think about you being stuck in Susan's house all week without any sort of escape."

His lips fall over my forehead and he cups a hand behind my neck. "The only thing I ask is that you shoot me a message before you come in, then again when you make it to the cottage. So I know you're safe. Then, just reverse that process on your way out. Deal?"

Emotion bubbles up inside me. "While you're gone, are those the only times you want to hear from me?"

He circles my waist and pulls me against him. "I want to take you with me. And I also want to plant a link in your brain so I can hear every thought in your head every second of every day because you broke my non-negotiables and I don't believe that happened just because Madge sniffed us out or even because you're worried about my parents. You're hiding something from me. Tell me what it is."

~43~

Spending time alone at the cottage is creepy. I've gone as far as driving out there twice in the daytime, but I refuse to go after dark. Mikey says the regular patrols of his family's property pick up when none of them are on the grounds and that he can have security come watch the cottage while I'm there, but *knowing* someone is out there is more unsettling than thinking every rustle of leaves is a murderer.

Half a dozen times, Mikey also offered to have Lily invite me to their big family estate where generations of them have celebrated holidays, but there's no way we'd pull off me being there as his friend and not his girlfriend. We'd get caught together. Even if that wouldn't be a big deal to his family, nothing can be done about the fact that I need to work. I'm surprised Dad hasn't stopped paying my phone bill yet, and as much as I hate using his credit card to pay for rides, I'd hate taking Mikey's money more.

My birthday is around the corner and I'll apply for a credit card of my own then, and go into debt if I have to. Anything to keep from taking a penny from anyone.

Mikey is coming home tomorrow night. I told him I'd meet him at the cottage, even if he didn't come back until after midnight, because spending today with Susan and Randall at a country club where they *celebrated* Thanksgiving with a handful of their friends left me feeling gross. I was the only minor there, which meant the only sober person. And when older people get sloshed, even their loose morals blush.

Avoiding the party that decided to come home with Susan and Randall, I sit on my bed and dig through my backpack. I have a paper due for my novels class next week and since I've read *Jane Eyre* a dozen times, I should be able to get the paper finished despite the tinkling glasses and raucous laughter. There's not a chance I'm leaving this room tonight. I'd be surprised if all the adults downstairs aren't naked and *entertaining* each other by now.

Setting the novel in front of me, I notice a yellow piece of paper sticking out from between the pages. I checked the book out of the school library a week ago and don't recall seeing anything inside it.

Fanning the pages, I see the flickering display of tiny yellow squares stuck to almost every single page. "What in the world?" I mumble aloud as I stop on one of the pages. Dead in the center of the page is a sticky note. *Tick Tock, Dani.* I flip to the next page. Exact same. *Tick Tock, Dani.* I rip the next page over and the note is the same. So is the next. And the next. I drop the book on the bed and scramble away from it. That book hasn't been out of my backpack since I checked it out. And my backpack is almost always in my sight. If I can't see it, it's either in my locker or in the breakroom at work. My *locker.* The only time this could have happened is at lunch on Friday.

Scrambling for the box of bags under my bed, I wrap one over my hand and then pluck all the tiny squares from the book, dropping them into one bag since there are too many to secure them all separately. These notes are handwritten, so surely there's DNA on them.

Adding the potential new evidence to the rest, I stuff the cracker box back under my bed and dump out the remaining contents of my backpack. Nothing else has been tampered with, except the backpack itself.

"Danielle?" Susan knocks on my door, the knob twisting because the people around here don't get that you shouldn't just barge into someone's room. "Danielle? Come down and join the party."

"So I can pretend to get knocked up by one of those men?"

"What?" She wiggles the handle again. "Come out, I can't hear you and I'm not going to scream back and forth through a door."

I stare at the items on my bed, the keychain Mikey gave me among the rest. It's dark already, but I'll feel safer behind the gate on his property than I do here. And not only because of Susan. The murderer is a teacher in my school. He's been close to me, talked to me, maybe even touched me.

Shoving all the items except the novel back into my bag, I grip the keychain tightly and open the bedroom door. Susan is still clothed, so that's good. She clamps a hand onto my arm. I pull away, moving down the stairs faster than she can. Without stopping, I rush straight out the front door and flip on the tiny light that Mikey attached to the keys. For something so small, it shines a wide path.

~

The door of the cottage creaks open and I press myself farther into the cold corner. When I messaged Mikey to tell him I was out here, he messaged back that he was on his way. It's been several hours but I'm not sure if that's too soon or just enough time for him to be creeping in.

I only turned the cottage lights on to make sure no one was in here, and then I flipped them all back off and huddled under blankets in the corner. I haven't moved since. Not even to turn on the heater.

"Dani?" Mikey whispers.

"Thank God." I shove out of the corner and tangle in the blankets trying to get to him.

"Hey." His arms wrap around me and he pulls me up out of the blankets, holding me tightly against him. I bury my face in his neck, tears hot as they rush from my eyes and soak into his shirt. I press myself into him, taking comfort in his scent while my mind races through everything I want to tell him, and yet nothing comes out of my mouth.

I never told him what he wanted to know before he left and right now, I just need him to hold me. He seems to know that. He settles us in the blankets, never letting go of me as he drags the heater close and flips it on. I tighten my arms around his neck and he tucks pillows under me, resting my back against them and staying close. He studies me in the darkness. I can feel his eyes on my face. "What happened?"

This whole time, I've planned on telling him everything. But now that he's in front of me, I can't force the words out. I hate that he even rushed here, but he said he'd been planning to come home tonight anyway. He wanted to be at the boutique in the morning to surprise me.

"Mikey," I latch onto his shirt, "I'm going to need you to take this off."

It isn't smart to cover all of my pain with the thick haze of lust that hangs between Mikey and me, but it feels better to kiss him than to cry. I only wish that when I fall asleep next to him, I'd stay asleep.

~

I'm awake early again, fear and anxiety raging against the contentment of being in Mikey's arms. I tuck my fingers into the waistband of his jeans and snuggle closer, the birds just beginning to sing their morning songs as I force contentment to win the battle in my chest. I don't want to face another day. I want to stay in this world Mikey built for us.

He moves against me, mouth working over my neck even though I don't think he's awake. I tilt my head back and his teeth scrape against my skin, a deep rumble quaking through his chest. "Dani, have you ever had a boyfriend?"

I laugh at his sleepy voice. "I've never even gone on a date before."

He lifts up onto his forearm. "Not for my lack of trying."

I tug on his waistband until he lowers back down beside me. "Why are you asking about my dating history?"

"Because I had too much time to think while I was gone." He runs a hand through my hair, fanning it out on the pillows. "You have a lot of fear about going public with our relationship. And it got me to thinking about why, and that led to me doing some self-assessment."

A swarm of stinging bees moves inside me. "And you don't want to be public now?"

His lips press against my cheek. "I do. Badly. But I think the reason I want it so much, and the reason I'm so insanely jealous, is because of a past relationship of mine. I wanted to blame you for casting a spell on me, but now I'm pretty sure I did this to myself by trusting someone that I shouldn't have."

"What happened?"

His hand slips under my shirt, fingers feathering over my back. "Eighteen months ago, I was in a relationship that was serious to me. I liked the girl a lot and thought she felt the same. Then she cheated on me. With Nick."

I sit up. "Is she insane? You're way hotter than Nick."

He rolls onto his back and sighs. "I'd like to think I'm better than him in every way. But I guess not, and I guess that whole situation did more damage to me than I realized at the time. I think I'm insecure now, so not being able to even say you're my girlfriend makes me feel rejected."

I stare at him. He stares back. "Can I take you on a date?"

I position myself on his bare chest and tuck his hand back under my shirt so he can rub his fingers against my skin. "I'm not sure if you read this in one of your books, but girls like it when their guy is vulnerable. And you don't have to be jealous when it comes to me because the girl who cheated on you most definitely regretted that decision. I won't make her mistake. So where are we going on our date?"

<h1 style="text-align:center">~44~</h1>

When I let Mikey walk me *almost* to Susan's door, he confessed that he'd already made plans to attend tonight's amateur car race with Angelo. The race he's bringing me to for our date. It's a weird choice for a date night but he's killing two birds with one stone, bringing me along for an already planned outing with his friend. I guess I should look at this as him wanting to include me in his regular life, but it's a little disappointing.

Mikey's hand brushes along mine as we take our seats in the stands. He's being reserved, not outing us even to Angelo when we met him at the entrance. The only time Mikey felt like a boyfriend was in his truck, when no one could see us. And that's my fault. I hesitated before I got out of the truck. Only, it wasn't for the reason he thought. One of the teachers in our school is a murderer and I need to tell him. But telling him ruins our date and he wanted tonight to happen so badly.

I let my eyes roam over the stands. The teacher could be here right now, watching us. "You okay?" Mikey asks as he spreads a blanket over my lap and leans into my ear. "In a little while, I'll tell Ang to get lost so we can have some alone time. Or maybe *we'll* get lost."

I lean into his shoulder. "I bet you can hold my hand under the blanket and no one will notice."

He slips his hand under the plush threads and laces his fingers through mine. "I *want* everyone to notice."

I'm ten days from my birthday. Close enough to eighteen that Susan can't ruin this for me. "The popcorn smells really good. A public boyfriend would know how to decode that statement, and then he'd get rewarded with a public kiss."

"On it." He jumps out of his seat. "Ang, you need anything? I'm hitting up the concession."

"All I need is this blanket." Angelo scoots closer to me. "You going to hook me up with some of your cuddles too, Meaty Thighs?"

Mikey plunks Angelo in the center of his forehead and then tugs the blanket out of Angelo's hand, tucking the loose ends under my legs. "Leave Dani's blanket alone. Stop talking about her delectable thighs. And I'll bring a cup of hot chocolate back for you to cuddle."

I bite my lip when Mikey winks at me. I turn in the seat to watch him dart up the stairs to where the concession and a few shops are set up inside a large concrete building.

"You know you're sharing this with me." Angelo untucks the blanket and slides against me. "Have you ever been here before?"

I shake my head and turn back around as the roar of engines rises above the crowd, cars beginning to circle the track. "I've never even watched a race on television. Are they racing already?"

He moves closer so I can hear his explanations over the noise. "This is pre-race, where they're just warming up."

Despite Angelo filling my ears with talk of pit crews, I find my head turning to where Mikey's name just rang out above the murmur of the crowd behind us. He's lifting a long-legged blonde into his arms, twirling her around and cupping her face the way he did mine when he kissed me earlier.

The girl in his arms is gorgeous. Tight jeans, crop top, and tall black boots. She takes a box of popcorn from him. My box. And he lets her. She opens it, popping kernels into her mouth while he smiles at her.

"…winter formal?" Angelo shakes my shoulder. "Dani?"

I turn back to him, air burning as it drags through my lungs. I look down, sure my heart is lying at my feet. Angelo's face drops into my line of sight. "So? Will you go to the dance with me?"

"Dance…" I flash to Mikey announcing he can't go with me. He didn't ask or say he wanted to, he only said he *obviously* couldn't. I thought it was because of me but…I'm not the stunning girl he's feeding my popcorn to.

Angelo's fingers grip my chin. "The dance, Dani?"

"Yeah." I swallow. "The dance."

"Yeah?" Angelo sits up and slides his arm around me. "I got a date!"

"Who with?" Mikey jumps over the back of his seat, landing beside me and handing me the already open popcorn.

Angelo's lips land on my cheek. "With Dani. We're going to the dance together."

Mikey's body goes still. "What did you just say?"

Angelo plucks the popcorn from my hands and gives it back to Mikey. "You're looking at the king and queen of Winter Formal. And since she's *my* date, *my* dime will buy her popcorn. And where's my hot chocolate?" He wiggles against me. "Never mind, I'm warm."

Mikey stares at me. I'm as still as him, in shock over Angelo but more so that Mikey dared to give me a half-eaten box of popcorn. I force my lips to move. "I'm sure the girl you first gave that popcorn to will go to the dance with you."

The muscle in his jaw spasms, his teeth clenching. "Sophie? My *cousin.*"

Angelo's arm snaps off my shoulder. "Sophie's here? Where?"

Mikey's glare sears through me. "Your *date* is sitting next to you. So you might want to stop drooling over your boss. Unless your *date* is as open as you are with how many people she likes to *date* at once."

The seat creaks, his long legs stepping back the way he came. Pain claws through me. "Ang, is Sophie a hot blonde?"

He clears his throat. "Um… yeah. But she's out of my league. And she's like twenty-five, so way too old for me to take to the dance."

I look behind us. Mikey is gone. I get out of my seat but Angelo grabs my hand. "I can't help being attracted to beautiful women, but that only means you're one of them. And I asked you to a dance, not to walk down an aisle with me."

I shake my head at him. "I have no idea what you yammer about half the time. I'm going to go find Mikey."

Racing to the top of the stairs, I search for Mikey's face in the crowd. He's tall enough that he should stick out, but I don't see him. Pushing through the bodies near the concession stand, ignoring the muttered curses and swatting at hands that grab me and tell me to get to the back of the line, I explore the entire building from the entrance to the restrooms located in the back right corner.

With a deep breath, I push into the men's room, eyes closed. "Mikey? Mikey Beller, if you're in here, I need to see you."

"Any of you Mikey?" A rough voice calls out. Three additional voices say no.

I turn around, getting bumped by another man. "Wrong room, girl."

"Yeah, I know."

Outside the men's room, I open my eyes and scan ahead of me. A door clangs to the right. I duck around the corner to see three people exiting a small metal door with a sign above it marking it as an emergency exit. That has to be where Mikey went.

Pushing through the door, I find myself in a poorly lit alley. The metal clangs behind me, making me jump. A voice laughs. My head jerks to the left where the end of a cigarette glows in the darkness. "I hope you don't think you can get back in that door. It's one way only. Unless you catch someone else coming out." The tip of the cigarette moves toward me. "Want a hit?"

I realize he isn't smoking a cigarette and back away toward the end of the alley where a dim fluorescent light hangs loose on the corner. Tires screech behind me but I can't turn around to see where I'm going, I have to keep my eyes on this man, and *hope* no one else is behind me.

The man's laugh echoes off the building as I slowly move away from him. The phone in my jacket pocket vibrates and I yank it out. "This is my friend calling. He's waiting for me," I lie to the still shadowed figure advancing on me. On the screen in my hand is a picture of Kira. Dead. *It could have been you.*

The door bursts open and I drop the phone, fishing for it while a giggling couple runs past me, the toe of the man's shoe clipping the phone and sending it skidding along the rough cement of the alley. I'm wedged between the building and a huge fence. The pot-smoking man takes another step, revealing himself in the dim light. "You missed your shot. They could have let you back inside since it looks to me like your friend isn't coming."

"He is." My voice shakes.

He slowly exhales, the smoke curling up over his spiked hair. He looks to be in his early twenties. "My friend is on his way, too. We're heading out to a party. You're welcome to go with us." Amusement flashes across his face. "You can even bring your friend."

I find the phone and do what you're never supposed to do; I turn my back on him. And I run.

Moving toward the sound of the street, I push my legs as hard as they'll go. It's brighter the farther I run, the alley opening into the parking lot that Mikey's truck should be in. I race through the aisles. He parked in the second row from the street.

The entire lot is full, except for one empty space in the second row from the street. I stop in the empty space, leaning my hands on my knees, my phone still tightly gripped in my fingers. It vibrates and I turn it over. It's another photo of Kira. In this one, her arm is still twisted behind her back and her face is sideways in the mud, but her lips are still pink. He took this picture as soon as he killed her.

Tears slide down my face and I gasp for air, hair prickling across my body as the breaths grow shallower. I stumble toward the street. My phone vibrates again. Another photo. Of me. From right now. *You're next, Danielle.*

<h1 style="text-align:center">~45~</h1>

I haven't left my room in days. I haven't gone to school or work, or even downstairs. After the couple who kicked my phone dragged my suffocating body off the pavement of the parking lot, the woman held my head in her lap while her boyfriend drove two blocks to the nearest hospital.

Nurses ran outside to remove me from the backseat and after I was in the emergency room with drugs forcing my panic to subside, I gave them Susan's information.

"Danielle?" Susan's voice floats across the room. "You need to get up today."

"No," my hoarse voice rasps.

"Yes." She pulls the covers off me, Randall pulling them over me last night the only reason I'm even under them. "I'm taking you to a doctor."

"No."

She sits on the bed beside me. "Your dad called again. I haven't told him about the hospital visit, but he seems to know something is going on because he's calling every day now. You need to talk to him." She folds her hand over mine. "With your history of psychiatric problems, it isn't healthy for you to stay in bed all day."

"I'm not the one who's crazy." My body is numb still. All I can do is stare at the ceiling.

She gets off the bed. "I can't deal with you. You're the most negative person that I've ever met. But you either get out of bed on your own, or I'm going to have Randall drag you out because this can't go on. You *have* to see someone."

My eyes flick to her. "I'm trying to, but that person doesn't want to see me."

192

When she leaves, I slide a hand under the pillow next to me and pull out my phone. There are messages from Angelo, Madge, and even one from Lily. But none from Mikey. I scroll past all the new messages and look at the pictures of Kira, tears welling in my eyes. The only person I can talk to about any of this doesn't want to speak to me.

I dial Mikey again, shock jerking me upright when he actually answers. I've asked for a video connection with him so many times, just so I can see his face again, and I can't believe it's actually happening. "What?" He isn't looking at the screen but a point behind it, his bare chest rolled out like a red carpet.

I swallow down the lump of tears. "I'm sorry."

"Tell that to Ang, not me."

"Mikey—"

"He's my best friend!" he roars, eyes staring directly at the screen. "My *best* friend."

The screen goes dark. I crumble back to the bed and release all of the grief into my pillow.

~

Randall is convinced Mikey did something to me and no matter what I say, Randall takes my refusal to go to school as proof that he's right. I sent Pam and the academy messages that said I have the flu, but Randall knows better.

"No one did anything to me." I take a small bite of the soup he brought, my stomach a knotted mess of queasiness.

He pushes a napkin across the comforter. "If that's true, then you won't have a problem going to the doctor and letting them examine you. Which is why I took the day off from work. I'm taking you to get an exam."

My eyes snap up. "I wasn't assaulted."

His shoulders shrug. "The doctor will be the judge of that, and at this point, your mother has let you wait too long. I told her you should have been checked that first night."

"I *wasn't* assaulted."

He lifts a foot and crosses his ankle over his knee. "How many times have I had to check on you because I heard you scream? And those pictures… That boy isn't going to get away with doing this to you simply because his last name is Beller."

I get off the bed and plop the bowl of soup onto the nightstand, spilling it over the sandwich he left there last night. "Get out of my room, Randall."

I slam the bathroom door shut and force myself into the shower. When I emerge, wrapped only in a towel, he's still sitting on the bed. I glare at him. "Do you mind?"

He folds his hands over his knee. "I spoke to your mom about a facility that we both think will be good for you. So pack a bag, and after we stop by the doctor's office for the exam, I'll drive you to where you can get the professional help that you need."

"Get. Out."

Susan and Randall want to have me locked away so they can keep milking Dad for his money. I'll be institutionalized and kept under their control, which means they'll leverage Dad for expenses related to my care. But I'm not a pawn in everyone else's life. Not even Kira's killer. If he wants me, he can come out in the open and get me. "I'm going to school today, Randall, so get out of my room. Now!"

~46~

I stomp into the academy. Late. Because I walked to the far side of Susan's neighborhood and had a car pick me up there. There's not a chance I'm ever getting in Randall's vehicle again.

Walking through the mob of students heading for their second class of the day, I hear Angelo's voice bellow down the hall. "Dani-girl!" I turn around and there he is, Mikey, standing beside Angelo whose arms are open wide.

"Wait." Angelo steps back. "You over those flu germs because I don't want to be sick and miss our big dance."

Mikey keeps walking when Angelo stops and I swing around, only to have Angelo's arms wrapping around me, my feet lifting off the floor as he spins me around. "You had me worried, girl. I thought I was going to have to find another date for the dance."

I push away from Angelo as he lowers me to the floor. "You should, Angelo. Find another date."

"There's the happy couple!" Madge puts her arms around Angelo and me, smushing all three of our heads together. "Winter formal is going to be so much fun. And I can't wait to see what dress Dani picked out. Please tell me it isn't denim."

Angelo reaches over and pinches my cheek. "I'd like to know what your dress looks like, too. A man has to match his girl."

My eyes flit to the hall that's now devoid of Mikey. "I don't have a dress."

"What?" Madge's high-pitched octave makes my ears hurt. "Then we have to go shopping right now."

I shrug her off. "I've missed nearly the entire week of school. I'm not skipping."

She shrugs. "All the good dresses are gone now anyway, so *whatever*, Dani."

~

I haven't been fast enough to catch up with Mikey today. He knows this school like the back of his hand, and I'm watching every male teacher as if all of them are child killers. But Mikey isn't at lunch and Angelo told me it was because Mikey is giving someone a swimming lesson.

Whether or not I'll only be pouring salt in my heart's gaping wound, I wind my way down to the basement of the school where a windowed corridor connects the gym housing the pool to the rest of the building. On the set of bleachers sitting off to the side, a group of girls huddles together, noisily whispering and giggling in Mikey's direction as his long arms propel his lean body through the water. His strokes are smooth and powerful, muscles popping across the expanse of his back in a shuddering display as he slices through the liquid with ease. I wet my lips. Two other boys are in the water but Mikey is the showstopper. Fluid, powerful strokes of mouthwatering delight.

I trace the outline of his tattoo, wishing it were me draped over his shoulder and wrapped around his arm. I wish I had *asked* him who the girl he hugged was instead of letting my self-consciousness get in the way. It isn't Mikey who is insecure. It's me. The girl who doesn't know if she wears her hair in a ponytail because it's easy, because she likes it, because she's lazy, or because I'm too worried that if I *try* I'll only fail.

Mikey slips from the pool, the temperature in this room increasing as he hoists himself onto the side, water raining down his body as he stands. A cheer rises from the group of girls. He looks up, flashing them a dimpled smile and raising a hand. Then his eyes drop to mine and the smile fades. He yanks a towel from the floor and runs it over him before disappearing through the locker room door.

Gathering myself, I steel my nerves and follow his trail of drips, leaning on the wall beside the locker room. Despite two boys still being in the pool, the group of girls leaves. They got what they came here for. I hope I do, too.

The last lunch bell rings and the locker room door opens. It's the two other boys who were swimming with Mikey. They went in five minutes after him. I step to the side as they walk past and wonder if there's another exit. When those boys went inside earlier, they probably told Mikey some girl with a blonde ponytail was out here waiting for him.

Pressing my palm to the door, thinking about entering this space a little more than I did when I entered the men's bathroom at the track, the wood pulls away from my hand and I look up. Mikey is a statue. Fully dressed, damp hair pushed back out of his face, and a hard line pressed into his lips. I swallow. "Can we *please* talk?"

He brushes past me. I grab his shirt sleeve. "Mikey, *please*? I made a mistake. I didn't know Sophie was your cousin and you know there's nothing between Angelo and me. We're only friends."

He jerks hard, removing himself from my grip, his long legs covering ground I have to run to cover just as quickly. "Did you ask Angelo what happened? It was one giant misunderstanding. He couldn't have told you anything different."

His hand reaches for the door, holding his arm out steady to block it from opening. "I don't talk to Angelo about you because I don't want to hear *anything* about the two of you. And you standing here telling me that you only made a date with my *best* friend because you're jealous and you wanted to spite me is even worse than you actually choosing him over me." His head turns toward me. "I thought we might have ended differently if you had the decency to *ask* me who Sophie was instead of jumping to conclusions, but we wouldn't have. Because there isn't any decency in you."

Tears flood my eyes and I shake my head. "That isn't true. I would never intentionally hurt you."

He pulls the door open. "You did. Intentionally. And now it sounds like you're going to break Ang open, too. Real *decent* of you to bail on him last minute, *Danielle*." He slams the door in my face.

My vision tilts, heart hurting in a way that feels like it has no right to do. Mikey hates me. And if I *don't* go to the dance with Angelo, Mikey's going to despise me even more.

~47~

Madge is wrong about all the good dresses being gone already. Of the few left in the boutique, what I always considered Arabella's best design is still on the rack. It's red, like the shirt I wore the first time Mikey took me to the cottage. Instead of plain bell sleeves, this dress has a slit running up the sleeves, the cords of the scarf-like fabric threaded through golden circles at the neck before diving down to form the plunging neckline. The bodice is tamed with a single golden hoop at the waist before fanning out into the flowing floor-length skirt.

I run my fingers over the threaded fabric, pain tracing a jagged path around my heart. I'll never have a chance to wear anything like this, let alone for Mikey. Tears sting my eyes, and a soft hand rests on my shoulder. "I heard you're feeling better." Mary's voice pulls me from my thoughts.

I blink away the tears, taking a steadying breath as I slowly turn to face her. "I am. Thank you for letting me have time off."

She presses the back of her palm to my cheek as if she's checking for a temperature. "You look a little pale, but that dress will still be lovely on you."

Heat flushes up my neck. "It'll be lovely on someone. I can't afford it, and I don't think I'm going to the dance anyway."

Her brows knit. "I just saw Angelo half an hour ago and he told me you were going with him."

My pulse rises, hands beginning to sweat. "I...missed so much work it isn't fair for me to take another day off."

She reaches behind me and pulls the dress from the rack, holding it up to me. "I have final say in what's fair, and you're only a high school senior once. So try on the dress."

"B-but I can't afford it," I stammer.

She nudges me toward the dressing rooms. "Humor me."

Closing the fitting room door, I stare at the dress for a long while before finally taking off my clothes and letting the silky fabric fall over my body. Unfortunately, it fits. But the sight of *me* in it doesn't. This dress was made for someone else. Someone whose face isn't plain, and whose hair isn't always in a stupid ponytail. Someone who is decent.

"Dani?" Mary knocks on the door. "Do you need any help?"

I wipe away the tears that keep wanting to fall and open the door. "Wow," Mary breathes. "You look beautiful, Dani. That dress was made for you."

I keep my eyes on the floor. "It's too dressy for me."

She takes my hand and pulls me from the room and out to where a three-hundred-sixty degree mirror surrounds a raised platform, urging me up onto the platform where a pair of gold shoes with red heels are waiting. "It's a dance. You're supposed to be dressy. Now try on the shoes."

I step into the shoes, not surprised when they fit but taken aback when she tells me again how beautiful I look. "Angelo is going to love you in this dress, Dani."

I meet her eyes. They're sparking with life. Because she knows that if I'm with Angelo, it keeps me away from Mikey. My mistake was the best thing that ever happened to her.

I slip the shoes off and bend to pick them up. "I should get back to work. I'll put the shoes back on their shelf right after I hang the dress back up."

She folds her hand on top of mine, prying the straps of the shoes from my fingers. "I'll have these up front waiting for you. After you change, bring me the dress and then pick out your jewelry. Whatever you want. And no arguing. All of this is my gift to you, and to my son."

My throat constricts. "Your son?"

Her face stills. "When you're dancing with my child, make Angelo mind his manners. You look well above your age in this dress but that doesn't mean you are."

~

I want more than anything to be wearing this sweeping red dress for Mikey, but he's done with me. And so is his mother. I still see the look on her face when she handed me the packages, once again telling me to be sure Angelo behaved himself.

This is my first dance. And my last. Tonight is my last everything. Tomorrow I turn eighteen, and in the early morning hours while the rest of the world sleeps, I'm taking the backpack I've already packed and I'm walking away from this place. Once I'm gone, Mikey and Angelo will be close again, and Mary won't have to worry that I'm out to get her son. All of their lives, even Susan's, will return to normal.

I don't know yet where I'm going to end up, but I picked up a burner phone when I left the boutique last night and did an internet search. There's a homeless shelter a few towns over, so I'm going to make that my first stop. I'll walk in with my signature blonde ponytail, but I'm walking out with short and spikey black hair. I bought the dye last night, too. After having pulled out my ponytail so my hair would cover my face. I paid cash and kept my head down. If Susan even bothers to report me missing, the store clerk shouldn't recognize a photograph of me. If Kira's killer was watching, he *can't* know what I bought. I made sure no one was around when I selected my items, and I placed a jacket over them in my basket until I was at the register alone.

"Perfect!" Susan beams, her perfectly manicured hands dabbing a touch more gloss over my lips. Since she found out I was going to the dance with Angelo, she's been a brand-new person. If I didn't know better, I'd think she likes me. She hired someone to come to the house to give us matching pedicures and had two others split between doing my nails, hair, and makeup. She called them her glam squad, and while I sat in a chair for five hours, they certainly transformed me into something glamorous. I don't recognize the person in the mirror, but that's something I'm going to have to get used to. Tomorrow morning is the last time I'll be Dani Madison.

The doorbell rings and Susan's eyes grow brighter. In her mind, dating Angelo is the next best thing to dating Mikey. "He's here. Now remember, dance at least twice with Michael Beller. He won't suspect anything, and of course you'll be with his friend, but believe me," her lips turn up, "you look simply too ravishing for *any* teenage boy to pass up."

She bought undergarments for me. Things that make me look like my chest is two sizes larger and my bottom two sizes smaller. At this point, I don't care. I'm not fighting with anyone. Not even Kira's killer. "Thanks, Sus…Mom. I'll be right down."

She leaves the room with an excited squeal. I walk into my closet, drop to my knees and pull out my backpack. Lifting my phone from the inside pocket, I text the murderer. "You're taking too long. So instead of you coming for me, I'm coming for you." I place the phone on the floor, press the pointy heel of my shoe to the screen, and let all of my weight stab straight through its heart.

~48~

With every muscle in my body resisting, I leave my room and walk down the stairs. Susan's is the first face I see, a smile that's even too big for Texas stretched across her face. I scratch at the back of my neck, the thick curls pinned all over my head like I'm a queen in some two-hundred-year-old dynasty bouncing oddly and itching me as I step.

She runs up the stairs and swats my hand. "Stop. You're going to mess up your hair."

"Sorry," I mutter, not bothering to tell her it's itchy because when I told her the pins hurt she told me there was a price to pay for beauty, and that price was usually pain.

Angelo is standing at the door, a long white limo parked on the street behind him. I give him a smile. His dark eyes spark, a low whistle thundering under his breath. "Dang, Dani. Beautiful is too light of a word for what you are right now."

I measure my breaths. *One. Two. Three. I can do this.* I force my resistant lips wider. "Thanks, Ang. You look really nice, too."

I'm not lying. His tailored black suit is trimmed in red satin and paired with a scrollwork red vest that shows underneath the open jacket. He looks dapper and about as handsome as a boy can be. A boy who isn't Mikey.

Susan shoves me toward him, forcing him to catch me as I trip. I glare at her. She smiles sweetly. "You two are so perfect together. His dark features really make your pale skin pretty, Danielle. Let's get some pictures of you." She snaps her fingers at Randall. He lifts his camera just as Angelo slides a red carnation corsage over my wrist, the gold leaves sparkling with a dusting of iridescent glitter.

"This is beautiful, Ang. Thank you."

He winks at me, eyes dipping to the pushed-up cleavage. "No, thank *you*."

I turn away from him and pick up the red carnation boutonniere that's on the table by the door. Susan took the liberty of calling Angelo herself to get all the details right because she was sure I'd mess up and get the wrong flower. "Don't thank me until we see if I can pin this on without stabbing you."

He slips a hand under his lapel. "I won't cry if you stab my fingers, but my chest is delicate."

His lighthearted nature always made me laugh before, but tonight, I can't seem to muster anything more than a tight smile. I pin his flower into place and turn toward Randall so he can get more photos. He steps forward, a rectangular black box in his hands. "I have a little something for you, honey." He opens the lid. A diamond bracelet catches every speck of light in the room.

Throat dry, I hold a smile steady on my face. "Thanks. I already have a bracelet, though."

"Don't be ridiculous," Susan snaps, ripping the simple gold strand I picked out at the boutique off of my wrist. Before I can rub the raw skin, Randall clips his bracelet into place. Susan lifts my wrist to inspect the bracelet. "Randall spent a fortune on this. I picked it out, of course. And we're lucky to have found something on such short notice." Her fingers trail over Angelo's lapel. "You sure kept a girl waiting long enough."

"Speaking of waiting…" I lock my painted nails onto Angelo's arm and move us out the door. "Some friends are waiting for us."

Angelo looks over his shoulder. "I won't keep her out too late."

I don't have to look to imagine what Susan's face is doing right now. It's bad enough I have to hear her words. "Stay out as long as you want. You kids are young, and the after-party is always the best part."

I pick up the pace, hurrying to get tucked inside the limo. Angelo slides onto the seat next to me, a wide grin splitting his face. I let go of his arm and smooth the fabric of my dress. "Yeah, I know, my mom is full-on crazy town."

He laughs. "She is. But this smile on my face is because you look *good*. And I just got permission to take you back to my place later."

I shift uncomfortably and Angelo settles in next to me as the limo begins to move. "You know I'm playing with you. But you do look good, like heaven opened up and dropped a star right down beside me."

Tightness builds in my chest. I busy my hands with pretending to need to adjust the corsage, just in case he gets any ideas about holding my hand. "You didn't have to splurge on a limo. We could have just ridden in your car."

"Not enough room in it." He waggles his eyebrows. "I wanted to take you out in style, and I was going to go with borrowing something sporty from the car lot, but Mikey managed to find himself a date, so we're doubling. So get those dirty thoughts out of your head, we don't need all this room for just us."

I suck in air, chest trying to constrict as my throat closes. Angelo grabs my hand. "You okay? What's happening?"

I press a hand to my throat. "Carsick."

He makes a face and rolls down the window, moving across from me and knocking on the glass. The driver rolls it down. "Hey, she's going to blow chunks. You have any bags up there?"

As if this happens all the time, the man's thin hand passes two bags to Angelo, who in turn hands one to me. "Is the air helping any?"

I nod, willing my heart to stop racing. The last thing I need is to flip out in front of Angelo or Mikey. Again.

Angelo places his hands on my knees. I move closer to the open window. "Madge is going to be mad. She said she got a different date for tonight because Mikey wasn't going."

Angelo leans back in his seat. "Even if she didn't have a date, he wouldn't go with her." I glance at him and he smiles. "Their relationship is only complicated on Madge's end. For Mikey, she's basically a click below cousin status. He's not interested. Unlike whoever his mystery date is. I didn't know he was coming to the dance myself until last night."

"So you don't know who he's bringing?"

His head shakes. "All I know is he said I'm going to love her. And that she's *his* date, so I'm to keep my paws off. Which means she's hot, but highly unlikely that she's hotter than my date." His eyes roam over me. "I *really* hope you don't get sick. It would be a shame to not spin you around a floor tonight."

~49~

An image of what Nym looks like filters through my brain, her centerfold arms wrapped around Mikey's neck as they dance the way he danced with me. I shove my head out the window, letting the wind catch in my face like a dog. Angelo moves to the seat beside me, rubbing my back. "We're almost to Mikey's. Hold on that long and we'll get you inside and let you lie down."

The limo slows, turning into Mikey's driveway and passing through the massive gates. I retreat back into the window. "I'm sorry, Ang, but I have to go home. If the limo stops here, I'll walk back."

He grins, arm draping around my shoulders. "Let us pick up Mikey and his girl, and then we'll drive you back to your place. I'm fine spending the night with you there. Maybe if you start feeling better, we can dance on your lawn or something sweet like that."

"No," I whimper as the house comes into view.

He presses a hand to his heart. "You going to do me like that? Mikey told me you've got moves, and I missed them at the party that night because I was…checking other moves. And now you hit me with this dress and won't even let me nurse you back to health so we can have one little dance?"

Tears pool in my eyes. "Ang, I *can't*."

"Hey now." He cups my face and plants a kiss on my forehead. The limo comes to a stop and he smiles. "I've got you. Just sit tight while I grab them real quick, and then we'll get you home."

I clutch at his forearm but I'm too weak to hold him. He sprints from the limo and disappears into the house. I don't even attempt to count. My pulse is too fast and too erratic for it to be calmed by sheer willpower alone. I lean against the seat, catching the cock of the driver's head as he stares at my Susan-designed cleavage through the rearview.

205

I stumble out of the car, keeping the heels of these shoes under me long enough to reach the back of the car. I press my shaking hands onto the metal. I have to get out of here.

Angling my body toward the closest patch of woods, I remove a hand from the stability of the car. Chatter erupts from the house. My head snaps in that direction, people filing out one after another, big and bright smiles on their faces as they fan out across the lawn. Angelo is in the group. Along with Val, Mary, John, Lily, several other people I don't know and one tall, gorgeous blonde that I do. While everyone else's eyes are trained on the door of the house, Sophie's are boring into me.

Sophie doesn't break her stare until cheers explode behind her. I lift my gaze. Mikey and his date are emerging. Her sequined blue dress hits her at the ankle, the flat silver shoes underneath catching light as she walks. Her hair is combed up on one side, and secured by an intricate silver clip. I stare at her face. "My grandmother is beautiful, isn't she?" Sophie echoes my thoughts from beside me. My legs go weak and I press myself against the car to keep from shaking. Sophie nudges me. Hard. "Thought someone should tell you who that woman is before you attack her. Or is it only my cousin who has to watch out for your sneak attacks?"

I meet her icy eyes. "Mikey told you."

She smirks. "Of course. But he didn't take my advice because here you are. With his *brother*."

I assume her advice was for him to run me out of town. I glance up to where he's standing taking photos with his grandma. "I didn't mean for any of this to happen."

She walks away, her place at my side filled by Mary. She presses a hand to my arm. "Angelo said you're not feeling well? Let's get you inside."

I pull my eyes away from Mikey. "I'm okay. I just got…carsick."

Angelo dashes up to us, handing me a bottle of water. "They're taking a few pictures and then we'll go. You going to last until then?"

I nod, pressing the cold bottle to the back of my neck where this stiff hair keeps itching me. A woman with amber eyes and honey hair walks toward us. "If she can stand there, we can get some pictures of you two. Try not to barf, Danielle Madison."

"She won't." Val shakes a finger at me. "I need proof that my son got a date as pretty as you."

~

I've now met Mikey's Aunt Sheila, Uncle Avery, Sophie, and several of his other cousins. And sitting across from his grandmother while she tells me that I'll have to help fill her date's dance card once her tired feet give out, I feel as if I've done *exactly* what Susan wanted me to do. Wormed my way right into the middle of this family.

I unwrap the mint Lily pressed into my palm before we left. I didn't get to know her as well as I would have liked to, but I'm going to really miss her. "I think we both might need help filling the dance cards of our dates."

Mikey puts his arm around his grandmother. He hasn't looked at me once. "You're the only girl I'm dancing with tonight, Grandma. Because you're the prettiest girl in the room."

She pats his knee. "I let you talk me into dancing with you one more time, but about one dance is all I have in me."

"We'll see." He stands, buttoning his jacket and covering his blue scroll vest. He bends at the waist, extending his hand to her. Her face lights up as her palm slides into his. He brings her knuckles to his lips, and then lifts her from the seat.

They walk onto the dance floor and Angelo slides his hand into mine. "Since you're still pale, let's go get our pictures taken. Maybe by then you'll feel better and I can take my little star out there and make her glow."

Ungluing my hand from his, I walk beside him through the winter-themed venue, clocking any male teachers from our school who are *chaperoning*. It's unlikely Kira was the monster's first victim. He probably had earlier victims that he didn't kill, escalating to murder once he got caught because dead kids can't tell on him. It's only odd that he'd be in a high school instead of where his intended targets are. Maybe he was kicked out of the primary schools.

"Ang, have any new teachers transferred to the academy lately?"

"Nah, most of them have been around for a while. Why? You thinking about becoming a teacher and looking for an opening?"

"Maybe. Do you know if any of the teachers taught primary school before coming to the academy?"

His head shakes as he lifts me up into a sleigh where a camera is set up for couples to have their picture taken in the prop. "I don't think I've ever heard you say that you wanted to be a teacher before. Not that you're much of one to talk." He wraps an arm around me and I stare into the camera for the last photograph that will ever be taken of Dani Madison.

"I've never had much to say before, but now I'm finally figuring out what I'm going to do with the rest of my life."

In the last twenty-four hours, I've come to terms with many things. One being that I'll never graduate. I'll never get a GED. And I may never be able to do more than travel from one homeless shelter to the next. But what I *will* do, is find the person who murdered Kira.

I climb off the sleigh and follow Angelo along the fringe, snowflakes suspended over our heads, the shimmery white decorations softly lit by a delicate blue glow. I glance around. Mikey is on the dance floor with his grandma. "Ang," I whisper, "I only ever meant to be your friend."

He puts his arm around me. "You are. Feel like you can handle the heat of the dance floor?"

I shake my head. He follows my gaze. "Then you leave me no choice. Have a seat and watch this."

I stand on the sideline, watching as Mikey spins his grandma in slow motion, her feet stepping around steady and sure. He's good with her. Gentle. The way he's always been good and gentle, until I hurt him. Angelo taps Mikey on the shoulder. With a huff, Mikey makes a show of being fake angry, he and Angelo shoving each other for the older woman's benefit. With a grin pulled wide over her face, she steps between them, playing her part and shaking a scolding finger at Mikey. He drops his head and walks away, shoving a hand into Angelo at the last second and throwing up his fingers to show his grandma it wasn't him. I laugh, until his eyes snap up and land on me. The humor goes out of him, and the look on his face makes everything inside me turn to ice.

Mikey goes in the opposite direction, moving through the crowd to the other side of the venue. I shouldn't bother him. My leaving here will give him his life back and he'll be okay. He'll move on and heal from the damage I've done. One day he'll even forget there was ever a girl named Dani to begin with. But none of that will explain to him why this happened, how sorry I am that it did, or that no matter the speed with which my memory fades from him, I'll never forget him.

Mustering the courage that I'm finally finding, I walk across the room to where Mikey is standing by the bar sipping on one of the non-alcoholic cocktails that are part of tonight's supposed fun. His suit jacket is slung over his shoulder and while I can't help but notice how good the vest looks on his body, I can't help feeling like red is more his color than blue.

I stop in front of him. He doesn't look at me but keeps his eyes fixed on something over my head. "I know you don't want to speak to me, so don't talk, just listen. I—"

His slamming glass cuts me off, his eyes searing into mine. "If you like Angelo, I'll give you two all the space you need. If you don't like him, you better tell him because you're *not* going to like what happens if I have to."

"Mikey, wait!" I clutch at his arm but he shrugs me off, the same as he does to Angelo who is closing in behind me. A sob jerks into my throat. Angelo's face goes hard as stone. "It seems we need to get some air and have ourselves a little conversation, Dani."

~50~

Tucked into an alcove on the outside of the venue, Angelo being kind enough to drape his jacket over my shoulders as we hide from the frigid wind, he wipes the tears from my cheeks. "You're crying over Mikey?"

I don't answer. He blows out a breath and runs a hand through his hair. "I don't know how I showed up so late to this party, but reality slapped me right in the face when I saw you two talking. You don't want to be here with me, you want to be with him."

I nod but the lump in my throat continues to keep my voice from working. Angelo's teeth clench. "One of you might have told me you had something going on before I got all up in your drama."

"I'm sorry," I whisper.

"You should be," he snaps. "I knew you were acting weird but you're always a little weird, and you're always back-and-forth standoffish with Mikey, so I didn't think it had anything to do with you having feelings for him. Or *him* having feelings for you."

"He doesn't," I choke out.

He lets out a cold, hard huff. "If he didn't, he wouldn't have stormed off like that. And now you got me sitting here looking like a chump because I snaked his girl."

Angelo gets up and paces. "You're the reason he's been walking around with a short fuse. I can't believe you let me hurt my brother like this."

I wipe my face. "Trust me, I'm not going to come between the two of you."

He flattens his back on the wall and looks up into the sky. "You already did, Dani. And I didn't even see it. And you sat tight-lipped on

210

the situation, and now…" He swipes a hand down his face. "He never told me he was putting moves on you. And the only reason I asked you to be my date was because I thought he *wanted* me to."

He bangs his head on the wall. "Look, I like you, Dani. You're smokin' hot and next-level in that dress, but because of how Mikey was continually bringing you up, asking me if I'd talk to you, sit with you, walk you to class, I thought he *wanted* me to fall for you." He faces me. "You're not exactly my normal flavor but Mikey hasn't ever steered me wrong. After this, I'm going to go right back to ignoring *all* his advice because this situation right here is all kinds of messed up. He's my *brother*, Dani."

I lift myself from the bench and give him his suit jacket back. "I'm not going to be a problem anymore. You can go back to dating girls who are your flavor, and Mikey can rebound with Nym. The two of you are going to be just fine, and right back to being best friends."

He follows me around the building, hand wrapping around my elbow. "Hold up. What did Mikey tell you about Nym?"

I drag in a breath. "That she's a hot little centerfold. Not plain like me. Or weird. Just a good, normal girl."

He chuckles. "Nym is good at a lot of things, but I doubt Mikey compared you to her because Nym is *my* girl, and you better believe Mikey straight up knows that. She's the whole reason I thought he was trying to steer me to you. Nym and I have an open relationship, and we're both a little more open than Mikey's comfortable with. He keeps trying to sell me on something more conventional."

I swallow, memory going straight to the party where Angelo disappeared with those girls. One of them was Nym. He grips my hands. "Don't be uncomfortable. Though you did make me rethink some things when you walked down those steps tonight, I've never even really thought about you like that. I mean, a little, but I mostly only ever wanted to be your friend too, Dani."

"Why does Val think Mikey is dating Nym?"

He smiles. "Mom caught my girl sneaking out of the house. Mikey just happened to be making an early morning stop, so he both initiated the bust, and then covered for me since I wouldn't have been caught otherwise."

I lower my head. Angelo tucks his hand under my chin and lifts it back up. "I don't know what kind of game you and Mikey have going on, and the longer I think about how *both* of you ruined my night, the madder I am, but I will *always* have my boy's back. If he wasn't hurt, he wouldn't have shoved by us like that. And to be hurt, he has to care about you. So go make things right with him, and then both of you get your butts out here and apologize to me."

~

Expecting his grandma to be tired and ready to leave the dance early, Mikey had a separate car waiting for them. Which Angelo found out about when we went back inside the venue and couldn't find them. Mikey left a message with the driver of our limo. A move that had Angelo clearly shaken. Not because Mikey left, but because he didn't bother telling his friend directly.

Susan's disappointment over Angelo dropping me off much earlier than even he expected to is palpable. It's a living thing all its own as I lie on my bed, the beautiful red dress hung on the back of the closet door. All of the jewelry I wore tonight is neatly arranged on the dresser. When I'm gone, Susan can take back Randall's diamond bracelet. As for the rest, I'm going to return it to Mary. The easiest way to do that is to leave it in the cottage for Mikey to find. I have to go there tonight anyway to remove all the research on Kira. I don't want there to be any reason for the killer to go after Mikey.

Fully dressed, a thick dark hoodie pulled over my head and my usual tennis shoes already on my feet, I wait for the sound of Susan's complaints to die off. Once the house is quiet, I climb out of bed, fold the beautiful dress and pack it into a trash bag, along with the shoes and jewelry. This is the simplest way to make sure it doesn't get soiled on the trip to the cottage.

Opening the bedroom door, I listen for any sound that Randall or Susan are still awake before easing down the stairs and out the front door. Once I reach the darkest section of the sidewalk, I turn on the light attached to the keychain that will also be staying at the cottage. I'll leave the four-wheeler parked there to make it easier for Mikey to retrieve, but I do have to bring this flashlight back with me. The only other light I have is the burner phone, and it's currently back at Susan's and already packed into the top pocket on my backpack.

Moving as quickly as I can through the woods, a branch snags in my still pinned hair and I yank it free, a mass of curls falling loose. I don't look to see how much of my scalp is left on the branch. I need to get this mission over with as quickly as possible so I can shower and begin what are sure to be the worst years of my life.

I glance up at the sky as I mount the four-wheeler. It's already past midnight. "Happy birthday to me." I start the engine and set course for the cottage, tears freezing to my face as I drive.

Inside the cottage, the icy air is barely any better. I don't bother turning on heat. I flip on the kitchen light and unpack the dress, trying to smooth the wrinkles out of the fabric as I drape it across the kitchen table. I spread the jewelry out beside it, place the shoes on the floor, and then move into the living room, shoving all of the notebooks and loose stacks of charts and paper into the trash bag.

Placing the dark plastic by the door, I open the laptop and begin deleting every file. I erase in every way I know how and hope Mikey never has a reason to hire Gideon. I can't imagine he would be curious as to why I erased everything. I think that once I'm gone, he'll be nothing but relieved.

Feeling as if I've done enough to erase myself from the cottage, I take the light off the keychain and leave the rest sitting with the jewelry. Then I exit the cottage and scan the darkness around me. From where I am, I can't even see lights from the house I know is out there.

Turning on my light, I walk toward the path Mikey uses to move between his house and here. What was once overgrown is now showing signs of use. I walk down the path, heading toward where I hope to at least catch a glimpse of the house. From there, I can whisper my last goodbye.

I train my light on the ground, cupping my hand over the end to let only a small beam shine on the pebbled ground below my feet. I don't want security to see me skulking through the woods in what seems like a futile attempt to reach the outskirts of the Beller home. It's doubtful they'll hear me, just like I won't be able to hear them. The wind is howling through the night, leaves swirling and branches snapping.

Tucking my arms close to my body, I try to ignore the stinging in my fingers. As long as they're not too frozen to hold the light, I'm okay.

And my nose has stopped running, or it's running but my face is too frozen to feel it.

A gust of icy wind pushes a set of pines to the left, their bows popping and snapping as they kiss the ground. For the briefest of moments, I see it. The light from what has to be the Beller home.

Warmth spreads through me and I find myself running toward the light, off the path and straight through trees. They poke and snag, pull and tug, reaching for my hair, my hoodie, and smacking me across my face. I don't care. I'll never be this close to Mikey again.

Turning my light off, I shove it into my pocket and tuck my hands under my armpits. There's only one set of pines separating me from the expanse of lawn that slopes down to the home. I stare at each visible window. They all appear dark. Even if they weren't, I don't know which one is Mikey's. And it isn't like I could just walk up and knock on the glass anyway. All I want is to catch a glimpse of him. To let this brutal wind carry my message to him. "I love you, Mikey."

"He can't hear you." The voice comes from my left. My mind goes blank, body unmoving as I process what's happening. "Are you just going to stand there, Dani?"

I step back and to the side. The voice sounds… "Lily?"

She laughs. "What are you doing out here? It's freezing."

I stumble over a root and fall on the ground. She laughs again and I pick myself up, barely able to feel what's hurting because all of me is hurting. "I'm being a perfectly rational creeper who is trying to catch a glimpse of a boy who probably isn't even home. What are you doing, Lily? It's *freezing* out here."

She brushes the dead pine needles off my shirt and then takes my cold hand in her warm gloved one. "I saw the light up on the mountain and wanted to come out and see who had a death wish. Now, follow me and be very careful. Step *only* where I step. I know where the blind spots are."

I go with her, brushing the remains of what used to be a curl out of my face. "Lily, I wasn't actually going to go right up to your house. I just wanted to…see."

She keeps walking, steps measured while she traverses the yard, skirting along the edge of the reach of the flood lights on the corner of the house. We stop at a window that's partially hidden by a tall shrub.

"Mikey's home. And you walked all the way here, through this." She waves a hand around to indicate the blustery weather. You have to at least come in and get warm." She hoists herself up to the window and slips inside. "Come on. And be careful or you're going to set off the motion sensors, and then we're both in hot water."

She presses a finger to her lips when I get inside. She moves through the house like a ghost and I do my best to follow her exact steps. We enter a hallway and she stops where the corridor dead-ends into a door. She faces me. "I thought it was cute the way you pretended not to like Mikey, but that was before, when he kind of thought it was cute, too. Now, I'm worried. About him. When I saw that light tonight, somchow I knew it was you, so if you mean what you said outside, this is his room. Go in and tell him to his face. If you didn't mean it, I'm calling security right now."

I swallow. "I didn't walk through this weather for no reason, but I also didn't come to bother him. I just wanted to be near him one last time."

She places a hand on my arm. "Don't let it be the last time, Dani. He likes you. A lot. And you just did the most romantic thing ever, so don't leave without letting him know you're here." She steps to the side and nods at the door. "He never locks his door so go on in and wake him up. Just…don't hurt him anymore. He was really sad when he came home earlier and I've never seen my brother like that. He's always the positive one."

I don't know what I thought would happen when I followed her into the house, but I can't come face to face with Mikey. I turn away from his door but it's too late. Lily is gone and I have no idea how to find my way back out of here.

Turning to his door, I let my hand rest on the knob. Sure enough, it isn't locked.

~51~

Mikey's room is dark. I follow the sound of his breathing, stubbing my frozen toe against the bed. Pain shoots up my leg and I limp closer, fingers finding the sleek rounded muscle of his shoulder. He's on his stomach, and now that I'm touching him, I want so badly to see his face. "Mikey." I shake him gently. He doesn't move. I lower myself onto the bed, letting my eyes trace his silhouette. His face is turned away from me and stuffed deep in a pillow, his bare back exposed above the mound of sheets at his waist. I'm freezing, and he's lying here as if he's on a beach.

I press my lips to his ear. "Mikey. Wake up." He bolts upright, head crashing into my face. "Ouch!" I hold my nose.

"Dani?" Mikey shoots one hand toward me, the other fumbling to turn on the bedside lamp. The room illuminates and he pulls my hands from my face. "Let me see. Is it broken?"

"I'll let you know once it stops hurting, and when I can actually feel all of my face."

He runs his thumbs down the sides of my nose. "I think it's okay. And I don't see any blood but I'll get you some ice."

"No." I wrap my palm around his wrist. "I'm cold enough, I don't need any ice."

He grabs a blanket from the bottom of the bed, revealing all he's wearing is boxers. He wraps the blanket around me. "Why are you so cold? And why are you here? I've been clear with you, Dani. I don't want to talk to you."

"I know." I stare at my knees poking out from under the blanket. "You have every right to hate me, and Angelo gave me a mouthful already about how I should have said something about my feelings for you sooner. Looking back, I wish that I did because the last thing I want is for you to think that I didn't completely fall for you." I look up at him. "I did, Mikey. Hard. Completely. In that all-consuming way that won't ever leave me." Tears rush my eyes. "You're my forever love, and I guess that's why I'm here, to make sure you know that."

His expressionless stare makes my insides churn. I bite down the agony and press forward with what he deserves to hear. "I don't know who I am, and I have no idea if I'll ever figure out who this person inside me really is, but I do know that this girl found the one person in this world who she could open up to." I wipe the tears from my face, the remnants of the thick makeup feeling cakey. "I'm truly and deeply sorry that I'm not a decent enough person to have ever deserved your friendship, let alone your affection."

"Dani." He shifts closer to me. "You *are* a decent person. I was angry when I said you weren't, but I didn't mean it."

I twist the blanket into my fingers. "What I am or what I'm not is debatable, except for the part where I'm sorry."

He lets out a soft exhale and wraps his arms around my blanketed shoulders. "I forgive you."

I shake my head. "All I need is for you to understand that everything was my fault. Please don't hold my actions against anyone else because you're going to find someone who is every bit as decent as you, and I couldn't bear to think that because of me, you wouldn't trust her."

"I trust *you*," he whispers.

I begin to protest but his mouth falls over mine. I shouldn't kiss him back but I want to. I throw the blanket off and curl my greedy arms around him, folding myself as close to him as I can get, my legs around his waist and the rest of me pressed tight against his chest, the taste of him igniting a blaze.

His hands cup my hips and I run my hands down his arms, across his torso and onto the waistband of his boxers. His head snaps up. "Are you sure?"

I run my lips from his jaw to his ear. "Positive."

He lowers us to the bed with a rumbling in his chest. "Stop me anytime, because I'm sure as hell not going to stop you."

~

My first experience wasn't anything close to earth-shattering, but tonight changed my opinion on what being intimate really is. When you're with someone you love, everything feels good and you never want it to end.

I lie beside Mikey, stroking my fingers over his broad chest. "Thank you. This day ended much better than I dreamed it could."

"Yesterday, you mean." His arm tightens around me as his lips press to the top of my head. "Happy birthday. Before you dumped me, I was planning a few things for today. I think I can still pull it all off, though. So today, my *girlfriend's* birthday is starting *and* ending good."

I close my eyes, a single tear sliding out. I wipe it away before it touches his skin, masking the movement by sitting up and pulling the sheets over my chest, as if he hasn't just explored everything I have. "I didn't come here trying to get anything out of you. I don't even celebrate birthdays anymore, with tomorrow being the anniversary…" I tuck my knees to my chest to hold the sheet up and reach for his hand. "I came here only to apologize, and to tell you that I love you, Mikey."

He sits up. "Sleeping with me isn't an apology. I forgave you before that, and I wouldn't have been with you if I thought that's what you were doing." His hand pulls my face to his. "I *only* let that happen because I thought all the drama was over now. That we both felt what it was like to be apart and were deciding *together* to make us official in every way."

I stare at the divot just above his perfectly soft upper lip. "I *do* wish it could be like that for us. I wish I didn't mess up and ruin this last week. I wish Susan was normal and that your parents didn't hate me." I fight the knot of emotion crawling up my throat. "If I could go back in time and do it all over again, I'd be different. Then maybe everyone around me would feel differently. But I can't change anything, so I've told you what I needed you to know, and now I have to go."

His body tenses. "Go where? How did you even get here?"

I clear my throat. "I walked."

His hand falls away and he sits taller, staring down at me. "You *walked*? From where?"

Avoiding the anger building in his eyes, I lower my head and begin pulling the remaining pins of pain from my mangled hair. "I came through the woods, but I didn't see any of the guards so your parents don't know I'm here. Lily does, though. And I'm sorry about that. I…didn't really have a plan. I just came, and then the next thing I knew, Lily was outside and ushering me through a window."

His fingers start running through my hair, helping to locate and remove the painful pins. "Don't ever do anything like that again. It's dangerous, and especially in a windstorm like what blew through here last night. You could have been seriously hurt."

I close my eyes while he massages my scalp. "Like I said, I didn't really have a plan. I was coming just to be near you, but never expected to get *this* near."

His arms move around me and his face lowers next to mine. "Are you regretting what we did?"

I look at him. "Not one tiny little bit. It was unexpected, but perfect."

He smiles. "Then let me make the rest of this day perfect. I'm not as slick as Lily when it comes to sneaking around this place, but I can manage to get you out to my truck without being seen. Then we'll drive to Susan's and let you change if you want, or we'll just get started on what I had planned for you today. It includes a shopping spree, so you don't have to go back home, you can just buy whatever you're going to need for the day. And for the night. I canceled my reservation, but I bet I can still find a suite for us. Someplace I can feed you cake totally unrelated to your birthday while we sit in a jacuzzi not celebrating anything."

I shake my head, the newly loosened curls splashing all along my shoulders. "I've caused enough problems. I just need to go now."

He throws the covers back and gets out of bed. "You haven't *caused* problems, you're *causing* problems." He opens a drawer and tugs on a pair of sweatpants. "I don't do this, Dani. I don't sleep with girls that I'm not in a relationship with and I thought I made that clear. Monogamous. Public. Those are my terms. Because I'm not *free love* and all the crap the rest of you are into. There's only one of me, and this one of me wants one girlfriend, who up until this moment I thought, *once again*, was you."

My breath hitches. "Your mom—"

"Did a really good job helping you pick out your dress." He cuts me off, chest heaving. "*I* asked her to help *me* pick out a dress for you because I knew you couldn't afford one. The very next day I had to tell her not to bother. Right after that, Angelo was here announcing to everyone how he scored you as his date for the dance. I sat through all of that, Dani, not saying a single word even though my parents were confused as hell and staring a hole through me. I haven't said a single word to *anyone* about *anything* this entire time, but I can't do this anymore. You can't be with me one second and then bail the next because you're making up problems that don't exist. My parents don't hate you. They're picking up on how I feel, and lately, that's all pissed off and sad, so *that* bothers them, but they don't care if we date. They're over their initial worry, and I'm over this." He motions between us. "I care about you and I'm not afraid to say that to you, or to show it to you and *everyone* else. So why are you so ashamed of me?"

I rush from the bed and cup his face. "I'm not ashamed. Of you, or of the way I love you so much it makes me flip out when you hug your cousin." The wall of resolve inside my chest crumbles and the flood comes out.

Mikey pulls me against him as I cry. "You were stunning in that dress, Dani. When I walked out of the house and saw you, I nearly tripped and took my grandma down with me." He nuzzles into my neck and holds me tight. "Sitting across from you in the limo, I wanted so badly to crawl inside Ang's skin so I could be the one next to you. I don't want to be forced to deny my feelings anymore. And the way you're crying makes it seem like you don't want to either. So *why* are you making us go through this?"

~52~

When I'm in Mikey's arms, I have no idea why I have a backpack full of hair dye and potential DNA evidence waiting for me. Every plan I've made seems illogical when I'm with him. I study my laces as I tie my shoes. "Tomorrow, I need to tell you some things I found out about Kira's killer. I think it's time to tap those resources you have."

"Okay." He tugs a shirt over his head. "And I didn't say I was going to *prance* you down the hall and out the front door, I said we'd walk. Quietly. So I don't disrespect the one rule my parents have for me."

"Because them catching you *quietly* breaking the *no girls in your room* rule is better than doing it noisily?"

He grins. "The two of them are rarely quiet, so yeah, me attempting to be is better than the fireworks display they're prone to setting off."

"Ew, gross." I pull my hoodie on and smooth my hands down the front. "That sets in stone that I *will* be going back out the window."

He sighs, going to his own bedroom window and opening it. "Here. I'll help you over the sill and then you can run straight back to the trees. When you get there, turn right and keep going until you see the garage. There's a door in the back, it's the same code as the cottage's door. Go inside and wait for me. It's heated in there so you'll be warm. I'm going to grab a two-second shower, pack up a few things, and then I'll be out."

He presses his lips to my forehead, hands lifting me unnecessarily so that I'm cradled in his arms. He places a kiss on my lips and then feeds my legs over the sill, putting a hand on top of my head to be sure I don't bump the window. My feet sink to the ground and I turn to face him. "I love you. I'm not saying it again so that you feel obligated to say it back. I know you aren't there, and mostly because I've made this whole experience so difficult. But you *are* my first love, Michael Beller, and I'm pretty sure you'll be my last."

221

He clears his throat. "I want to work on our relationship and grow with you, Dani, and I'm not far behind how you say you're feeling. Now run to the garage and I'll be out there in about five minutes."

I dart away from the window, the frosty morning air causing my shoulders to shiver. Inside the safe harbor of the pine boughs, I look back at the house. Mikey's window is closed. I turn away, kicking my feet into overdrive. I only have a five-minute head start.

~

Mikey

"Dani," I whisper, moving around the garage. I assumed she'd wait at my truck but she's not there. "Are you hiding unnecessarily? No one is up yet but us."

She doesn't answer. I walk over to the door and open it. "You better not be standing out here in the cold." She isn't. "Dani?" I shout, only the sound of my quickening pulse answering. "Dani!" I run out into the woods behind the garage. "Babe? Where are you?" Visions of her sprawled on the ground with a broken leg after having tumbled over a rock in the dim light pound in my head. I shouldn't have let her go into the woods. "Dani!"

"Michael!" Dad's voice booms through the trees and I hear his body crashing through them the same way mine is.

"Dad." I feel my hands shake as he comes into view. "It's Dani. Did you see her?"

"No." His chest heaves. "She's out here? Why?"

"She was…" Doing her best to not have to come to the garage with me. "As stupid as I feel for even saying this because right now I can't think of a single reason *why*, I love her. And she either loves me too, or she's a better liar than her mom ever was."

I could comb through the woods to make sure I'm not wrong, but I know in my gut that Dani is just fine and on her way back to Susan's. My bike is faster than the one I left for her and she's had less than a ten-minute head start, the first part of her journey being on foot. But I'm not taking any chances on missing her.

Not answering any more questions from my dad, or Mom who is

just now catching up to us, I stomp into the garage and get in my truck, firing it up and not caring that I'll hear from Dad later about the squeal of my tires.

I don't slow down at my own gate or the one leading into Dani's neighborhood. Barreling down the streets, I keep my foot on the gas until I reach the end of the cul-de-sac, driving my truck up onto the grass beyond where the pavement ends before skidding to a halt and slamming the truck into park.

I check the gate. No Dani. I move through the woods around the gate in case she's in here hiding from me, but I highly doubt she's had time to make it back here yet.

The roar of an engine hits my ears. She's driving her four-wheeler right up to the gate, and she's making good time. My decision to bring my truck and cut her off on this end was the right call.

I stand against a tree and watch her jump off the bike, her frantic hands pulling a black bag from the compartment under the four-wheeler. She runs to the gate and when she stops to open it, she sees me. "Mikey."

"This isn't my garage, Dani. Did you get confused on where you're supposed to be right now?"

Her face goes slack and she slowly steps through the gate, dumping her black bag and walking toward me. "I don't want to go out and celebrate today. All I want is to take a long shower and get all this makeup and hair goop off of me, and then I just want to…not remember that this is my birthday."

I shake my head, arms folded across my chest and not moving from my tree. "You're not pinning this on me, Dani. You're not going to make it sound like I'm being an insensitive jerk. If that was the case, I would have planned a huge surprise party for you and tricked you into going. I didn't. I knew before this morning that today would be tough for you because of what tomorrow is. So all I did was plan for *us* to be *together* for the next two days so you could have any emotion you need to have and I'd be there for you. And hell yeah, I was going to slip in any special thing I could because the day you were born deserves to be celebrated. That's not me being a jerk, it's me *caring* about you. But you don't know anything about that because you don't care about me."

"I love you," she insists.

I step away from her when she reaches for me. "Hollow words, Dani. You kick me every chance you get."

She looks at the ground. "Susan hired this team of people to work on me so I'd look the way I did at the dance. It took them five hours to do that. And I've cried about thirty times since all the plaster went onto my face, and I walked through a windstorm, and fell, then barged into your room with actual leaves stuck in my hair. You literally picked one out right after…" Her cheeks turn bright red. "I just *really* wanted to take a shower before you looked at me again because I feel like a monster and the more the sun comes up, the worse that feeling becomes."

I run a hand down my face. Her explanations never quite make sense but I have this nagging soft spot that makes me want to hug her and love her even though I *know* she's lying to me. "You could have said all of this earlier. Instead, you lied to me. I was frantic when I couldn't find you in the garage. I jumped straight to worst-case scenario, Dani. I thought you were hurt out there so I *searched* for you. I woke up my entire family shouting your name."

"I'm so sorry." She reaches for me again and this time I don't move. Her hands slide across my biceps. "I knew you'd come after me, that's why I ran so fast and drove your four-wheeler all the way to the gate, but it never occurred to me that you'd think I didn't show up because I was hurt."

"Something that could have been avoided if you'd just talked to me." The vein in my neck throbs. "I can't take one more lie, one more accusation, one more time of having you blow me off like I'm nothing. You *slept* with me, told me you loved me, and then left me. Do you even realize how messed up that is?"

Her body moves close to mine. "I *desperately* love you, Mikey. So yeah, I know how messed up the things I do are. I'm not remotely good enough for you. And I dread the day when someone better comes along, someone who deserves your heart, and you see how much they eclipse me. I'm scared of that day coming, and *every* one that will come after it."

I remove her hands from my arms and lace my fingers through hers. "It will feel less scary if you just *stop* running away from me. If something is bothering you, speak up. Don't run off and *then* tell me you're embarrassed that you have leaves in your hair. There are four pretty big showers in my house. You could have used mine, with or without me in it. Instead, while I was enjoying myself, you were miserable."

Her lips tip up. "I said I was embarrassed, not miserable. It was fairly dark in your room so for the most part, I didn't think about the way I looked, only how you felt."

My mouth captures hers, reminding her of just how good everything we've shared felt. She tilts her hips against me and a rumble rattles inside my throat. I break away from her lips, staying close enough to feel her raspy breath washing over my face. "Dani. You still have leaves in your hair."

~53~

In what feels like a historic moment, Dani not only lets me inside her house, but she walked down the street with her hand in mine and hasn't let go of me. Her palm is firmly affixed in mine.

"Thanks." I press a kiss to her temple as I close the door behind us.

She shrugs. "Your funeral. The instant Susan sees us together, she's going to take out a billboard to announce that *the* Mikey Beller is dating her daughter. It's going to publicly ruin you."

I scratch my chin. "The billboard is a good idea. I was only planning to add it to the school's morning announcements."

She laughs while tugging me toward the stairs. "Danielle!" Randall's flustered red face runs down the hall. "Where do you think you're going? And where have you been all night?" His eyes narrow on me. "Let go of her and get out of this house."

I do let go of her, but not to leave. I step toward him. "I'm going to need your tone to level down when you speak to my girlfriend, or I'm going to lose the very little cool I have left and end this power trip you're having in a way you're not going to like."

Dani's hand wraps around my arm. "Let's just go up to my room."

"Absolutely *not*!" Randall's jaws jiggle with rage, spittle flying from his mouth as he keeps his eyes trained on Dani, not me. Coward.

"I asked you nicely to speak to her with respect, and now we're going to have to go outside so I can make you."

"No," Dani pleads, tugging on me, but I stay where I am. This man needs to learn a lesson. Even when I'm pissed at Dani, I don't yell at her like this.

"What on earth is going on down here?" Susan's voice stumbles down from the top of the stairs. "Oh!" I hear the ring of her recognizing who I am just seconds before her footfalls scurry toward me. "Forgive us. The mornings around here can be a little crazy. Are you going up to Dani's room?"

"If he takes one more step I'm calling the law!" Randall shouts.

Susan wraps herself around my middle as if she's protecting me. "You will do no such thing. Leave this poor boy alone."

I pry her arms from around me and step toward Randall. He backs up. "Mikey, don't," Dani urges.

For her, I stop. "When your cops arrive, send them upstairs. Where I'll be. With Dani."

I allow Dani to pull me up the stairs. She races into her room but I stand in the hall. Randall is now screaming at Susan, who is yelling back at him. Dani pulls on me. "Will you just get in here? He isn't going to bother us anymore now that Susan is involved."

I look at her. "He wasn't going to bother us before she got involved. But now I'm worried about Susan."

Dani's eyes roll. "They're both blowhards. They do this all the time now. I think Susan is about sick of him and this is how she's running him off."

I take one more beat of listening to them argue and then slip into Dani's room, closing the door behind me. "So you and your mom both have a hard time being direct and saying what you mean?"

She pulls her shirt off. "Don't you dare compare me to her in any way. But because you already did, I'm going to go wash you off of me and then make you *try* to be slick enough to put it right back."

I follow her to the closet. "Now that you're finished running away from me, I doubt there's going to be a time I'm *not* all over you."

She kicks her backpack under a shelf and pulls the red shirt with the bell sleeves off a hanger before pressing her lips to my cheek. "Not here. *Never* in this house. So wait here for me. I'll wash the debris out of my hair as quickly as I can."

Dani disappears into the bathroom and I step back out into the hallway. Susan and Randall are still yelling, but their voices are finally getting lower. I can still hear well enough to know that what little Dani has told me about living here is correct. Susan is representing me as some sort of messiah while Randall harps on Dani being too young and too naïve, adding in accusations against Susan for being too lenient and ambitious.

"Susan really is fine." Dani's hand reaches from her doorway. My eyes rake over her, a curse slipping from my lips. She's standing there in nothing but a towel.

I move her backward and shove the door closed behind me. My fingers trail along her collarbone. "How am I this lucky?"

"It gets better." She smiles, loosening the towel that's holding her hair captive and letting the wet tendrils fall down her back. "Not one single piece of nature hiding anywhere in it."

"Then I can kiss you and you're not going to be embarrassed?" I ask, hands already moving up to anchor her against me. She leans her head back and lifts her mouth. My fingers flex against her bare hips. "I'm going to need you to get dressed. We'll go to the cottage or my truck, whichever you're good with."

Her arms slide around my neck, eyes sobering. "Do you remember me mentioning that I might transfer to public school?"

I nod. "Vaguely. Why? Do I need to make an announcement in two schools?"

She sighs. "Funny, but no. It's just that, if we do this dating thing for real, it's going to end up being a long-distance relationship and—"

"Nope." I lift her into the air and plop her onto the bed, my body pressing over hers. "You're not making up another pretend obstacle that I have to pretend is serious."

Her arms tighten on my neck. "Nothing is pretend. Everything is going to get harder. And I might also be dyeing my hair."

I slide my hand under her towel. "You're so random, and I like it."

Her towel pops open and I grin at her. She bites her lip. "Let me guess, towels are pretend obstacles."

I lower my mouth onto her. "Something like that."

Her bedroom door clicks open and I whip the end of the comforter up and over the side of the mattress, covering her before launching off the bed and storming toward Randall. "Ever heard of privacy?"

He backs toward the door. "I knew this is what you were doing. She's a child!"

"Compared to you, yeah!" I clamp one hand on the door and place my other squarely in the center of his chest, shoving hard enough that even over the sound of the slamming door, I hear his body crash into the far wall of the hallway. I click the lock and stomp into Dani's closet. She's right behind me, pulling clothes off hangers and onto her body. I fit a hoodie over her head and feed her arms into the sleeves. "Does he come in on you like that all the time?"

"No. And I'm usually not naked in bed either." She runs a comb through her wet hair. "You didn't hurt him, did you?"

I ignore the question. I hope every bone in his disgusting body is broken. "I *never* lock my bedroom door and my overbearing parents haven't *ever* walked in on me. They knock and wait."

"Yeah, well, in this fun little house of horrors you either lock the door or that happens. But usually, it's Susan coming to tell me I'm too fat for you to like me." She faces me. "Still want to let her take out that billboard?"

I plant my hand in hers and move us out of the room. The drywall has a little crack in it but Randall is gone. "I'm going to rub every mouthwatering inch of you in Susan's face, take out my own billboards, and go ahead and make announcements in every school in the state."

~54~

Now I have another favorite moment to add to the growing list of my happiest life moments. Only this one spans nearly an entire day. And makes me thankful that the air mattress in the cottage's closet is still usable. Dani's birthday wish was to confine ourselves to that room.

After we got to the cottage, the only low points to our day and our night, were when our stomachs demanded we leave the warm embrace of the bedroom. Dani always insisted on helping with the food instead of letting me serve her, and even with her being there to distract me, I couldn't ignore the fact that her beautiful red dress was spread across the table. Each time my eyes fell on it, I'd feel the sting of having not been with her when she wore it. And something about the way she intended to return what was meant to be a gift gnaws on a nerve.

Counteracting my unease is Dani's explanation about not having intentionally taken a date with Angelo. She wasn't trying to spite me. And in four hours, I'll walk into the academy holding her hand. Maybe *then* all this unrest will subside and I'll ask her what I nearly asked her this morning after I kissed her goodbye on Susan's doorstep. I want Dani to move in with me. Now. Instead of waiting for graduation, we'll go ahead and get an apartment because the way she reacted to me hugging my cousin is proof that Susan's hateful words have made a direct hit. I want to get her out of there and into a place where I can keep trying to figure out what she loves, what she hates, and what makes her smile reach her eyes.

I've put a lot of thought into how to proceed through what's going to be a tough week for her emotionally. Today is the anniversary of Kira's death and Dani is going to need extra care. I told her we didn't have to go to school today but she insisted that she needed to. There's something at the academy that she wants to show me. So I'll find ways to distract her while we're there and be prepared to take her to a private place if she needs to cry.

Over the course of time, I'll find ways to give her the birthday gifts I've been collecting, along with some new ones that are coming to mind now that we're officially official. I just won't call them birthday gifts. They're girlfriend gifts.

"Lily." I gently shake my sister's shoulder. "Get up. I need your help."

"Go away." She stuffs a pillow over her head. She's a night owl but somehow manages to function during daylight hours. *If* she gets to sleep in.

I kneel beside her bed and tug the pillow free of her grip. "I can't. I need you to help me buy Dani a gift before school."

She fights me for control of her pillow. "You already have ten gifts for her in your closet. 'Lily, find out what size shoe Dani wears.' 'Lily, find out what size shirt Dani wears.' 'Lily, find out if Dani collects anything.' Grr!" She rips the pillow from my fingers. "You do know I'm studying for my nursing exam right now?"

I muss her hair, a grin on my face over how well she mocks me. "I know your massive brain needs sleep, but I bought all those gifts *before* Dani was my girlfriend." That announcement gets Lily's attention. I let my grin slip into a smile. "Now I need to buy a gift for my *girlfriend* Dani, and I need my little sister to help me because I'm just a big dumb lug."

Lily slings her legs off the bed. "A big dumb lug who's finally dating a girl I actually like. Have you called any stores to see if anyone will be open in time?"

I straighten. "I called a florist and have an eighteen rose bouquet being delivered to the school at noon, and Dad's jeweler said she'd open for us so we can shop and get back in time for me to pick Dani up."

Lily's face goes slack. "Jeweler?"

"It's not what you're thinking, but I do have something special in mind that I need your opinion on, so hurry up."

~

Finding the perfect promise ring for Dani took longer than I expected, mainly because Lily said I couldn't buy *all* of the rings in the store. Picking just one didn't seem good enough, but then I found the one that's currently tucked into my console, wrapped in a silk inlaid box until the time is right for me to ask Dani to move in with me. When I ask, I want to promise her that if she agrees to move in with me and down the road we break up, *I'll* be the one to move out. She'll stay in the apartment for the remainder of the lease. A lease I'll be solely paying for. Which is another reason for the ring. I want her to know that my intentions are to finish growing up with her, until one day we find ourselves growing old together.

I didn't have time to drop Lily off back at home so she's waiting in the truck while I knock on Susan's door. Lily doesn't like to go to school early and would rather sleep in and have my parents bring her later, but I think she's also anxious to see Dani. Their relationship will blossom now, and that's another thing that draws me to Dani. She genuinely likes my sister, and Lily genuinely likes Dani.

"Did you ring the bell?" Lily yells through her open window.

"Yeah," I call back to her, that gnawing feeling I've been having growing stronger. Susan's house is too quiet. I take out my phone and dial Dani's number, pressing a finger to the doorbell again and then rapping my knuckles on the door. No one answers anywhere.

I hold my phone up to Lily. "Try calling Dani from your phone." I wait while she dials, turning back to the house when her head shakes to say she's not getting an answer either. I pound on the door. "Dani!"

Footsteps patter inside the house and the door finally opens. It's Susan, a satin robe barely pulled around her and an eye mask shoved onto her forehead. She attempts to smile but only manages to squint at the sky. "What time is it?"

"It's time for Dani to leave for school," I answer, barely managing to mask my annoyance. "She's waiting for me so can you please get her for me?"

Susan waves me inside. "You can go on up to her room. Randall's already left for work so he won't be around to bother us."

I move past her and take the steps two at a time. "Dani?" I knock on the bedroom door. Nothing but silence. I check the knob, it's unlocked. Closing my eyes, I slowly open the door. I've seen every delectable thing she has to offer but I only get that view when she's offering it, so I keep my eyes tightly closed in case she's changing, and step forward. "It's just me."

Waiting for a few beats, I pop my eyes open and look around. The lights are out, the bed is made, and Dani isn't here. I check the bathroom to be sure and then plod back out into the hallway, that gnawing feeling beginning to feel like rats on a feeding frenzy. "Dani!"

Susan tops the stairs, masking a yawn. "She's not in her room?"

"No."

She tugs her eye mask off and stands beside me, looking behind me into Dani's room. "Well, that's odd. Maybe. I'm not usually up this early so I have no idea where that girl gets to in the morning." She slips her hand around my bicep. "Want some breakfast?"

Jaw so tight it's clicking, I remove her hand. "What I want is to find your daughter."

Susan follows me through the house, checking each room and calling Dani's name. I'm growing more agitated by the second. We even walk through the basement, Dani isn't here.

Muscles straining in a mix of anger and worry, I get back into my truck, body tense. "Dani's not here."

"Then where is she?" Lily looks around. "I thought you said she knew you were picking her up."

"Yeah, well, Dani isn't exactly reliable when she tells you she'll be waiting for you somewhere."

I slam the truck into gear and back out of the driveway, heading into the cul-de-sac. Lily folds her arms. "Where are you going?"

"I need to check something."

I walk through the patch of woods to the gate. Dani's four-wheeler is still parked where I left it this morning. "What's this?" Lily asks, unearthing a trash bag from the dead leaves by the gate.

"Someone's littering," I mumble, looking around and walking back toward the truck.

"This isn't trash." Lily pilages through the bag. "Oh my gosh."

She drops the plastic and it clicks in my head that I saw Dani drop a black bag yesterday morning. I pick up what Lily dropped and sort through the pages. "This is Dani's."

"Why does she have that stuff?"

I swallow, confused as to why all of Dani's research is in this bag. If she had this with her yesterday morning and made sure I avoided noticing it missing from the cottage last night, she wasn't avoiding meeting me in the garage simply because of her appearance. Something bad is happening.

"Dani's friend was murdered. Today is the nine year anniversary of Kira's death."

~55~

I knew it was a long shot but Lily thought Dani might turn up at school so I came, and I've waited by her locker instead of going to class. When I'm not at her locker, I'm stalking the halls, calling her, and scanning every classroom for her face. She isn't here.

Her flower delivery just came and I picked it up from the office, stalking back to her locker once more. Everyone keeps asking who the flowers are for but they all already know, and I'm not so sure *that* isn't the reason Dani hasn't shown up. While I stand here worrying about her, she could just be avoiding walking through these halls holding my hand. If she's avoiding this, she's never going to wear my ring.

Slamming the flowers against the lockers, I release the bouquet and walk out of school, driving straight back to Susan's house. What I now know is Randall's car is parked in the driveway. I whip in behind him, blocking him in, and dash up to the front door, doing exactly what I did earlier after no one answered. I ring the bell and pound on the door simultaneously.

The door opens and I keep my face blank as Randall's eyes narrow. "Is Dani here?"

His stubby arms fold over his attempt at having a puffed chest. "No."

I motion for him to move aside. "You wouldn't tell me even if she was so I'll go check for myself."

He stays put. "This family has had enough of your temper. Leave. And that means exit from my doorstep, and from Dani's life."

I lean into his face. "Even if you were her dad, I wouldn't listen to you. If Dani doesn't want me here, *she* can tell me to go. Now move, or I'll move you myself."

235

He blusters and blows but all I focus on is his body language. He isn't moving. My hands clamp over his shoulders and I shove him aside, launching myself once again up the stairs, taking them two at a time. My feet stall outside Dani's room. The door is open and the room looks the same as it did this morning.

I jog back down the stairs and check the main house again, clocking Randall's whiny voice on the phone. He called the police and is reporting that I assaulted him. Just for that, I should assault him.

Confirming this house is still devoid of Dani, I walk out onto the porch where I presume Randall is waiting for the cops to show up. "Do you know where Dani is?" He doesn't respond. "When you see her, you better tell her I was here. She'll already know I'm pissed, so you can leave that part out. And when the officers get here, tell them I'll be at my house. If they want to stop by to ask about me hurting your poor little fragile feelings, they can call ahead to make sure I'm not busy."

~

Taking a trash can from the kitchen into my bedroom, I start trashing all the little items I've been buying for Dani along the way. A new pair of tennis shoes like the ones she's always wearing, a red flannel since she looks exceptional in red and winter is here, a charm I had made to look like a jar of peanut butter back when I thought peanut butter was her favorite food in the world, a box I made and stained myself and then filled with hair ties so she can keep wearing that long, beautiful hair of hers up in her signature ponytail, and now this stupid ring.

"What are you doing?" Lily whispers from the doorway.

"Getting rid of this stuff."

"Brother." She walks up beside me and rests a soft hand on my forearm. "Dani will turn up, and she'll probably have a good explanation. Don't throw her gifts away."

I pull the promise ring out of its box. "Dani probably will turn back up soon, but I'm not going through this with her over and over. Here." I hand Lily the ring. "I'm done with Dani, and I make you a promise to never chase a girl again. So take that ring and if you don't want it, throw it away. It's not even worth the hassle of returning it."

Her eyes drop. "Madge and Angelo just got here. They're worried about you, especially after finding Dani's decapitated roses in the hallway at school."

Lily thinks my bad attitude is an overreaction, but I know it isn't. The knot that's been festering in my stomach is now a full-blown tumor. Its name is Dani. I want to rip the world apart to find her, but I also want to forget she ever existed.

Sitting here being forced to look at Angelo is only magnifying my emotions. If he didn't steal her from me at the racetrack, maybe Dani and I would be in a better place and she wouldn't be forgetting that *I* exist.

"I don't get it," Madge whines for the third time. "If Dani is too stupid to see what a catch you are, then why do you care if she fell off the edge of the earth?"

"It's called feelings," Angelo snaps at her. "We all know you don't have any, but some of us care about people other than ourselves."

She makes a face at him. "Like *you* know anything about having feelings. When we hooked up, I distinctly remember you saying how great it was to be *with a girl who can keep her emotions detached.*"

My head snaps between them. "You two hooked up? When? How did I not know about this?"

Angelo plops his elbows onto his knees. "We kept it to ourselves. Same way as you kept this whole being down with Dani thing to yourself."

"I did *not*," I growl, restating some of the things I said prior to him snaking her right out from under me. "'Dani is hot.' 'I'm going to ask Dani to go to the movies with me.' 'I can't work at the car lot with you anymore because I want to work at the boutique with Dani.' 'Dani is really cool, she's deep, she's not like other girls…'" I throw my hands up. "Any of that sound familiar?"

His eyes bulge. "Yeah, but then you also started working at the car lot more than you ever have, and you stopped sitting on our side of the table after Dani started having lunch with us, and if you *did* sit with us, she'd get up and leave! You also told me to keep up with Dani, make sure she was okay and that no one was bothering her."

"Because Madge's stupid Bunny Clique are all bullies and I didn't want them messing with Dani."

"They're not *my* bunnies," Madge nips. "They're yours. And if you didn't treat Dani like a *special* little bunny, none of the originals would have messed with her."

I drag my hands down my face and sit back in my seat. "I'm not going to fight with either of you about this. Madge just confirmed that I didn't keep my feelings for Dani a secret, so both of you leave me alone." My head feels too heavy for my neck to hold it up anymore. "Dani doesn't feel the same about me and that's it. End of story."

My parents storm through the front door, two uniformed officers behind them. Mom's furious. "Michael, you have visitors."

I groan. I didn't actually think the police would show up here. "I didn't assault anyone. I *gently* moved Randall aside because he's a moron and I really don't feel like arguing with idiots today."

Angelo looks from me to Madge. "Is he calling us idiots?"

I get off the sofa, glaring at them. "Yes."

I follow my parents and the two officers into the dining room and plop into a chair across from the two uniformed officers. The female one is frowning at me. "Mr. Tricot has bruising on his torso. Can you explain how he got that?"

"Can you explain who that is?" I ask.

"Michael," my dad warns.

I blow out a breath. "I only know him as Randall, so is that who you're talking about?"

The woman nods. "He's at the hospital as we speak, having his other injuries checked."

Both of my parents sit forward and I shake my head at them. I don't need a lawyer. "If he has *other injuries*, then he must be a real delicate guy. Maybe he tripped. Because though I would have loved to, I didn't hit him, and therefore I have no idea how he got bruised up."

"He says you shoved him." The male officer speaks this time.

I mimic with my hands while I describe what happened. "He was standing in front of me like the dumpy slug that he is and I placed my palms *gently* on his shoulders, dug my fingertips in nice and good so he didn't fall and hurt his poor little self, and slid him over." I sit back in my chair. "If my fingertips bruised his shoulders, sorry, that's my bad. I'll send him a fruit basket."

This time Dad chuckles, and Mom slaps his knee under the table. He wipes the smile off his face and the officers nervously glance at him and then back to me. "You're describing what happened today?" the woman asks.

I nod. She pins me with a glare. "What about when you were there before? When he caught you in a compromising position with his underage stepdaughter."

"Danielle?" Mom asks.

I glance at her and sit forward, placing my elbows on the table. "Dani turned eighteen on the day Randall, without knocking, walked into the bedroom of his *girlfriend's* daughter. Dani had just gotten out of the shower and the way that man barged in on her, he deserved more than what I gave him. And write down in your little notebook that I'm also only eighteen, so we can go ahead and cut the implication that I was in her room doing something inappropriate. I wasn't. And when you talk to Dani, she'll confirm that. Do you happen to know where she is?"

The male officer sighs. "We're going to speak with Miss Madison to see if her story matches yours."

I sit back in the chair and fold my arms. "Which means you don't know where she is either. Did you talk to her mom? Dani was supposed to be waiting for me to pick her up for school this morning but she wasn't there. Her mom didn't seem to have any idea where Dani was, and Dani hasn't answered any of my messages."

The woman makes a show of checking her notebook. "Are you saying Miss Madison is missing?"

I look at my parents, acutely aware that Madge and Angelo are sitting in the living room tuned into every word being spoken behind them. "Do I not speak English? Is there a reason no one understands the words coming out of my mouth?"

Mom presses a hand into my arm, and she and Dad both stand. "We're done here. If there are any further questions, direct them to our lawyer. And start looking for Danielle now. It isn't like her to not do what she says she's going to do."

I let out a snorting huff and everyone turns to me. I shrug. "I'm worried about her, but I'm also mad at her. So before I become any more pathetic, someone should figure out where she is because maybe it really is only me, and every single person I happen to know, that she's avoiding."

~56~

I go back to the living room and brace myself for the interrogation I'm going to get when my parents walk back into the house. Madge sits next to me and pets me like I'm her dog. "Stop." I shrug her off.

"Fine," she bites. "I just thought I could cheer you up."

Angelo's head shakes. "We can't cheer him up, Madge. We're just idiots who can't understand his plain ol' confusing English."

I roll my eyes and then cringe when my parents walk back into the room. They sit across from me, saying in unison. "Whole story. Now."

I motion toward the dining room. "I just told it. Randall is a jerk, and Dani wants nothing to do with me."

"Do you think she's upset because of how you treated Randall?" Mom asks.

"No." I groan. "He's trying to make up for her mom's lack of being a parent and he does it in overbearing ways that make Dani uncomfortable."

"Is he mean to Dani?" Dad asks.

I shake my head. "Her mom is horrible to her, but Dani never implicates Randall. She just overall doesn't like him, and he doesn't like me even though I've never done anything to him." Everyone in the room makes a noise. I glare at them. "*Before* he walked in on us when Dani was completely naked."

This time only my parents clear their throats. I scrub my hands down my face. "Yes, Dani and I are sleeping together, it's kind of a new thing. No, we weren't getting busy in that house. Neither of us are down for that. Randall is just a blowhard, and he puffed one too many times. So I shoved him. Hard. But he didn't go completely through the drywall so I don't think I bruised the baby."

"Michael," Mom's voice is soft. "This isn't like you."

I look up at her. "I've never had to navigate being in love before. I thought you just loved people or you didn't. And more than wanting to know if Dani does or doesn't love me back, I want to know she's okay. And if she is, someone needs to tell her that there are better ways to dump me."

Mom sits on the opposite side of me and picks up my hand. "We could see that you and Dani were drawn to one another. Both of you, and sometimes her a little more to you than I realized you were to her. She's supposed to be working today so I'll run to the boutique and let you know if she shows up."

Dad places a hand over my shoulder. "And we'll call the lawyer so we can get ahead of this Randall situation. In the meantime, try not to smash anyone else through a wall. Not unless they really deserve it."

Mom slaps his arm and drags him away. It would be funny if I wasn't infuriated to the level that even Angelo is shortening my fuse. "I need to make a call."

I go to my room and look up Dani's dad, finding a phone number for his office and from there tracking down his direct line. He doesn't answer. "Mr. Madison, this is Michael Beller. Your daughter is missing. If you've heard from her today, I need to know. If you haven't, call me back anyway. I need to tell you what a pathetic person you are to have abandoned Dani like you did. There's nothing wrong with her except she has a sorry excuse for parents."

Worry settling into my bones, I make a call to the academy to confirm that Dani's records haven't been transferred anywhere. They haven't, and Mom just messaged to say Dani hasn't shown up for work. I walk back into the living room and both Madge and Angelo pretend to not notice. I fold my arms. "Be salty all you want, but Madge, you need to drive me over to Dani's house. I need you to knock on her door and see if her mom has filed a missing person's report. I'm pretty sure family has to do that."

Angelo glances up at me. "You really think it's as heavy as all this? Like you don't want to give it a day and see if she turns up?"

"No."

"Fine." He stands. "Come on Madge, I'll lick your Mikey-is-in-love-with-someone-else wound later."

~

Hunkering down in the seat of Madge's car, I watch as she stands all bubbly at Dani's front door. Both Susan and Randall are there, and I can tell by their blank faces that Madge is overselling the whole coming-here-to-check-on-Dani-because-she-didn't-show-up-for-school bit.

"What did you expect?" Angelo reads my mind.

"If she gets in the door and finds Dani in there, I'll kiss her and make her happier than you did when you boned her."

"Dude, you really got to stop with the whole *you stole my girl* drama. And you also need to calm the hell down because you're freaking me out, and you're the one who always keeps me from freaking out."

I tune him out, watching Madge's expression as Randall steps forward and says something to her. She stumbles backward. I open the car door and storm toward them.

"No, Mikey!" Angelo is right behind me. "I got you front, back, and sideways but this is not the time to go all loose cannon. Dani's been gone like twelve minutes. Chill. Out."

I keep myself trained on the door. "What did you say to her, Randall?"

His face turns red and he pushes Susan into the house. "Call the law! We need that restraining order. Today!"

I rush at him. "Restraining order?"

Madge latches onto my arm, dragging me backwards. "Don't, Mikey. We need to get out of here."

"Why?" I look at her. "I'm not going to let anyone hurt you, so calm down and tell me what he said."

Her head snaps side to side. "It's not me. It's you. They said you did something to Dani."

"What?" Anger billows up through my veins. "Get in the car, Madge. I'll be right back."

~57~

Before Dani came into my life, I was rational. Calm. Laid back to a fault and not apt to get into any physical altercations. Now I'm on round three with Randall and I slugged one of the officers who showed up to arrest me. Before Madge could reach my parents, I was in the back of a police car.

When my dad arrived, he very nearly slugged the same officer I hit. Then there was lots of shouting, phones buzzing, and now I'm at home pacing my living room. "She's definitely not in that house," Angelo confirms. While I was punching Randall, he ducked by Susan and scoured the house. "Her backpack is in her closet, packed with some clothes and a couple of jars of peanut butter. And this." He flops a bag onto the table. "Black hair dye. Weird, right?"

I open the bag. Two do-it-yourself dye kits are inside. "She said she might dye her hair."

"With this junk?" Madge makes a face.

"Why was Dani going to dye her hair?" Mom asks.

I shrug. "She just said she might. How long do I have to sit here instead of being out looking for her?"

Dad clamps a hand on my shoulder. "You're not doing much sitting, and I really wish you would because I've been where you're at, son. You're too emotionally charged to be out anywhere, which is why I called your aunt Sheila. She's calling Sophie and they'll find Dani. Now, sit down and help us understand exactly what's going on."

He points to the stack of research that Lily found in the trashbag this morning. "Dani's friend was murdered when they were nine. Today is the anniversary of that. And this is all the work Dani has been doing to try to find out who killed Kira."

243

"So Dani would have a reason to be upset and hiding out today?" Mom asks.

"No." I groan. "Maybe. I don't know. She's hard to reach sometimes, but she's been opening up so much lately that I don't know why she'd ghost me like this. Not after…" I begin to pave again. "We talked about this. I told her she can't do this. She can't shut me out."

Dad sighs. "You mean you don't *want* her to shut you out. But she can, and she might be. That doesn't mean we're not going to help you turn the world over to find her, but it does mean you need to consider that when you find her, she might not give you the answer you're hoping for."

"Unless we find her, she's not giving any answers." Angelo plops a phone onto the table. It isn't Dani's.

"Where was this?"

"Top of the backpack." He points to the hair dye. "Any way you slice this, it's not adding up. Who leaves home without their phone?"

I shake my head. "This isn't hers."

Dani's red dress floats into my mind and the rats begin to chew through my stomach. This phone is a burner, and it isn't password protected. I look at the device history. "She was going to run."

"From what?" Lily asks.

"Everyone," I whisper.

~

My parents' lawyer says that a restraining order Susan and Randall are requesting will most likely be granted. Assault charges won't stick to me so I'm not worried about that, but the news that Dani's dad showed up out of nowhere is unsettling. Apparently, he got the ball rolling on the police looking at Dani as an actual missing person. For that, I'm grateful. I don't even care that he's also pushing for a search warrant to be executed on my truck. I don't have anything to hide, and Susan and Randall are half right in reporting that the last time they saw Dani, she was with me and we were walking into the cul-de-sac. The last time *I* saw her, she walked into their house.

Dani's dad hasn't called me and I find that odd. I've contemplated calling him again, but the lawyer keeps telling me no. Everyone keeps telling me no. They expect me to just sit by while others work to find Dani. But though I do think Dani intended to run, she didn't go through with it. Her backpack is still in her closet.

"Keep an eye out!" I yell to Ang over my shoulder. He's on the back of my bike. I convinced the others that we should scour the woods because Dani walked in here before. They're all coming in the larger utility vehicles but I'm faster, so Ang and I will head out to the gate and then work back to the cottage while the rest of them pick along the trail from this end and meet us there.

The nip of the air sends a chill through me as we race toward the cottage. It's dark already and the headlights aren't illuminating far enough to the sides of the path. If Dani came out here, she could have stumbled off into the thickest parts of the woods and gotten lost. "We're going to have to get dogs in here."

"I was just thinking that," Angelo calls back.

If Dani came in here and got lost, she's been out in the cold since I went shopping for her ring this morning. She'll be hypothermic by now. Unless she's at the cottage. It's up ahead and completely dark. "I'm going to run in and check for her, she was out here one other time without any lights on."

"I've got it." Angelo slides off the back of the bike. "Go on out to the gate and work your way back. I'll clear the cottage and give Sophie a ring to see how fast we can get some dogs in here."

We bump fists and I roar off in the direction of the ravine, eyes scanning as I go. It stung when Meisha cheated on me, but while I committed to her and was serious about it, I didn't feel anything for her that comes close to what I feel for Dani. Dani has upended who I am at the core of my being, and I *have* to find her. Even if doing so means she's going to finish destroying my heart.

~

When I get close to the cottage, I hear it. Even over the roar of the four-wheeler engine. Shouting, and something farther away that's beating the air. I race toward the noise, sliding to a halt in front of the cottage where Madge is screaming and being barely contained by my mom who is sobbing, limbs shaking as she stares into the cottage. Dad is beside her, holding her up while she holds onto Madge, his phone at his ear and his mouth yelling into it.

I stumble off my bike and trip toward the door. Dad's stiff arm punches out, keeping me from it. But not far enough away to not see through it. Angelo is kneeling beside a body, hands pumping against the naked chest while Lily breathes into Dani's mouth. They're both covered in blood. "No!" I scream, fighting the grip Dad now has on me. "Dani!"

I fight Dad. He shoves me to the ground. Mom collapses and screams for him to let me up, her voice pleading. "He *needs* to see her. Think if that were me in there."

He releases some of the pressure from my back and I surge out from under him, knees skidding over the floor as I fall beside Dani, my hands pressing against her cold cheeks. "Dani, wake up. Look at me, baby." My tears wash over her. "Dani, please."

"I don't know if she has a pulse." Angelo keeps his chest compressions going, tears falling from his eyes as Lily sobs through every breath she gives Dani. "She's so freaking cold. So cold."

I take over for him, blood smearing over my own hands as I pick up the count. "Lily?"

She presses her fingers into Dani's neck. "I…I don't know. I can't tell."

I breathe for Dani, going back to pumping her chest as both Lily and Angelo pull away. I can't tell where the blood is coming from. It's smeared over her chest, some fresh and some dry. "Come on, baby. Give me a pulse." I breathe for her again, focusing on what I've learned in CPR classes because I can't bear to meet Lily's eyes. I don't want to hear her say that Dani is gone.

The rumble of beating wings fills the fog in my head, a haze of movements and words happening all around me as I'm shoved away from Dani's body. I push to her, follow the paramedics out when they take her, and get pulled off the chopper just before they lift her body into the sky.

It's Dad. He has ahold of me again. "Get off me!" I shove him with all my might.

He staggers backward but doesn't let go of me. "They found a pulse. So let them treat her without you in the way. We'll meet them at the hospital." He pulls me toward the four-wheelers and I bend sideways, stomach heaving as a shockwave of nausea doubles me over.

When I'm finished, I straighten, chest still heaving. I point to the cottage. "What in the hell was that?" I point to where every good memory I had was just destroyed. "What. In. The. Hell!" I shout.

Dad drags me into a hug. "I don't know, son, but we're going to find out what happened here, and who did this to Dani." He pulls back and looks into my eyes. "I *know* you didn't do that to her. I *know*."

"I know it, too." I sob, clutching his arms. "Dad, I didn't do that."

~58~

I can't get Dani's beaten face out of my mind. Someone hit her. They stabbed her. And she was completely naked, so they probably did more damage to her than what I even saw.

"How's Dani? Any news yet?" I ask as soon as the door opens to the room I'm being held in at the police station. Shortly after I arrived at the hospital, the police came. Because I was told I'm not family and therefore wouldn't be allowed to see Dani, my lawyer advised that I should go home. I decided to come here instead. I want to talk to the police because they're going to help me find who did this to Dani.

The lean detective massages his thick mustache. "If Miss Madison dies, we're looking at a murder charge. You have anything to say about that?"

I wipe my face, a strand of relief flooding through the sludge of emotion inside me. "She's alive, then." I look at my lawyer. "Work on getting me in to see her."

Rylan Sears nods, his fingers flying over his phone while I go back to staring at the detective. The smooth-faced one leans his elbows on the table. They've both told me their names but I don't care to bother with remembering them. "What do you have? Who did that to Dani, and where are they?"

"She was in your cottage." The man's elbows move closer together, his hands folding under his chin. "You left her in pretty bad shape."

Rylan straightens. "My client agreed to answer your questions because he wants to help you find whoever did this to Miss Madison. So ask a question, because baseless accusation isn't why he's sitting here."

"Well my accusation is hardly baseless." The detective smirks. "She was found in his cottage and he admits to being the last person with her."

248

I nod. "Yeah, and I already told you the last time I saw Dani was when she walked into her mom's house. Have you looked into Randall, the mom's boyfriend? And Dani's dad? He hasn't spoken to her since she moved here and today he's suddenly right in the middle of everything? Today, on the anniversary of Dani's friend dying? The one *he* found."

The detective with the mustache jots a note onto a pad of paper and looks up at me. "Do you recall if Miss Madison had her cell phone on her when she walked back into the house?"

I shrug. "I don't recall seeing Dani's phone at all that day, or that night." I'm not telling him about the burner.

He taps the table. "You don't know if Miss Madison had her phone the last time you saw her? Don't you kids always carry your phones?"

My eyes narrow. "Dani was never on her phone much, and I didn't know she was going to go missing so I didn't think to take an inventory of what she did or didn't have on her."

"So, you don't know how that phone came to be smashed up and tossed outside your gate?"

"You found Dani's phone?"

The smooth-faced one readjusts. "Tell us about the pornography. How many times did you take nude photos of Miss Madison?"

I press the heels of my hands into my eyes, catching the awful scent of Dani's blood. "You have two seconds to tell me what you're talking about. There are nude pictures of Dani on her phone?"

Mustache clears his throat. "Her phone is too smashed to recover anything, but you sent her this." Paper scratches over the table. "Right after she got this, her parents say she started spending all her time with you. Were you blackmailing her?"

I drop my hands from my eyes and stare at the paper, *Danielle Madison's Greatest Hits* in the center of the page. I flip the paper over and slam my hand over top of it, lifting from my chair and leaning toward them. "Where. Did. You. Get. This."

"Her mom turned it over to us. Mr. Tricot was home the day you delivered it and he said Miss Madison was upset, and she has been ever since."

"Dani is upset because her best friend was murdered and the worthless police department never found the man who killed that little girl. She's upset because her dad abandoned her, and her mom is a pathetic excuse for a parent. And my fists have already told you what I think about *Mr. Tricot.* I didn't deliver this paper to Dani. She's not afraid of me, but the two of you better be." I turn to Sears. "Get my dad in here. Now."

~

I know where my ability to become irrationally unhinged comes from. My dad. One whisper about the accusations in this room and the *evidence* the police have, and ballistic doesn't describe how Dad reacted. Mom was worse. And none of the chaos is because I'm being accused of hurting Dani. It's because Dani *was* hurt, far worse than any of us could have ever imagined, and the police are looking in the wrong spot. I wanted to give Kira justice, and give Dani peace, but now I think I only made it all worse.

"So in all those swabs and samples they've been taking at the hospital," Mustache yells at my parents, "you're telling me we're not going to find your son's DNA on Miss Madison?"

I push off the wall where I've been watching the fighting unfold. "For nearly all of the twenty-four hours before I last saw Dani, we were together. And were intimate quite a few times. So yeah, you're probably going to find me all over her. But *I* didn't try to kill her. Who did?"

Smooth-face opens the folder that's been sitting in front of him. He takes out a single photograph and slides it across the table. It's a picture of the inside of the cottage. The spot on the floor where Dani had been lying. Tears burn in my eyes and throat. Dad flicks the photo away. "We were there. We remember what it looks like."

"When were you there?" The man looks between us. "You know, I've been thinking how curious it is that your son doesn't seem to have any scratches on him. I guess they could all be on his torso. Because a strong young girl like that would fight back if someone was trying to strangle her."

Dad and I both tug up our shirts to prove we're not hiding anything, and Mom motions for us to put them back down. "What do you mean Dani was strangled?"

The detective taps a finger to his temple. "Never mind. I forgot that the hospital, they see a lot of drug overdoses, so they're trained in what to look for and they found…" He taps the crook of his neck. "This little mark right about here. A place a needle was probably pushed right in." His eyes land on mine. "Were you trying to overdose her? Or only incapacitate her so she couldn't fight you back."

I lunge over the table and grip his shirt in my fists. "You're telling me someone stuck a needle in Dani? And then they beat the hell out of her? And then *strangled* her? And you're just now mentioning it!"

Dad scuffles with the other detective as Mom pulls the Smooth-face one away from me. He straightens his collar and fishes back into his folder, taking out another photo. "Do you recognize this?"

I glance at the shirt with pieces of animated fruit dancing on the front. "No."

"You never saw Miss Madison wearing it?"

"Dani didn't wear stuff like that."

His arms fold. "Then how did it get twisted around her neck?"

I snatch the picture from the table, every drop of my blood draining into my feet. I thud back into my chair. Everything had been so chaotic at the cottage that I didn't pay attention to the fabric Lily had peeled from Dani's throat. I never let it register that the clothing had been used to strangle her. No one did.

"Kira." My voice strains. "I think this shirt is Kira's."

<h1 style="text-align:center">~59~</h1>

I lie on my bed, scrolling through all of the connections Dani was making in Kira's case. There was something new she found out because she'd said that she wanted to discuss it and tap into my resources. Then she disappeared before she had a chance to tell me what she had discovered. That means Dani was close to fitting the final pieces together, and somehow, the killer knew.

I get off the bed. I can't wait here any longer. I have to find a way to sneak into the hospital. Dani needs to know she's not alone, and that I'm sorry I've been so focused on our relationship that I forgot that first and foremost, what she needed was my help.

Skulking to my window, I see that the two security guards are still stationed outside. My parents say this is for my own protection but I'm an adult, they have no right to hold me prisoner. I don't care if going to the hospital will only get me arrested, Dani never had a chance to be a child and is barely surviving turning eighteen. For all I know, she might not have survived it.

Early this morning, I took a hot shower and washed all of Dani's blood off of me. I got dressed again right after but I haven't left my room until now.

Trudging into the living room, Lily's red-rimmed eyes run toward me, her small arms circling my waist as she clings to me. I hug her. She looks up at me, tears dripping from her lashes. "I'm so sorry."

I press a kiss to her forehead. "Me too. Thank you for helping Dani. You and Ang probably saved her life. At least I hope she's still alive."

"She is." Sophie leans on the corner of the fireplace, her face showing none of her usual self-assuredness. She looks as downtrodden as the rest of us. "Between the police and Dani's parents, we're having a hard time getting anyone close enough to put eyes on her, but I do know Dani is alive and stable."

Hot tears race down my face and I hold Lily even tighter. "I need to go see Dani. Where are my parents?"

Sophie clears her throat. "Outside. There's a visitor at the gates and they've gone down to greet them."

"Cops again?" I growl.

A small smile tugs at her lips. "Not yet."

I take Lily to the couch and sit down, letting her curl into my side while she continues to cry silently. Sophie follows us. "The police don't want to arrest you, but they also can't be seen as favoring us and let's face it, Mikey, the few facts we have don't look good for you."

"Except for the part where I didn't do it," I snap.

She holds up her hands. "No one here thinks you did, but that isn't stopping Dani's mom from blaspheming the Beller name to anyone who will listen. Which is why we're keeping you here, and it's why Zyair is working his connections to dig into Kira's case. Why didn't you ask him for help, anyway?"

I rub my face. "Dani didn't want to involve anyone else, and now I'm thinking the real reason is because she knew she was close. But somehow, the killer must have known that. He had to have been following her."

Lily's eyes fly open wide. "You think he's watching us, too? All of us?"

I pull her back against my side. "No, but I don't want you sneaking out of the house anymore at night. Dani said you came out on her because you were curious. Don't do that again. If you see something, call security and have them check it out."

A pain traces the back of my skull and I move Lily off of me, standing on legs that are suddenly feeling like they need to kick someone's face in. "Our security team. One of them would have had no problem ambushing Dani at the cottage."

The front door opens and all three of us look up. My parents enter, with another man trailing behind them. Sophie's head snaps back around and she gets up, leaning into my ear. "That's Dani's dad. Do *not* say in front of him what you just speculated."

I march across the room to the man who caused so much pain in Dani's life. "Isn't this convenient? You just *happened* to show up for your daughter now?"

"Michael," Dad growls.

I shake my head, staring Mr. Madison right in his ice-blue eyes. "I called you, and you didn't bother calling me back. Just like all the times you never bothered calling Dani back."

His face flushes red. "Because I wanted to stand in front of you and hear it from your own mouth. Did you hurt my little girl?"

I lean toward him as far as Dad's blocking arm will let me. "No. But you did, when you forced her to come here and live with that disgusting excuse for a mother. But is that all you did to your *little girl?*"

"Enough." Dad's voice booms. "Everyone is hurting and the last thing we need to do is rip each other apart." He lowers his arm from my chest but steps in front of me so I can't get to Dani's dad. "Like we told you outside, Michael had nothing to do with what happened to Dani. If it wasn't for him insisting upon us searching the woods in the middle of the night, we wouldn't have found her when we did."

"Not in time, anyway," Mom adds. "You said you came here to talk and that you had both questions and answers. I suggest you start using your words to do something other than accusing my son of attacking Dani."

~60~

Dad personally vets all the security detail who work our property, so he doesn't believe any of them could be a murderer. Nevertheless, I whispered my speculation to him and he's having Sophie run with that angle while he forces me to sit and have a conversation with Mr. Madison—a man Sophie is also digging into.

"So you think Kira's killer tried to kill Dani before she could expose him?" Dan Madison asks.

I nod, glaring at him over the dining room table. "Dani thought the man could be a serial killer and that other cases would all link back to him. With the way she was attacked, I believe she was right, and the man decided to end her the same way he ended Kira."

Tears form in his eyes. "Kira wasn't stabbed. Dani was. And…I don't recall there ever being drugs found in Kira's system. Maybe there were and the information wasn't released, but I talked to her folks a lot during that time and I don't remember them ever saying…maybe a toxicology screening was never done."

He looks perplexed, and I'm torn between wanting to have compassion for him and wanting to beat his head into the table. "The shirt that was found around Dani's throat was the exact same shirt design as Kira's," I point out. "Regardless of the other stuff, that shirt isn't a coincidence. Dani's a lot bigger than a nine-year-old so she wouldn't have been as easy to control. I assume that's where the drugs come in. But she still would have fought so why don't you take off your jacket and show me your arms."

He does, nostrils flaring as he unbuttons his collared shirt and tugs it all off. "The only thing I'm guilty of is sending my little cupcake here. Right into the hands of a monster."

I lift from my seat. "Then why did you send her here? You were married to Susan so you *know* what kind of a monster she is, but you still forced Dani right into her arms."

He sinks into his chair, head down. "I had a scare with a biopsy. It ended up not being cancer, but in the interim, not knowing if I'd be getting a death sentence, all I could think about was what would become of Dani if I died." He looks up, his eyes full of tears. "She was such a bright and happy child. Her giggle was contagious. Then after that day…" He sniffs. "After Kira died, I never saw my little girl again. Dani was lost and I've tried so hard to get her back."

"Dani isn't lost," I snap. "The trauma changed her. That's what trauma does to people. And Dani had to deal with those changes all on her own because people like you kept wanting her to just get over it and go back to being the version of her that you liked better because the pre-traumatized Dani was easier for you to deal with."

His jaw ticks. "I never told her to get over it. I wanted her to cope. To have a *whole* life instead of fixating on something she wouldn't ever be able to change."

"You left the country without her!"

He swallows. "Because nothing else I did weakened her all-consuming obsession for crimes against children. Evette suggested a radical change, and the only way I wouldn't rescue Dani from having to live with her mother was if I was too far away to run to her when she called me. And she *did* call. Evette monitored my contact with Dani because I'm telling you, I was so broken I wouldn't have been able to hear one whisper from her without running straight here and taking her back home with me."

I lean over the table. "But you didn't. You listened to Evette, and now Dani is fighting for her life. You're more than partly to blame for that."

"Michael," Mom scolds.

I shake my head, jabbing a finger in the man's face. "He doesn't get to sit here acting like he's consumed with guilt so he can get sympathy from us. He *should* feel guilty. Do you know how long it took me to get a smile out of Dani? A real, honest-to-goodness genuine smile? And don't even get me started on the way she thinks about herself! And it's all because people like *him* keep telling her to be something other than what she is instead of just experiencing who she actually is!"

Anger pushes me away from the table. I can't be that close to him without wanting to hurt him. "There's nothing wrong with Dani. She's intelligent, beautiful, and she happens to care about other people more than herself. She wants to help make this world a better place, so no other children have to suffer what Kira suffered." I pin her dad with a glare. "So no other children have to go through what *Dani* went through."

Angelo walks through the door, Val behind him. "Any word yet? How is she?"

I give my brother a hug. "Thanks to this guy, she's alive. Thank you for what you did for her, Ang."

"Of course." He wipes his nose. "Um, when can we go see her? There's this dance I want to see about taking her to."

Lily smacks his shoulder. "Have you met Mikey lately? He doesn't joke, he punches."

I roll my eyes at both of them and look back at Dani's dad. "I want to see her. You can make that happen."

He nods. "I was with her before I came here. She was awake twice, but she refused to open her mouth. Police, nurses, doctors, her mom, me, none of us have gotten a single word out of her."

"Maybe she *can't* speak," I snap. "She was strangled. There's probably damage."

His head shakes. "It could be psychological, but the doctors have told me they don't see any physical reason for her to stare at the ceiling like that. She doesn't appear to have been raped," His eyes flick to mine. "Nothing rough, as far as they can tell. So outside of contusions, only the cartilage in her sternum and ribs is separated. The *strangling* was nearly as superficial as the stab wound."

My eyes narrow. "Let me stab you and see how superficial it feels to you."

"Enough." Dad's teeth grind. "I'm not going to tell you again. The man is distraught."

Angelo takes a step backward. "Wait, you're Dani's dad?"

Mr. Madison doesn't take his eyes off of me. "She's angry with me, so I can only imagine what she said about me, but until the past months, Dani and I have always been close. I love her very much."

"You have a funny way of showing it." I turn to Ang. "Do you have your keys? The parents took mine but we're still going to go see her."

He tugs his keys from his pocket. "I'll grab a baseball bat and dare anyone to stop us."

Mom's arms fold. "The parents are standing right here, and you're not walking into a hospital with a baseball bat."

Val steps in front of the door. "I second that."

Mr. Madison clears his throat. "No matter what anyone chooses to believe, I do love my daughter. I was on my way here to spend her birthday with her, but my plane was rerouted due to a storm and…" He sighs. "Look, Michael is the one who let me know Dani was missing. Not Susan. And now that I've heard the version of events from this end, things make better sense. So I'd like to make you an offer, Michael. I'll get you in to see Dani, but if she speaks to you, you *have* to tell me what she says. Every single word."

~61~

According to Dani's dad, her heart rate was low due to hypothermia, not blood loss. The stab wound on her chest wasn't deep, and her doctor speculated that Dani might have fought her attacker hard enough that if the man had a knife pressed to Dani's chest, she basically thrust up into it and stabbed herself. During CPR, the wound had broken back open and that's why it appeared that she was bleeding out.

"If you hadn't gotten to her when you did, instead of slowing her heart enough to save her life, the hypothermia would have killed her."

I scratch my jaw. "Why would this killer drug her, strangle her, beat her up and who knows what else, and then just leave her there to freeze to death? I mean, I'm glad she's alive, but why did he take this risk?"

Dan glances at me from the driver's seat of his rental car. "The toxicology report isn't showing any drug in her system but there are several that wouldn't, especially if it's not part of the standard screening. But the prevailing theory is that she was given a small dose of something that would make it easier for her to be transported to the cottage. Not an incapacitating dose, just enough to make her pliable. Since there's no devasting injury to her neck, the detectives believe she may have regained full consciousness during that particular part of the assault, and that's when the stabbing occurred. The person either hit her hard enough to knock her out, or strangled her until she passed out. Either way, she has defensive wounds on her hands and arms so she fought at some point."

He isn't saying it, but I feel the accusation. He still isn't fully convinced I'm guiltless. "I didn't hurt Dani. At all. When it comes to us, she calls the shots."

"You got that right," Angelo mumbles from the backseat.

"Shut up, Ang."

He flicks the back of my head. "All I'm saying is that girl has you tied into a bow. Whether it's a pretty one to be tied on a package or a lethal one shooting an arrow depends on if she gives you a kiss or not."

Her dad slams on his blinker and turns into the hospital parking garage. "I don't want to hear about my daughter kissing anyone."

Angelo leans up between the seats. "So this dude strangles her but Dani wakes up, fights him, and accidentally gets stabbed. Maybe that's why he left her there without finishing the job. He wasn't planning for blood, and then all of a sudden, there's a bunch of it. He got flustered."

I nod. "He thought he'd be slick and attack Dani on the anniversary of her friend's death because he knew she'd be vulnerable and that she'd recognize the shirt. He thought she'd be too afraid to fight back even without being drugged."

Dan parks, a heavy sigh heaving from his chest. "Nine years to the day after he took Kira from us, he tried to take my Dani." He looks straight into my eyes. "I've failed my little girl enough, so please don't make me regret getting you in to see her."

~

Dan's plan is to sneak me into the hospital by having me masquerade as his stepson. He showed me a picture of William and even though our hair is close to the same color, I don't see how I'll pass. "You'll be fine." He plops a tweed hat on my head and ties a scarf around my neck.

"Aw." Angelo adjusts the scarf. "Mikey, you're *so* pretty."

I shrug. "If this is what it takes so see Dani, I'll wear it. And you can call me anything you want, just as long as you don't call my girl."

Dan looks at Angelo. "I saw the dance pictures. Dani looked beautiful and I'm still a little confused on why she was with you and not him, but we'll talk about that later." He nods to the vehicle. "I only have one stepson so you'll have to wait here. I don't want Susan to know I'm letting anyone in to speak to Dani. I need to play both sides of this thing to get the answers I need." He pats my cheek. "Ready, pretty boy?"

I follow him into the hospital and onto the elevator. I stand against the back wall with my head down. "Dani mentioned once that she thinks the person who killed Kira is a businessman."

Dan glances at me. "Why's that?"

"The pattern of child murders. She pointed out that there are clusters within one hour of major travel hubs. She had a theory that it was someone who travels for business, she just wasn't sure what kind of business."

He huffs. "That doesn't really narrow anything down."

I shrug. "Something about what she was doing spooked him, so I'd say it's getting narrow."

Dan shakes his head as the elevator door opens. "I don't think you should push this with her. Just comfort her, let her know that she has someone other than the father she's angry with and the mother she can't stand."

We walk down the long corridor and I keep my head down but peep up through my lashes to what's ahead of us. Randall is standing outside of a room, staring into the window while Susan walks off sniffing in the other direction. Dan sighs. "Stay a few paces behind me and I'll draw Randall away. I should be able to keep him talking for a while, I knew his grandfather, we lived across the lake from one another until… Well, until I took Dani away from that community." He drags in a breath and faces me. "Randall was fond of his grandfather's boat, I'll bring that up, but don't stay with Dani for too long. I doubt Susan knows what William looks like, she apparently didn't even remember meeting Randall or his grandfather before, but she most certainly knows *you*."

I slow my pace and lower my gaze while Dan approaches Randall. "How's our girl doing?" I hear him say with much more civility than I'd ever show Randall. I inspect a poster on the wall while they talk, only moving forward when their feet begin to move away from Dani's room. "Go on in, William," Dan calls over his shoulder. "I'll be back shortly."

I pull a hand from my pocket and wave an acknowledgment, keeping myself angled away from them while I slip into Dani's room. Outside of a steady beep, the room is quiet. Dani's head is turned away from the door, her chest softly rising and falling. I walk toward her bed, hand instinctively moving to pull the blanket up over her hospital gown. "Dani," I whisper, allowing my fingers to graze along her cheek. "Dani, it's Mikey."

Her head snaps around, eyes wide. I move away from the bed. "I'm sorry. I just wanted to—"

"Mikey!" She launches herself up and I get to her just in time for her arms to leap around my neck. She pulls me tightly to her, her mouth on my ear. "Randall."

"What?" I try to pull back but she doesn't let me.

"Randall." She repeats in a hoarse voice. "He grabbed me as soon as I closed the door. He had a knife and told me not to scream."

I lean against the bed rail. "*Randall* attacked you?"

She pulls from my neck and looks into my face, her words rushed and whispered. "He forced me out of the house and made me open the gate. I went because I thought I could scream and get to you, but he did something." She rubs her neck. "I didn't feel right. I tried to scream but then I remembered you left in your truck." She cups my face, tears and anger reflecting in her eyes. "I don't know all of what happened, but I do know he killed Kira and said he was leaving my dead body as a present for you. I fought as hard as I could, then I woke up here and everyone keeps saying you did this to me, and Randall's sitting there the whole time…"

"Shh." I hug her to me. "He won't get near you again. I'll take care of this."

"Kill him." Her teeth grind and I pull back. She repeats the words. "Give me a gun and I'll shoot him myself."

I press my lips to her forehead and pull out my phone. "Ang, call my parents and get them here. No one but us gets in Dani's room. Randall is the one who attacked her. I'm going after him."

"Dude," he whispers. "Randall, her mom's boyfriend Randall?"

"That's what she just told me."

"I'm looking at him right now."

"What?" I spin toward the door. Dani's dad is watching us. "What in the hell are you doing here?" I shout at Dan. "You're supposed to be with Randall!"

"He had a meeting he was late for. But Dani…you're talking." He's looking at his daughter, tears streaming down his face.

"Angelo, do you still have eyes on Randall?"

"He saw me. He's running."

"Follow him. I'm coming."

I turn to Dani. "Ang has eyes on Randall, I'm going to go help run him down. Tell your dad exactly what you just told me, and then the two of you call my parents. Got it?" She nods, the motion shaking tears from her lashes. I tuck her back into the bed and press a kiss to her lips. "I love you, Dani. You're my hero, and I love you so much."

~62~

Leaving Dani is hard but it's time for me to be *her* hero. Ang directs me to his location and I enter the stairwell just above him. "Up!" he shouts, lungs straining as his legs push. I take off up the stairwell. Randall jumped on an elevator and got ahead of Ang, but Angelo wasted no time catching back up. Randall won't outrun us.

"Check the floors," I shout down to Angelo. I might miss a door closing and we don't want Randall giving us the slip.

A woman and her child are huddled on the landing above me. The boy points as his mother rubs her elbow. "He shoved my mom."

"I'm going to stop him from hurting anyone ever again."

I dash up the stairs and push out a door at the very top, skidding to a halt on the roof. Straight ahead and to each side of me are ventilation systems where Randall could be hiding just out of view. I move slowly, ready for him to pounce.

Circling to my left, I round the first ventilation system and head for the one in the middle, scanning as I go. Ang bursts through the door behind me and I hold up a hand, motioning for him to slow down and help me corner Randall.

Ang moves to his right as I disappear behind the center unit. I reach the far side just as Ang is moving into position on the furthermost unit. A shadow bolts from behind it. We both take off. "You're caught, Randall! There's nowhere to hide!"

"Stop running, you coward!" Angelo's temper flares. He doesn't love Dani like I do, but something about her has changed both of us. Almost like our lives had never really been whole until she showed up.

Randall crosses the helicopter pad and we close in. He spins around, searching, backing toward the edge of the building. "I didn't hurt her. You leave me alone! I didn't hurt that stupid little twit!"

I ball my fists at my sides. "You're done, Randall. Dani is too smart for you, and she just told me everything."

He scrambles onto the building's ledge. Angelo and I slow our pace.

"I'm sick," Randall sputters. "It's an illness. I can't help myself. I try but the voices…" He hits himself in the head. "I can't help it. The kids, I see them, and the sickness comes over me. Don't you see it? I'm sick!"

Angelo stalks closer to him. "We see. And all the men in prison are going to see what kind of monster you are."

"Monster?" Randall throws his head back, body swaying with swagger instead of the fear he displayed only seconds ago. "Those girls *want* me. Running around in their cute little shorts, smiling and giggling just to get my attention." His gaze drops to us and my stomach rolls. This psychopath actually believes nine-year-olds are flirting with him.

I move closer. "You're demented."

He squats, balancing his pudgy body on the ledge. "You're just jealous. Danielle wanted me. She's been *begging* me to take her all these years, but I didn't want her, and she didn't want *you*." He laughs. "Just listen. I can hear her now. I can hear all of them. 'Come get me.' 'Play with me.' '*Take* me!'"

Ang and I continue our slow advance. Randall straightens, eyes snapping wide as if he's just realizing he has no escape. "I…I didn't touch her. Danielle Madison is unclean." His mouth bends in disgust. He paces two steps along the ledge, talking to himself now. "She's not pristine, and all of my girls are perfect. Soft. They're smooth and they fit me like gloves." He lifts his hands in front of his face. "Gloves. They're gloves. They make me wear gloves because they want to be gloves."

"This dude needs to be locked under the insane asylum," Angelo growls.

"No," I answer. "He doesn't get an insanity defense. He's going straight to the darkest prison where *all* the inmates know exactly what he is."

Randall beats his head. "No! I'm sick! I need help! Don't you see? Don't you hear them?"

He swings around as if the air itself is talking to him. I'm not buying it. "You premeditated what you did to Dani. You wanted me to find her dead body and go to jail for it. And for your own sick pleasure, you strangled Dani in the exact same way you strangled Kira. But you calculated wrong. You needed Dani strong enough to walk on her own because you're too weak to carry her, and by the time she got to the cottage, the drug you gave her was wearing off. She had just enough fight in her to show you she's eighteen, not nine, and you bailed because that's what cowards do. Now Dani is going to put the nail in your sick little coffin."

Ang and I are so close we know what we're doing without using words. At the same instant, we both lunge forward.

In the split second before our hands reach Randall, he smiles. I wonder how far down he was before he regretted that decision. Before he regretted all of his life's decisions.

We look over the edge. Randall is sprawled on the cement eight stories below, his limbs at unnatural angles. Angelo pushes away from the side first. I take one more long look at the dead body below me and then fall in at Angelo's shoulder. My best friend glances at me. "He deserved that."

I nod. "Jumping was the best decision he ever made. I just hope he was alive long enough to feel every bone in his body shatter."

~63~

Graduation is a right of passage. The first big achievement in most people's lives. I always knew I'd be happy to have the milestone behind me, but in light of this year's events, today holds a meaning deeper than milestones and achievements.

I sit in my row, diploma in hand, and watch my fellow students cross the wooden planks of the stage. "Danielle Madison." My girlfriend's name is announced and I launch to my feet in a roar of cheers and whistles. Angelo stands with me, fingers in his mouth as he whistles so loud he nearly drowns out the cheers coming from behind us. My parents, Lily, my aunts and uncles and all of my cousins are here. Most importantly, Grandma is here to witness this day, her longtime life-partner Willis is on her arm. Of all the people in my life, she understands love better than any of us. And she *loves* Dani.

"Congratulations." I rush to the bottom of the stairs as Dani exits the stage.

"Thanks." She laughs, waving to my family in the stands. "Did you tell them to scream like that?"

I shake my head. "From the sound of it, they're more excited about your diploma than mine." I hold her hand, so thankful for the months we've been given. Her dad relocated here and she moved in with him once she was discharged from the hospital. Still, we've spent most of our days together and somehow found a steady rhythm. We even make regular trips to the cottage.

Everyone in my family, including Lily, wanted to destroy the cottage. That's what was done to the old farmhouse where my mom once endured a traumatic experience. But instead of tearing the cottage down, Dani asked us all to go there with her. She had us relive the good

267

memories, even sharing her own, and explained to us that the cottage isn't at fault. "I'm not afraid to be here, and no one else should be either. Because if we let bad people take sources of joy from us, then they win."

I loved Dani more that day, and my love grew again when she asked me to give her swimming lessons. But I've never loved her more than I did last week, when we moved into our apartment. Or as I do now.

Keeping Dani on the very last step below the stage, I drop to my knee in front of her. Her face goes slack. "What are you doing?"

I smile. "Giving Susan that billboard." I slip the promise ring from her finger and replace it with a new one. "I know you don't want to be the center of attention, but you're the center of my whole world. I want to live my life with you, Dani. I want to follow our dreams right into the days where one of our grandchildren will take you to a school dance. I want to love you through every high, through every low, and through every case we end up working once we get our investigator licenses. I love you, Danielle Madison." I kiss her hand. "Will you marry me?"

She reaches around her neck and unclips a chain, pulling it from the red top with the flouncy sleeves that I like so much. Dangling from the gold chain is a ring. "I was going to give you this at the party later. It's my promise ring to you."

"Speak up! We can't hear you," Angelo shouts.

She laughs, tears falling from her eyes. "Yes!" she shouts. "I said yes!"

A Note From The Author

"Devotion is diligence without assurance." ~ Elizabeth Gilbert

Thank you for reading *Dawn Of Devotion* – the third book in the Beller Ties set! The fourth and final book releases on September 1, 2022, and is Lily's story. For early release news on this and other future books, join my newsletter here https://mailchi.mp/c9aefdb4dab7/leedawna-books

And be sure to visit my website at https://leedawnabooks.com

As we near the end of the journey for the Beller family, I reflect back on where this all began—with barely more than a whisper from my husband. He said I should write a book and after I finished telling him all the reasons I couldn't, each member of the Beller family invaded my head. They've lived with me for many years now and I hope you enjoy their stories as much as I do.

I'm lucky enough to have a fantastic editor in Anita from Proof Positive. She understands what I'm trying to say even when I don't, and lights the path to having my manuscripts become whole and complete. If there are mistakes, they're all mine.

I thank my husband for igniting the creative spark, my son for his continual support, and my readers for the joy you add to my life.

Billie, I'll never walk through a swamp with anyone but you.

ABOUT THE AUTHOR

Lee Dawna is a thriller, suspense, and romance author living in the rolling mountains of West Virginia. An avid traveler and outdoorswoman, you may bump into her along a remote trail where a meandering stream whispers her next story.

Connect with her on:

Instagram https://www.instagram.com/leedawna_author/

Twitter https://twitter.com/LeeDawna_Author

Facebook https://www.facebook.com/leedawnabooks

Book four of the romantic suspense Beller Ties set releases September 1, 2022.

Book two of the Hinton Thriller series releases October 31, 2022.

Join my newsletter for early release deals! https://mailchi.mp/c9aefdb4dab7/leedawna-books

Check my website for author specials! https://leedawnabooks.com